THE P

THE PALACE OF EROS

Delver Maddingley

First published in 1994 by
Nexus
332 Ladbroke Grove
London W10 5AH

Typeset by TW Typesetting, Plymouth, Devon
Printed and bound by
Cox & Wyman Ltd, Reading, Berks

ISBN 0 352 32921 1

*To my friends at Nexus, who declined
the opportunity to make personal appearances
in this work of fiction – though Fido, the office
mascot, nearly gets a walk-on part on page 24.*

This book is a work of fiction.
In real life, make sure you practise safe sex.

ONE

HOT COPY

Helen had always been a first-rate fuck – frisky, tight-cunted and oozing with lustful juice. Yet, as she sat there so primly at the computer keyboard, you could almost imagine she'd never had a man inside her knickers, or that those little breasts swelling inside the front of her thin, high-necked black sweater had never thrilled to the feeling of hairy hands swarming over them and tugging the tiny nipples into aching hardness.

It was hot and muggy in the little office. On this blustery March morning the window-sash rattled in its frame and the rumble of traffic, mingled with the shouts of stall-holders, was wafted up in gusts from the North End Road below. As he had not yet got round to having the central heating system repaired, the Captain had brought in an array of shin-scorching electric fires and hair-deadening convection heaters to keep his young editorial assistant sweet and sweating. With all that overloading they would be lucky if they didn't blow a fuse and lose whatever Helen had copied since the last time she remembered to save the text she had typed.

The Captain leaned back in his chair and looked at her. There could be no doubt that Helen Lascelles had come on wonderfully in the three years since he had first possessed her skinny body. Well, it had been skinny then – narrow and bony but alive with an extraordinary, lewd energy and the agility of your born whore. When she came back into

1

his life so usefully last summer, he had been struck by her development from the tired-eyed, crooked-toothed, nail-biting adolescent slut he had screwed at Cunlip College into a promisingly pretty young woman. To be sure, she still retained a hint of sleaziness and corruption – just enough to signal her sexual nature and arouse any cock that came within range. Now, only five months after their reunion, she looked prettier than ever. Her limbs had filled out just enough to be described as slender rather than skinny; slender and shapely.

He moved over and stood behind her chair. Her short, yellowish hair smelt delicately spicy as he rested his stubbly cheek against her smooth one. The large red earring pressed coldly into his neck. He let his hands hover for a moment on her shoulders before sliding them down to cover the soft breasts. Beneath the thin sweater her nipples hardened. She crossed her legs and the short red skirt rode up over her black tights.

Helen was typing from a neat handwritten transcription of one of those anonymous classics of erotic literature which may be examined under supervision at the British Library by holders of a reader's ticket. Fortunately the Captain's old friend Muriel MacDonald, a *bone fide* scholar and habitué of the famous reading room, had proved eager to undertake this chore. His own academic credentials, bogus but impressive, were hopelessly tarnished since his enforced departure, more than a year ago, from his post as Keeper of Reserved Collections at the Banesville University Library, Southern California.

He glanced at the green letters on the monitor but at this range he could make out no more than the title in capitals at the top: *TWO FLAPPERS IN MONTE CARLO*. This, the Captain was aware, was a sequel to *Two Flappers in Paris*, an engaging tale already published by a rival firm. In that story the narrator, known as 'Uncle Jack', persuaded a gullible headmistress to let him take two of her pupils out for the day – Evelyn, a sixteen-year-old English girl he had met on the cross-Channel steamer and her chum Nora. The action of the novella took place in a

Parisian brothel to which Uncle Jack escorted his young charges. There the girls received theoretical and practical instruction in the basics of sexuality and enjoyed their first orgasms. But Uncle Jack was a man of honour and returned them to their school intact. In the sequel, the Captain knew, this state of affairs would be rectified.

Reaching down to Helen's waist, he tugged at the bottom of her sweater and lifted it until it was clear of her breasts. She stopped typing, raised her arms and allowed him to remove the garment completely. A natural body fragrance was released by this operation. For a moment the Captain's palms lingered in the slightly moist concavities of the girl's armpits, flattening the yellow curls that were allowed to flourish there. Then they wandered down to the little white swellings with their tight, dark red peaks. He kissed her right shoulder.

'Helen,' he murmured, 'I hope your spelling's as good as Miss MacDonald said it is. You do know the difference between *areolas* and *aureoles*, don't you? And between *palpitating*, which is what I can feel your heart doing, and *palpating*, which is what I'm doing to your boobs right now. Those are probably the commonest howlers in our competitors' books, and I don't mean just the crap ones. I won't stand for that kind of sloppiness in the Honeymooners Library.'

'Funny you mention it,' Helen replied. 'That's exactly what Mummy's always saying.' Many years ago Helen's mother, Cicely Lascelles, had taken up writing erotic novels under the pseudonym Lucette Arrowpoint, so as to be able to send her daughter to Cunlip College in the absence of paternal contributions to the fees. 'Yes, I reckon I can get those things right. And I can tell the difference between your *glans* and your *glands*,' she added, reaching behind her to squeeze the rising bulge in his trousers.

In general, the Captain's knowledge of men and affairs was extensive but somewhat furred at the edges. At school his English teacher had accused him of sciolism, but he had never got round to looking the word up. However, with the exception of the odd oddity like *scio-* whatever it was, he

3

felt that when it came to his native language he was well qualified to lay down the law. He would be watching Helen like a hawk and would enjoy taking it out on her if she so much as let a split infinitive slip through the net. And if that made him a scholiast . . .

Helen twisted her head and looked up at him. 'If you think I'm illiterate,' she smiled, reaching for *Pg Dn* on the keyboard in front of her, 'why not have a quick spot check of what I've been doing? Look, here's an interesting place to make a start. Uncle Jack's got these two silly sixteen-year-olds to the hotel in Monte Carlo but in spite of all the fun he had with them when he took them to that brothel in Paris, he's finding it a bit difficult to break the ice. So he takes them to an expensive private club near the casino to see a blue movie. Go on – take it from here.'

The Captain pushed Helen's chair forward on its casters so that he could lean over her and read the text on the screen while continuing to play with her bare breasts. Excited by the present situation more than by his expectations, he began to follow the adventures of that old reprobate, Uncle Jack.

We took our seats at the back of the room, just to the right of the aisle, my darling Evelyn on my right and the delightful Nora on my left. 'Oh, Uncle Jack,' whispered Evelyn, 'everyone here seems to be really rich. But if the men are so old and fat, why are their wives so young and lovely?'

'I think I know why,' little Nora offered. 'The wives didn't come from well-to-do families. But they had these good looks, so they were able to get really rich husbands while the men were able to buy themselves beautiful young wives. Isn't that right, Uncle Jack?'

'Nearly right, you little dear,' I replied, running my fingers through her long yellow hair. 'Only most of these ladies aren't really the men's wives at all. Why, they're not even ladies in the proper sense of the term.'

The lights were dimmed and instinctively Evelyn and Nora drew up closer on each side of me. I took advantage of this to allow my hands to wander, gently and

4

with infinite care, first to their slender hips and then down so that I could stroke and fondle the outsides of their thighs and of their soft young bottoms through the thin skirts. Evidently pleased by the touch, each girl slightly raised the cheek that I was squeezing as though inviting my hand to pass more completely underneath!

All three of us were recalling the film we had been shown in Madame R's establishment that glorious afternoon in Paris, the film in which the cunning hermit, Father Rustique, had delighted the charming and naive little Alibech by showing her how he put his 'devil' into her 'hell'. This had been Nora and Evelyn's graphic initiation into the secret of copulation, and the lewd sensations it aroused in them as well as in me had been satiated as far as possible by an afternoon of debauchery in which everything had been accomplished save the actual ravishing of the little darlings. That was the object to which our present sojourn by the sea-side was to be devoted.

'Are we going to see something like "The Devil in Hell" again, Uncle Jack?' asked Nora.

'Hush, dear,' I replied, not wishing the couples sitting just in front of us, however loose their own morality, to get wind of the girls' innocence. 'What we are going to see will probably be a good deal more realistic than that story of the hermit in his cave.'

Meanwhile the film began to be displayed.

As he read on, applying, as he did so, a regular massaging pressure to Helen's breasts, the Captain recognised the silent movie watched by Uncle Jack and his little companions as the continuation of a silent film described in one of his favourite novels, *The Altar of Venus*. In that book the narrator had held his breath and watched, with stiffening prick, as a pretty young Parisienne called Eva was lured into service in a Bordeaux bawdy house under the false promise of work as a showgirl. The climax of the movie presented in lovingly photographed detail the sale of Eva's virginity for five hundred francs to a sadistic client.

5

Now broken in, Eva was still engaged at the low-class waterfront brothel in the film being viewed by Uncle Jack and his young charges. It appeared that this second film was to show the use Eva was put to the day after her defloration. The Captain's eye ran down the screen of the computer, taking in the description of Eva's humiliation at the hands of the madame and her whores. They subjected her to a series of degrading domestic chores and were continually beating her for supposed derelictions of duty during her first day in this evil house. Every now and then he lifted his right hand from Helen's soft tit with its tight little nipple to reach for the keyboard and scroll the text down. When the action of the tale seemed to be warming up he paused to read more slowly.

The repeated depictions of Eva's bare bottom [Uncle Jack's story continued], now marked from the floggings she had endured at the hands of her tormentors, were having their effect on the audience, and on none more than my young companions. With a shuddering sigh, my darling Nora lifted her left buttock for a moment. When she lowered it I realised that she had eased her thighs wider apart, permitting me to curl my fingers up so that their tips just tickled her little pussy through its silken covering.

Suddenly the screen was filled with bustling activity. A great warship had tied up in the harbour and drunken *matelots* were seen, first swarming down the gangplanks to throng the quayside and then carousing in the downstairs salon of the *maison close*. Through the fog of cigarette smoke we could see that a raised platform occupied the far end of this room. In the middle of the platform stood a bed.

There now appeared on the screen, in a florid script, a message which, translated to English, read about as follows: 'STILL SORE FROM HER BRUTAL DE-FLOWERING, YOUNG EVA IS FORCED TO MAKE HER STAGE DEBUT'.

In the film the drink-crazed sailors threw their pom-

pom-adorned berets into the air, whooping with lecherous appreciation, as Eva, looking timid and dazed, wandered into the room and mounted the platform. She was dressed in bridal white, but would hardly have been allowed to tread the aisle of any church in that mockery of a wedding dress. Her pretty face was not covered but framed by a short veil hanging from a head-dress of orange blossoms. Instead of a modest gown she wore a loose, sleeveless, low-cut white tunic that did not quite reach to the tops of her white stockings. This tunic was secured around her tiny waist with a cord which caused it to flare out over her hips. Behind Eva strode the madame, attired as a circus ringmaster and cracking a vicious whip.

As well as arousing the tipsy mariners, the scene also had its effect on us and the rest of the somewhat more refined audience watching the film. Everyone seemed to be shifting in their seats and gasping, some of the women quite noisily. On my right, little Evelyn squeezed up against me and grasped my thigh. Whether her touch or the spectacle on the screen was the major provocation is hard to say, but my tool lengthened along the leg of my trousers until its tip nudged against the side of her hand.

Unheard by the audience except in the ears of their imagination, the sneering madame cracked her whip, urged on by the sailors. Eva began a stumbling, embarrassed dance on the edge of the platform. The whip curled round her waist and dislodged the bow with which the girl's garment had been negligently tied. The tunic fell open. Although the plump little breasts were still covered, the rest of her almost virginal beauty was disclosed to the gaze of both sets of beholders: the actors within the cinematographic performance and those watching it with bated breath. For a moment we, the watchers of the film, were dazzled – the whole screen was filled with the whiteness of Eva's body shown at short range, from her dimpling navel down to her garters. Between her slightly separated thighs, below a little

7

cluster of curly blonde hair, the flower of her sex was partially visible.

The scene was emotional, and not a sound was heard in the room except the whirr of the film as it was fed into the projecting machine. Evelyn lifted her hand slightly and placed it over my rigid member. My own fingers, which had slyly crept up under her skirts, slipped inside her drawers to finger the humid flesh for which I longed. At the same time Nora, who must have sensed that her friend was developing a close intimacy with me and had no intention of being outdone, leaned more closely against me, resting her right cheek on my left one. I now had a finger at the tight, unopened pussy-entrance of each of my little darlings. All three of us kept our eyes fixed on the screen throughout these manoeuvres.

And now Eva was once again displayed at full length. A crack of the madame's wicked bullwhip induced her to gyrate her hips reluctantly but suggestively, shrugging her shoulders and allowing the open tunic to fall to the floor. Apart from her white stockings and the head-dress with its little veil, the poor abused girl stood there in all her naked beauty. At the madame's behest she turned and bent down until her face rested on the bed. Once more the camera vouchsafed us a really close view. Eva's delicious bottom was exhibited in all its glory, the split peach of her sex pouting lewdly between the buttocks where they curved down to meet the tops of her thighs. The whip flicked across the screen and left a dark line which crossed obliquely from right thightop to left buttock, not sparing the tender fruit with its shading of soft down.

The lustful sailors had surged forward and were clamouring at the edge of the platform. Madame cracked her whip and raised her hands to appease them. For a moment the picture disappeared, to be replaced by a caption:

'STEADY LADS. THERE'S ENOUGH HERE FOR THE WHOLE FLEET. YOU PAID YOUR MONEY

AND YOU SHALL HAVE HER, BUT NOT ALL AT ONCE. LET'S HAVE SOME DISCIPLINE – UP YOU COME NOW, THREE AT A TIME.'

Three hefty *matelots* leapt on to the stage, divesting themselves of their bell-bottomed trousers even as they threw Eva down on the bed. Despite her screams she was held down on her back by two of the men. The third knelt between her forcibly parted thighs. His enormous cock, its foreskin drawn back and head exposed, projected in rigid, menacing erection. He mounted her. For the second time in her young life Eva's sexual flower was about to be plundered without mercy.

Her white flesh formed a pathetic contrast with the hairiness of her ravisher's thighs as he groped with one hand and endeavoured to place the head of his cock in the strategic spot.

'NO! NO! NO! – OH! YOU'RE HURTING ME! – OH, DON'T! PLEASE DON'T!'

And her exclamations rose in a shriek of anguish, indicated on the screen in script beginning with small letters, which increased in size, terminating in immense letters that covered half the screen.

The brutal sailor had found the entrance and was about to force the lock which had only once before been opened. He thrust hard at her – the girls on either side of me shuddered and squirmed as the screen was filled with the spectacle of the whole length of his cock plunging into her tight, girlish cunt. 'Look, Uncle Jack!' gasped Evelyn. 'His devil is pushing in and out of her hell like a steam engine!'

Eva's white-stockinged legs flashed up in the air, but to no avail – the lucky sailor was fucking her ruthlessly, cruelly, eager to unload a cargo of spunk wich had been building up in his balls during many months on the high seas without land or a woman in sight. And, as he fucked, one of his shipmates mauled her breasts and

9

sucked her nipples while the other one stuffed a fat cock into her mouth.

The trio rang the changes with their reluctant prize until all three had enjoyed her rosy nipples and achieved full stiffness between her lips with which to ravish her cunt. Successive parties of three took their places on the bed until Eva's reluctance began to give way to what might have been exhaustion but looked suspiciously like the languor of sexual fulfilment. Some of the men who had begun by taking their pleasure between her legs still sported rigid poles when they withdrew. These connoisseurs of the slow dance saved their sperm until it was their turn to be taken into her mouth; their buttocks quivered as they inundated her throat with the freight of boiling spunk. Others, their taste for more normal modes of enjoyment perhaps perverted by the exigencies of life at sea, found their release in the forbidden rear passage of the lovely girl's bottom.

As the action of the film became faster and more furious, my two little 'nieces' abandoned almost all restraint, encouraged in this by the dimly discerned behaviour of other members of the audience. Evelyn's hand had found its way right inside the front of my trousers and her fingers were gently squeezing my hard tool. On my left, Nora had unbuttoned her blouse and eased down the shoulder straps of her bodice, camisole and richly laced chemise, so that a snow-white breast, tipped with coral, presented itself to the attentions of my lips and tongue. I sucked it as if it had been a delicious bonbon, doing my best to keep the screen in sidelong view.

Meanwhile my own hands had not been idle. Delightfully conscious of the contrasting textures of Evelyn's silky, astrakhan-like curls and Nora's crisper little blonde ones, I had parted their pouting lips and slid my fingers up and down the moist slits for some minutes until the juice was pouring down to saturate their petticoats. The tips of my index fingers had then hovered over the swollen cherries emerging from their protective

10

grottos, those buttons which serve as the thermometers of feminine pleasure.

By now the film was drawing to a close. No longer were the impatient mariners respecting the madame's commands. Mutinous and tipsy, they took the platform by storm and rioted all over the bed. Every orifice of Eva's body was used to slake their lusts, and she was buried beneath a heaving tangle of brawny backs, hairy legs and bouncing buttocks.

Suddenly the salon was empty. The crew had been summoned back to their ship; all their wantonness was forgotten under the influence of the tight naval discipline to which they were accustomed. Eva lay worn out on the soaked sheets.

The camera showed a truly scandalous view of her thighs, slackly open, and the plundered treasure between them. White foam bubbled from the opening of her vagina and poured down over the undersides of her bottom cheeks, filling the rift between them and pooling on the polluted bed.

As we gasped at this lubricious spectacle the viewpoint changed. Now the whole screen was filled with the girl's pretty features as she lay exhausted after her ordeal. Spunk was spattered all over her face. Great gobs of it could be seen in the blonde tresses of hair which were spread over the pillow. The bridal veil attached to the little head-dress of orange blossoms, now sadly crushed and awry, still formed a poignantly charming frame to this picture. Her lips were slightly parted; white semen flowed from the corner of her mouth.

Eva opened her eyes to gaze up at the camera and at us, the spectactors of the film. One eye closed in a knowing wink and more spunk flooded from between her pearly teeth as she flashed a smile at us. The word '*FIN*' replaced this image on the screen and the entertainment was over.

Or so everyone thought. But the house lights had hardly been turned up long enough for the audience to rearrange their clothing and extricate themselves from

11

compromising entanglements with their partners when the screen was illuminated once more, this time by a spotlight. (My own engagement with the two little flappers on either side of me was sufficiently concealed by their skirts and by Nora's hair, which hung down over the bare breast I had been sucking. I continued to frig them gently, always holding back when I sensed that they were on the brink of spending on my hands.)

Silence fell on the house once more as a small figure skipped into the circle of the spotlight. A round of applause went up. It was none other than the actress who had played the part of Eva in the cinematographic display. She was wearing the mock-bridal attire that had been used in the film, at once demure and lasciviously suggestive.

She smiled and bowed in acknowledgement of everyone's applause, perhaps, except mine, whose hands were otherwise employed. Then she turned to face the screen. Lifting the back of her short tunic she tucked the hem into the cord around her waist. The living flesh of her lovely bottom was exposed to public view. She bent forward and reached a hand back between her legs to part the cheeks for us. When she straightened up she kept her back to us for a moment while hitching up the tunic in the same way in the front. Then she turned to face us.

The film in which she had performed so impressively had, of course, been devoid of colour. But now the creamy smoothness of her limbs and belly, themselves contrasting interestingly with the whiteness of her costume, was set off to fine effect by the triangular patch of golden fur she stroked and flaunted for our delight.

With a sprightly step, 'Eva' descended from the dais which supported the screen and advanced up the aisle between the rows of spectators. Some of these were rapturous and others seemed to be somewhat embarrassed. Speaking for myself as I sat there with my hands between my flappers' thighs, I could not wait for the girl to reach our end of the room. To see the principal performer of a moving picture in the flesh had long been a

12

secret dream of mine; it was about to be realised with more flesh visible than I had thought possible.

And now the girl drew level with us. She must have thought we made an interesting trio, for she stepped towards us with a saucy smile. Framing her blonde triangle in the inverted V of her fingers, she thrust her hips forwards as if offering us the tempting fruit with its pink bisecting line. With her free hand she took Nora's left one and guided it to the fluffy mound; delicately she ran the flapper's finger tip down the slit and up again. For a moment she worked it against the hidden bud. Once more she ran it downwards, and this time the lips parted to let it glide between them. At the bottom of the run 'Eva' whispered something I did not catch. Nora blushed and grinned. I saw her push her finger up to the knuckle into the young Thespian's cunt. As she did so I felt a stream of warm juices flooding over my own fingers from Nora's open sex.

I began to fear that the audience would leave their seats and gather round us at the back of the room. But gently holding Nora's wrist, the actress pulled the finger out. With a naughty wink she raised it to her own mouth and licked it clean. And then she pranced back down the aisle, her bottom sustaining many playful slaps from the gentlemen seated on either side. For the last time she stood in the spotlight to take her bow before blowing us a succession of kisses and skipping off into the darkness.

Back in the hotel room Evelyn and Nora could hardly wait to tear off each other's clothes and hurl themselves on the bed. 'My sweet little darlings,' I said as I began to undress, eager to make complete women of them. 'When you are eighteen and the girls at school let you join the Lesbian Society you were telling me about, what exciting tales you will have to tell them.'

Nora smiled at me. 'Oh, Uncle Jack,' she said. 'You will think it very naughty, but we have already been allowed to join the society.'

'How was that?'

13

'Gabrielle – she is our head girl – caught us doing some of the things you and Rose showed us when you took us out in Paris. She said it wasn't our age that mattered but how much we knew.'

I made them lie side by side on the bed so that I could admire their sixteen-year-old charms while I completed my undressing. Nora, stripped naked, would have been a worthy model for a sculptor's chisel. Just a nice height, just sufficiently plump without being too much so, she was made to perfection. One would have loved to die smothered by the soft but powerful grip of those full and rounded thighs, between which her fair downy-bush framed a flower so pure, so fresh, so tempting and so fragrant it seemed a crying shame that she was still *virgo intacta*.

My little Evelyn was not quite so well built as Nora. But if her forms were less plump they were more graceful and more full of nerves, which made them equally alluring. Evelyn was all energy and activity, while at the same time being just as passionately voluptuous as Nora, who, for her part, would rather be passive and tenderly submissive to refined caresses. At the base of Evelyn's flat belly luxuriated a fine thick dark brown bush, sheltering in its shady folds a fountain in which I longed to quench my greedy thirst.

I allowed the girls to join together in a passionate embrace, urging them on with resounding smacks to their firm young bottoms. However, my own state of arousal was such that I could no longer delay my own satisfaction. When I intimated to them my strong desire to place my devil at long last into their hot, delightful hells, they responded with alacrity.

'Oh yes,' cried Evelyn. 'After all the excitement of the film I just can't wait to be treated like that lovely girl Eva.'

'Well, my dear,' I replied, 'it will not be possible to arrange quite the same treatment for you. I have no intention of bringing ruffians in off the boulevards to defile you, so you will have to make do with your old

14

£5 off

when you purchase a 50ml or larger bottle on the following brands

THE PERFUME SHOP

EMPORIO ARMANI

GIVENCHY

RALPH LAUREN

DKNY
DONNA KARAN NEW YORK

Showtime
KYLIE MINOGUE

Sean John

Calvin Klein

LACOSTE

DAVIDOFF

BOSS
HUGO BOSS

Terms and Conditions:

Voucher only valid at The Perfume Shop locations in the UK.

This voucher entitles you to a saving of £5 on a 50ml or larger fragrance when you purchase one of the following brands in a single transaction Davidoff, Calvin Klein, Boss, Lacoste, Givenchy, DKNY, Emporio Armani, Kylie Showtime, Sean John or Ralph Lauren fragrance.

Offer valid from 3rd November 2008 - 26th November 2008.

This voucher cannot be used in conjunction with any other voucher, offer or discount card.

This voucher cannot be redeemed online against our website.

This voucher cannot be redeemed against Vivaboxes, giftsets, or bodylines.

Only one voucher will be accepted per customer per transaction.

No cash alternative.

This voucher will be retained via the cashier at the time of redemption.

Subject to availability.

Offers available while stocks last.

Please do not try to redeem this voucher against any other products as this may cause delay or embarrassment at the till.

Only original vouchers will be accepted - photocopies are not valid.

To find your nearest The Perfume Shop call 0845 601 1950 or visit www.theperfumeshop.com.

999013570009

uncle. What is more, instead of being shared by five dozen sweating sailors, you will have to share me with our darling Nora here.'

'Will you really have enough for both of us?' Nora enquired.

'Of course he will,' Evelyn reassured her. 'Surely you remember how he distinguished himself in Paris? You haven't forgotten why Mademoiselle Rose called him *Monsieur Quatrefois*? Or how much of that sticky juice came out of him when you stroked his – his prick' (she said the word shyly) 'to make him spend? Why, it shot up four or five feet into the air. When he had finished spending there was a long line covering the towel from just under his chin right down to where you had been playing with his rude parts – remember?'

Both girls laughed at the recollection and I gave them a solemn undertaking.

'We have all night, my dears,' I said. 'By snatching some sleep now and then when I begin to flag, I can promise I shall have satisfied both of you at least four times by the morning. But I know you are desperate for it right now. Because I've only got one cock I can't spend in both your cunnies at the same time, so I'm going to make sure that at least you have an equal share in making me come this first time. There is one little problem, though.'

'What can that be?' asked Nora, and I thought I noticed her winking slyly at her friend.

'It's bound to hurt a bit the very first time I put it in. But . . .'

'Not at all,' laughed Evelyn. 'You see, Uncle Jack, we're not virgins any more.'

I was devastated. After all the pains I had taken with their venereal education and all the consideration I had shown in keeping my promise to respect their physical integrity in Madame R's establishment, how could these two youngsters have given themselves to another man (or boy? or *men*?), knowing as they must have done how hotly I desired to be their first lover? The pretty flappers

15

laughed all the more at my hang-dog air. Nora explained.

'You see,' she said, 'the girls in the Lesbian Society have this India rubber thing they strap round their hips so they can do it like a man. That was our initiation – they called it deflowering us. It did make us a little sore at first but I'm sure it was for the best. Here we are, not virgins though we've never been had by a man. And it won't hurt a bit.'

This story had inflamed me even further until I could barely contain my sperm. A heavy drop of clear juice had formed on the tip of my instrument and was detaching itself to hang from a silken thread between my legs. I made the girls kneel side by side on the bed, their heads down on the pillows and their bottoms stuck well up with their sexual parts pouting out between the tops of their thighs. By inserting a finger into each of them (confirming, incidentally, the loss of their virginities) and churning the fingers about I caused the cunts to gape wetly.

My right knee I placed between Nora's calves and my left one between Evelyn's; my hands rested on their outer buttocks. By leaning slightly to my left I was able to slide into Evelyn without difficulty. The sleeve of flesh tightened provocatively around my stiff prick. I thrust in and out a couple of times before drawing right back and leaning across to spear Nora. The darling quivered and deluged me with her juices as I plunged deep into her long-desired cunt.

Soon I established a frenzied rhythm, shifting easily from one girl to the other and back again and never poking either of them more than two or three times before disengaging. So rapidly did I work that, as they told me afterwards, they both felt as if they were being stimulated continuously, while I myself almost seemed to be enjoying a deliciously uninterrupted fuck.

As I pumped away more and more furiously I found time to wonder which of my lovely 'nieces' would be the one to receive the outpouring of my loins and whether

16

the other would be disappointed. I need not have worried. The first jet of semen squirted into Nora. But before its even more violent successor could race up my interior tube I was out of Nora and into Evelyn, stretching her pretty lips with the purple head of my tool just as the second load gushed forth. Back in Nora's sopping cunny I discharged an even heavier package. From then on I lost count and almost lost consciousness. I seemed to be coming in a continuous stream. No longer could I make any effort to see that it was all delivered to one receptacle or the other; it flowed and spouted all over their bottoms and thighs and drenched the brocade cover of the bed. Yet even with this prodigious (and, I must confess, exciting) waste, my later investigations with fingers and tongue persuaded me that far more spunk had been deposited in each of my darling flappers than had been spilt externally.

'If that film ever gets made,' the Captain remarked, 'remind me to audition for the part of Uncle Jack.' With cupped palms he kneaded the pebble-tipped softness of Helen's breasts, delighting in their resilience as they slid up and down and from side to side on her narrow chest. This was as far as she had typed. He was now in fine condition to devote himself wholeheartedly to her rather than to her work. He kissed a mole on her shoulder before leaning over and dragging the little right breast upwards to his mouth. The nipple responded fiercely to his sucking and Helen gasped.

'Let's do it properly,' she said, breaking away from her employer's embrace. 'You get me so worked up, I can't wait for it.'

She stood up and crossed the floor to the couch beneath the window. The skimpy red skirt dropped to the floor and the Captain knelt to ease down the tights and panties over her hips and bottom. As the pubic mound came into view, hardly darkened by the slight shading of silvery-yellow fluff through which could be seen the delicate vertical slit, he sniffed at her warmth and ran the point of his tongue up

17

the length of those puffy lips. Helen flinched as he flicked
at her clitoris. She flopped back on the coloured shawls
that draped the couch and parted her thighs lasciviously,
opening herself with her fingers and toying with the little
bud the Captain's tongue had brought to sudden stiffness.

By this time he had struggled out of his lower garments
and dived down to bury his face in the wet warmth so
eagerly offered to him. The girl's gleaming pink labia
seemed to close over his mouth and nose like an anaesthe-
tist's mask. He inhaled her sexual perfume, musky but
fresh, and lashed into her with sweeping strokes of his
tongue. At the top of each stroke he used the tip to prod
the engorged clit several times before slicing down and
plunging deep into the vaginal opening.

While his tongue was thus engaged, he could see nothing, his eyes being pressed against the base of Helen's
belly. But he allowed his hands to run over the cool
smoothness of her flanks, relishing the contrast between
the slightly muscular leanness of her thighs, the yielding
softness of her buttocks and the relative sharpness, though
sheathed in velvet-like skin, of her narrow hips. All these
subtly contrasting sensations, of course, were what one
might call external skin sensations. The Captain was fascinated and inflamed by the far greater contrast they col-
lectively made with the feeling of crisp, dry fuzz round the
bridge of his nose and the pulpy membranes in which he
was beginning to suffocate.

As he panted and spluttered into her vulva, Helen was
suddenly seized by the throes of orgasm. She clamped her
powerful young thighs together against his ears, threaten-
ing to crush his head like a nut. He felt the muscles of her
bottom tighten and her pubic hairs stood up on end. His
mouth was awash with the tide of lust that poured from
her cunt as her outstretched fists pounded against the
covers of the couch. And as she writhed and wallowed, his
firm prick swelled with impatient longing.

No sooner had the girl's thighs slackened than the Captain disengaged his lips and tongue from her hot and still
pulsing sex and began to drag his body up the length of

18

hers. The tip of his tongue led the way, lingering in the hollow of her rather large navel and dodging sideways to take in a long nipple and a fragrant armpit before licking over the neck and jaw and thrusting between her lips. During this upward progress his hairiness brushed over her smooth skin, which still glowed with the erotic flush that had raced down from her throat to her crotch beneath a thin, gleaming film of sweat. He saw her nostrils widen and her eyes light up at the proximity of her own cunt-cream smeared all over his face.

It was now necessary for him to raise his body and stoop his head right down in order to continue kissing her while bringing his hot loins into alignment with hers. The raising of his hips entailed by the action allowed the erection he had dragged up the couch to spring free. The knob splashed stickily into Helen's flowing juices and the whole length of the shaft pressed against her slit. Simply by easing back a couple of inches and then leaning forward the Captain was able to slip the cockhead into her opening. Once lodged there it seemed to grow of its own accord, doubling its thickness and distending to fill her belly to bursting.

A second orgasm was sending its powerful waves through the girl's body and these waves were communicated through the stretched vagina to the Captain's member. He lifted his head and gazed down into her dark, dreamy eyes. 'Know what?' he whispered. 'You're wanking me with your cunt.'

Helen had to wait for a brief interval between the orgasmic waves to reply. 'You know me by now,' she said. 'I've got these incredibly strong muscles down there. If I come with a guy inside me I sometimes squeeze him right out like a champagne cork. Hold on tight now and see if you can give me the feeling of being properly fucked by a live cock instead of a dead dildo. Come on, now – give it to me hard and fast.'

In a great burst of passion the Captain began to fuck her furiously. The spunk boiled in his loins, gathered itself in a mass of unbearable sensation and exploded into the

19

depths of the twitching cunt. Helen screamed aloud as he gushed into her. He was convinced that he actually climaxed twice with no intermission to the pulsing flow of sperm.

At last he had emptied himself. As he lay sprawled on top of Helen, his slowly shrinking prick still bathing in her flooded quim, he caught snatches of a raucous voice raised above the traffic noises in the market below: 'Hey Sharon – gentleman here wants a nice soft pear. Just let him have a feel, will you, love?'

TWO

THE VISUAL ANGLE

He must have dozed. When the buzzer ripped through his consciousness his limp member was resting cold and sticky on one thigh while his other leg was still stretched over his editorial assistant's bare bottom. Helen was fully awake, unsure whether to risk his displeasure by climbing out from under him to deal with the insistent buzzing. The Captain glanced at his watch and remembered he was expecting a visit from Anne Amory and Carla Merryweather.

He untangled himself from Helen and dragged his jeans on, not bothering to pull up the zip. Helen hurried with her clothes to the little adjoining kitchenette. The Captain shouted into the entryphone and pressed the button to admit his visitors; as the atmosphere in the room was heavy with sex, he raised the sash of the dusty window. This let in a cool draught and the roar of traffic and chaffering from the market down below, where busty Sharon was still trying to tempt gentlemen to finger a nice soft pear.

Anne and Carla entered the office, slightly flushed from their ascent of the steep stairs. In the case of Anne, the flush seemed also to be partly a symptom of embarrassment; her violet eyes avoided the Captain's gaze, he noticed, when he approached to kiss both girls on the cheek. 'Well now,' he said, 'you haven't changed a bit, my dears. If anything, you look lovelier than ever.'

And indeed, the two girls now displayed all the youthful freshness that had first attracted him to them, as well as a

21

new-found poise. This poise was more marked in Carla than in her chum. Carla, to be sure, had shown a kind of precocious sophistication even when she was only sixteen and the Captain, in his capacity as temporary odd job man, was taking full advantage of the young ladies of Cunlip College. Her friend Anne Amory had always been a little bit awkward; her charm lay in her ability to use this awkwardness as a come-on, and the ability was very evident now as she simpered and smiled coyly at the Captain. The pretty pair must by now be nineteen, he calculated, and, as he had already observed, in their different ways they combined the girlish attractions he had enjoyed in their Cunlip days with the riper allurements of early womanhood.

Carla Merryweather stood there looking quite the young lady. She wore a smart two-piece suit in charcoal grey over a white blouse that buttoned up to the throat. Her tights or stockings were vivid red and her shoes black. Her raven-black hair, which the Captain remembered cascading down over her shoulders, was now piled up on her head and fixed there professionally. Anne, with her blonde fringe and pretty curls hanging loose to her shoulders, had gone for an agreeably contrasting effect, as the Captain saw when she slipped off her lightweight raincoat. A crisp, light blue dress with a broad black belt gave her something of the appearance of a nurse, although the black mesh that emphasised the shapeliness of her ankles, calves and knees might have been deemed unsuitable attire on the wards.

'Helen, bring some coffee up to the studio, will you,' he called to his assistant, leading his two visitors to the door by which they had entered the office and up the narrow, uncarpeted stairs to the second floor. Ahead lay the door to his on-the-job living quarters. To the left was a large room to the front of the building, directly above the first-floor office. They entered.

It was necessary to get the girls relaxed and ready to go, so he sat them side by side on a little couch and sank into an armchair facing them. Anne and Carla took in the details of a professional or semiprofessional photographer's studio: a dressing table, lights, tripods and umbrella-like flash reflectors, a tangle of cables, a large screen of crinkly foil beside a frame draped with pink paper. There was also a jumble of costumes and props, among them a fierce-looking stuffed Alsatian. The curtains were closed and the room rather dimly lit by a couple of spotlights directed at a small dais.

'Lovely to see you again, my dears,' the Captain began. 'We haven't met since you helped me to look after those dreadful Americans a couple of years ago, have we? How are you keeping, then?'

'We manage to find a fair bit of fun,' replied Carla, rather doubtfully. 'You know we're sharing this flat in Earl's Court, don't you? I mean we're sharing it with a couple of blokes, but we have our own rooms, mind, and keep ourselves pretty much to ourselves on the whole. Well, Anne and me share one room and the guys have the other two most of the time. We make ends meet, just about. Anne draws benefit and stays at home to do the cooking and stuff while I go out temping. But it's great that you've got a bit of work for us. Thought you said it was something to do with publishing, though.'

'It is,' he explained. 'That was the office you saw downstairs. We haven't actually gone into production yet, but our first batch of paperbacks ought to be out by May, in plenty of time to catch the best of the beach trade, see. What I do up here is illustrations to go inside some of the books and pictures for the covers. It's a spot of modelling I'm offering you. When the weather warms up a bit get in touch again and I'll have some outdoor work for you. Maybe for your flatmates too.'

'What sort of books, then?'

The Captain sat back and looked at them across his joined fingers. 'Well, we're bringing them out under the imprint "The Honeymooners Library", which'll give you the general idea. They're novels, spicy ones. That's why I call the office my Palace of Eros. Yes, quite spicy.'

Little Anne gave him a bashful glance. 'What they call "romantic"?' she asked. 'You know, those bodice rippers?'

'Well, no,' he replied. 'They're a little bit stronger than

that. It's a competitive industry, so we've got to grab our readers by the balls, if you'll pardon the expression. Catchy titles, stunning covers and above all some first-rate illustrations to spice it all up.'

'So what are these saucy books like?' Carla pressed him.

'There's going to be a lot of variety. Newly commissioned work and reprints of old erotic classics are the main things, of course. Some of them will be quite sophisticated and literary – you can get away with really intellectual stuff as long as it's got plenty of sex. But until we've made our name we can't afford to be too subtle. I wanted to move straight into the mafia end of the market with a dreadful thing called *Teenagers and Dogs*. See Fido over there? The stuffed Alsatian? He was going to feature in the cover picture. But we were warned off anything with animals – our legal people didn't like it.'

At this point Helen appeared with the coffee and biscuits. The visitors rose and embraced their old Cunlip contemporary; it was through her that the Captain had been able to make contact with them. Before she left the studio she winked at him and told him to stamp on the floor if he needed any help with the pictures.

Evidently nervous, Anne nearly choked on a biscuit crumb. The Captain was afraid she wanted to back out of this assignment, but her friend Carla did all she could to encourage her and to promote an atmosphere of lively abandon. 'Isn't it exciting to be with the Captain again?' she said, squeezing Anne's knee. 'There's always so much talk about him from Melanie and Miss MacDonald and that crowd that it's hard to believe we've only fucked with him once. At least, I think we have. Remember the time?'

Anne blushed. 'Course I do. It was Melanie's dorm feast. We'd all had a bit too much to drink.'

'We played that game when he had to keep moving from girl to girl, remember? Wasn't it your cunt he finally shot his load in?'

Anne glared at her indignantly. 'No way. I wouldn't have let a stranger like he was then do that to me. When I felt him getting too lively I twisted sideways so he popped out. It was Helen who got flooded with all that white stuff.'

24

The Captain confirmed this. 'She was so tight in those days – well, she still is – so tight she gripped you like one of those things for sucking the air out of wine bottles. Lucky to pull out of her the first time round. The second time I knew I'd had it the moment I got stuck in. She just gripped me and it all burst out. But I remember it was Anne's little tits I was looking at when it happened. They still as pretty as ever, then?'

Carla was getting into the spirit of this conversation over the coffee and biscuits. She lunged at the front of Anne's dress and started scrabbling at the buttons. But the Captain could see that the blonde girl wasn't quite ready yet for this kind of horseplay. He asked them both to sit demurely side by side with their cups in their hands while he took a perfectly innocent photograph. But Carla was already aroused and not to be easily diverted. 'Pity we can't do it with that dog,' she said. 'We make a lovely pair of teenagers, Anne and me.'

The Captain couldn't help agreeing. In support of this last proposition he went over to a table where he rummaged for a moment in a large folder. Returning to the girls, he handed them a set of five sepia-tinted photographs. 'Remember these?' he asked. 'Some of those old-style pictures we took to fool the Americans. And fool them they certainly did – they never challenged their authenticity, you know. Just as well they didn't recognise your faces when you and the others had to entertain them.'

Anne perked up at the sight of the photos for which she and her friend had modelled on that tipsy occasion. 'Oh, look,' she laughed. 'There's that cute little Darcy. We're all got up like old-fashioned school kids, with Miss Muttock as teacher.'

The five pictures all showed the same static pose from different angles so that none of the interesting details was missed. The group was dominated by the standing figure of the slim and lovely Miss Muttock, formerly principal of Cunlip College but forced into premature retirement by a scandal involving the Captain and a number of the girls. This lady was attired in a mortar board and black academic gown which had fallen open to reveal her pale nudity. Her loins were thrust forward lewdly as she stood with feet straddled wide apart and pulled open the lips of her fanny.

Between her legs on the grass (for this was an open-air occasion) lay three young people, two of whom were Anne Amory and Carla Merryweather. Anne and Carla were lying facing each other on their sides, their heads behind their former Principal's feet, their waists between them and their legs projecting in front. The two girls, however, were not touching each other. Between them, but pointing in the other directon, a young lad sat with legs outstretched supporting himself on his straightened arms so that his face was close to the standing woman's cunt.

The three youngsters were dressed, or partly dressed, in the school costume of those far-off days. Anne and Carla wore voluminous white blouses with long black gym slips and black woollen stockings; the gym slips had been pulled right up above their navels. The black (or sepia) contrasted strikingly with the shining whiteness of their bellies, bottoms and upper thighs; these white expanses furnished a further contrast with the darkly fleeced delta adorning Carla's crotch and Anne's tiny triangle of blonde fur. To enhance this spectacle they had lifted the knees of their upper legs so that they lay there with open thighs.

The boy, his hair parted in the middle and slicked down, was equipped with nothing but a black waistcoat and jacket with a broad white Eton collar. But by flicking through the pictures, Anne and Carla soon reminded themselves that this was not quite his only equipment.   all came back to them as they recalled the lewd event. Propping himself up, the lad was extending an eager tongue which almost reached Miss Muttock's gaping vulva. But if his tongue was eager, that was nothing compared to the state of his slim, stiff penis. The girls, facing inwards, had laid their cheeks on his thighs. They too had extended their tongues but in their case the tips actually reached the goal. As if supported by their feathery touch, Darcy's penis stretched between them, a droplet of clear liquid visibly gathering on its tip.

mmodest though this posture was, his young supporters' private parts were not completely exposed to the probing eye of the camera. Their perineums at least were hidden, but not in a way that could help to calm Anne's racing heart as she stared at the photos. The boy's fingers had reached between the tops of the girls' thighs and rested on their bare bottoms; each of the four buttocks was seen to be dimpled by a pair of his fingertips pressing into it. The pressure he thus exerted had given him a firmer purchase as he used his thumbs to plug their cunts.

The Captain could see that by now Anne was not only blushing but trembling from the effects of these saucy pictures. When she had posed for them she had probably been too tipsy to realise what she was doing; now, two years later, her self-image was under assault from the indiscreet past. He glanced at Carla and inclined his head meaningfully. Carla placed a hand on Anne's thigh, squeezed it and smiled broadly.

'Didn't we have fun?' she giggled. ' feel all damp down there just from looking at them. How about you, Anne?'

She moved her hand under Anne's dress, sliding the hem up as she stroked the white flesh between the girl's stocking top and the tiny triangle of white cotton material which had come into view. Anne's response was to throw her arms round Carla's neck and bury her face in her bosom. At the same time it seemed to the Captain that she parted her thighs almost imperceptibly and edged her bottom slightly forward to the edge of the couch. Her knickers were drawn tighter over the bulge of her sex and a marked division appeared between the two plump outer lips. Where the material was dragged into the central rift, it rapidly darkened with a spreading stain.

Anne's resistance was now broken. Her more self-confident friend had been game all along. Spurred on by the sight of his prick, which had grown, forced its way out of his open flies and reared its head up into proud erection, the two girls proved even more eager to model for him now than they had been on that earlier occasion.

First he got them to stand on the dais side by side, each

27

with an arm round the other's shoulder. Carla opened her smart jacket, unbuttoned her blouse and slipped one strap of her bra down so that she could coax a breast out of its black lace restraint. Anne reached across with her free hand to pinch the nipple, which stuck out between her thumb and forefinger. Her own dress was hitched up round her waist and she had pulled her knickers halfway down her thighs. Carla's fingers were playing in the silky blonde hair at the base of Anne's belly. The Captain came over to adjust the postion of this titillating hand so that, without obstructing the view, the middle finger was able to dabble among the folds of pulpy pink flesh. This operation allowed him, without alarming the unsuspecting girl, to stick a finger of his own into that tight young cunt.

Having arranged the lighting to his satisfaction, the Captain moved a tripod mounted with a medium-format Hasselblad into position, peered down into the viewfinder with satisfaction and took a number of shots as the girls moved about slightly without losing the basic pose. He would select the best one for professional purposes and put the others in one of his private albums. No book, as yet, existed which could be suitably illustrated by this scene. Still, he could surely get one of his authors to write one around it.

Next he went for a cover picture. Covers, as he explained to his models as they changed behind the couch, had to be a bit less provocative than the illustrations inside. Keen though he was to extend the limits of public taste he could not afford to alienate the patrons of the supermarket chain Bigbuys, contracted as his main retail outlet. Bums were permitted, but not nipples or pubic hair; Carla's playful offer to shave hers off was laughingly dismissed.

The book he had in mind was the one Helen was copy-editing for him, *Two Flappers in Monte Carlo*. Carla put on an ankle-length skirt of white chiffon, white gloves and a white straw hat with a mauve band around its crown. A little top that went with the skirt was donned by Anne. It had padded shoulders and long sleeves. He made the pair stand facing a backdrop which carried a blown-up repre-

28

sentation of the exterior of the celebrated casino. Anne stood to the left of Carla and rested her hand on Carla's right shoulder. Carla's gloved right hand grasped the handle of a furled silk parasol; her left one lay on her friend's bottom, which looked very bare beneath the little white jacket that reached to just above the small of her back. Instead of placing the camera directly behind the two chums, the Captain stood it somewhere to the right, so that the curve of Carla's right breast would be visible with just a hint of nipple – not enough, he hoped, to upset the Bigbuys clientèle and spoil the book's commercial chances.

When a few shots were successfully in the can the girls were about to slip out of their abbreviated Edwardian finery when he stopped them. 'What we can't show outside has to go inside,' he said. 'The next one can be a frontispiece. Turn round and face the camera. First let's have one with you standing side by side again, but this time I want Carla to put a hand on Anne's tummy – no, it mustn't hide the fur – and Anne to reach round behind Carla and under her armpit to fondle her tit. That's it. Great. Right, next you must face each other, sideways-on to the camera, and embrace. Yes. Make sure I can see that tit, Carla. That's the way – pull it sideways so it's sort of on the outside of Anne's bodice.'

By this time both girls were enjoying themselves immensely. He judged the time was ripe for the main business of the session, a shot of little Evelyn and Nora being fucked by Uncle Jack. Or maybe a couple of shots.

If he was to play the part of Uncle Jack himself (and who else was available at this pressing moment?) he would need Helen to operate the camera. He directed Anne and Carla to follow his example by stripping down to their skins. They both seemed surprised to see him do this and poor Anne was clearly in a state of some confusion. She kept glancing towards the door as if hoping that escape would be possible if proceedings became too hot for her.

In response to a couple of blows on the floor administered with one of the shoes he had taken off, the Captain summoned his young assistant up from the office. Helen knew already what was required of her. She made straight for a camera he had set up beside a bed in a corner of the studio which had been got up to look like part of a hotel bedroom. Carla encouraged Anne to get up on the bed with her; the Captain made them kneel side by side, their faces down on the covers and their bottoms sticking up in the air. Having adjusted the lighting and checked that the focus was right he let Helen begin by photographing the two bottoms. Just where the buttocks curved downwards to meet the smooth tops of the models' thighs, two plump quims pouted out at the camera, one fringed with silky, dark brown curls and the other adorned with fuzz so fine and fair that it was normally almost invisible. On this occasion, however, its owner's recent activities had fetched forth some drops of moisture which gleamed like jewels in the studio lighting.

Telling the girls to make room for him, the Captain jumped on the bed to kneel between them facing the camera. His prick stood up hard against his belly. He did not really know if this image would be acceptable for a picture inside the book. Even if it would be, for some reason he felt uneasy displaying himself like this to all and sundry. By squeezing the head of the member he forced it to droop. It was still fat and twice its usual length, but now curved downwards, hanging over his heavy balls without actually resting on them. He had pulled the foreskin modestly over the tip, which was now reasserting its wish to show itself ready for action.

As he knelt there, he placed a hand on each of the two pretty behinds. The index fingers fitted over the arseholes and along the central rifts of their sex. 'Ready, girls?' he asked. Without waiting for a reply he plunged the tips of the fingers into their vaginas and told Helen to activate the shutter.

For the next picture, 'Uncle Jack' made sure that the girls were kneeling right on the edge of the bed so that he could stand between the projecting calves of 'Evelyn' (played by Carla). His cock had reared up to full stretch once more. He parted the juicy cuntlips and penetrated her

30

without provoking a word of protest. The blonde 'Nora' whimpered slightly as he cupped a hand under the pouch of her sex and tickled her clitoris with his forefinger while jamming his thumb up her love channel as far as it would go. He found her wet and tight, tighter on his intrusive thumb than Carla was on his prick. Then he pulled halfway out of both of them to expose the sticky wetness on him for the benefit of the camera.

If ever an illustration needed to be one of a pair, this was it. The Captain disconnected himself from the kneeling girls and rapidly shifted his position so that Carla accommodated two of his fingers while Anne received the well-lubricated head of his cock. Having forced the entrance, he ran it up the full length until his pubic hairs scoured the soft curves of her bottom. Anne, who had squealed at his first shove, now sighed, closed her eyes and pushed back against him. Helen moved the tripod and splayed its legs wider, enabling her to point the camera upwards and take in a view of two bellies and pubic mounds with the rogering fingers and penis working them to a frenzy.

This time the Captain could wait no longer for the release of his pent-up lust. To give himself a firm purchase as he thrust, he pressed the flanks of the young ladies tightly together, his left hand on Anne's hip and his right one between Carla's thighs, the inserted fingers dragging her sideways by the cunt. He rammed and bucked against Anne's bottom until he was on the point of bursting. With one final thrust he drove right up into the girl's belly; she cried out as he jabbed against her womb, then sent a succession of muscular contractions shimmering down the tightness of her vagina until his sperm exploded and sluiced in great waves into her panting body. Before he withdrew completely Helen made him hold the pose for a moment while she took a close-up of the point of juncture, showing the masses of spunk oozing from the tight seal of flesh and beginning to slip down the inside of Anne's left thigh.

The three participants in this lustful scene rested side by side on their backs, gasping to regain their breath and composure. The Captain lay in the middle, cradling the heads of the two friends in his armpits and gently fondling their breasts. He was surprised that their old college chum Helen had so little to say to them, or they to her. Could Helen be jealous? Perhaps a likelier explanation was that Anne and Carla had always been so close to each other; their relationship might be a very exclusive one, off-putting to outsiders of the same sex.

Meanwhile Helen was drifting around the studio and had stumbled on the forged photographs of the two girls with Darcy O'Flammery and Mary Muttock. An intense look came into her eye. 'Let's all do it like this,' she suggested. Then, leaving her black sweater in place, she proceeded to strip off her short red skirt. She had not bothered to put her tights and knickers back on after the recent bout with her employer. In no time she was standing over the bed, dragging the trio to their feet and spreading a blanket for them on the bare boards of the floor.

Using the pictures as a guide and reminder, the Captain sat up with his legs stretched out in front of him like young Darcy. To his left, Carla lay on her left side with her left cheek on his thigh; Anne assumed a similar position on the other side and he felt both of them breathing on the slackness of his moist genitals. Their nipples pressed into the smooth skin of his sides like hard peas. They raised their upper knees in silent invitation for him. He discovered it was not easy as might be supposed to imitate Darcy's pose; if he had tried to begin his fingering of both cunts simultaneously he would have fallen backwards. Accordingly, he first grabbed Carla by the crotch with his left hand; his fingers curled over her buttocks while his thumb slid into her buttery quim. Then it was Anne's turn. With Anne, as usual, he experienced the added thrill of her lovely, juicy tightness. The pad of his thumb played around for a while among the sweet fleshy folds, brushing a couple of times over the distended bud of her lust, before forcing its way in. He moved it from side to side, stretching the elastic muscles of the canal, and Anne moaned softly. The constricting sheath was slippery with the sperm he had so recently deposited there.

The Captain was less lithe and athletic than Darcy. The girls could hardly be expected to support his full weight on their pussies. His back was aching. 'Get on with it,' he pleaded, gritting his teeth.

Helen Lascelles placed a foot on each side of the statuesque group, edging forward until her plump mound with its fair, downy hair and prominent pink lips hovered an inch in front of the Captain's mouth. Realising that he was having difficulty holding himself in position, she relinquished the hands-on-hips attitude adopted by Miss Muttock in the pictures and instead reached behind his neck to cradle his head and press it against her sex.

Just as the point of his tongue tasted the sharp but syrupy juice gathering between the lips of her fanny, two other tongues went to work, lapping away at his limp manhood. The slight movement of their heads occasioned by this operation communicated itself down their bodies and seemed to terminate in a twitching of their bottoms and cunts. His fingers struck up a lively dance both outside and inside. Soon the hot blood started to pump into his prick, which uncurled itself from the cushioning scrotum and reared up, a shining purple-tipped column scaled by two lascivious tongues.

`Anne and Carla licked his cock and used their fingers to toy with his balls; the Captain lashed into Helen's slit with his tongue and ransacked the other two cunts with his fingers, relishing the contrast between Carla's capacious passage awash with her own fluids and Anne's narrower vessel still foaming with his semen.

All four of them were working flat out. But Helen, with a knowing wickedness that belied her years, pointed out that it would be fun if they tried to adjust the pace of their activities in order to target a simultaneous orgasm.

This proved to be by no means easy. They all seemed to be talking together, urging the others to go faster or slower and hardly able to tell who was addressing whom.

From her superior position standing above them, Helen had a good oversight of operations and soon assumed control. Calling out for silence, she explained that the only thing needed was a shout from each of them to indicate imminent climax. Whoever was ministering to that person's pleasure would then have to hold back until Helen saw that all four, including herself, were ready for release. She would then give the signal.

At it they went. Very soon the Captain found it almost impossible to contain himself any longer. 'Stop!' he cried. The two tongues locked rigid against the base of his cock and the two hands maintained a steady pressure on his balls, just enough to hold him in tensed equilibrium.

Carla was the next to plead for respite. He held her firmly between the fingers spread on her bum and the thumb lodged up her quim. She trembled. He felt her nipples lengthening and digging into his side.

Then it was the standing Helen. She squeezed his face tight against her pubic mound, begging him to take it easy. She was peering down under her left arm, watching Anne for the first sign that the blonde girl was approaching her peak. The only movement now was the frenzied churning of the Captain's right thumb in Anne's bubbling insides and the twitching of the girl's body. Beads of sweat had formed on her skin; the muscles of her flushed belly and slight limbs quivered and strained.

Anne was too far gone to articulate her condition. As the lust exploded within her she tugged at the Captain's scrotum and let her tongue lash wildly at his stem. 'Come!' yelled Helen. 'Everybody come!'

Fingers and tongues unfroze. Everybody came. The lens of the abandoned Hasselblad 500C/M stared blindly at this passionate scene. Only the eye of the security camera above them, disguised as a fire alarm, witnessed and recorded for later scrutiny the fountain of sperm that shot up vertically from the upright phallus to spatter the Captain's chin and the underside of his tongue as well as the youthful pussy into which that tongue was thrusting.

The next Tuesday morning he took his work upstairs to bed with him for an hour or so. He also took Helen, leaving the answering machine to cope with any business that

might develop. He was getting very close to Helen, much
closer than he had been to Gloria when she was first his
research student and then his assistant at the Honeymoon
Palace Motel. This was in spite of the fact that he didn't
really like Helen. His taste was really for delicate, refined
and rather squeamish girls. Helen might be described as
delicate; she always seemed to have this slightly shagged-
out look. But the main thing about her was that she was a
slut, though a devoted one.

The work he took to bed with him was the scruffy manuscript of one of the most illiterate and execrably typed
novels that had so far been submitted to the Honeymooners Library. The title was *Fucky Days* and the author
had signed the covering note 'Annon'. This 'Annon' was
likely to be female, like the narrator of the story; the Captain doubted whether such an unsophisticated writer would
have attempted to get inside the head of a character of the
opposite sex. No, this stuff was probably straight auto-
biography, a literal transcription of her 'fucky' existence.

The Captain plodded through a tedious and rather taste-
less account of how this female got up one bright morning,
then went to the loo, then had a fucky of breakfast, then did
the washing-up and then tidied her flat. Then she ventured
fòrth to see what the day had to offer. It was only when
she was standing at the bus stop that he perked up a bit.
He had been reading on automatic and had failed to latch
on to the way this girl had dressed herself. Or perhaps the
writer had failed to divulge this rather crucial information
until she had her standing there waiting for the bus. Helen
was asleep at his side, so he couldn't consult her. From this
point the Captain scanned the text more attentively.

This bloke standing next to me give me a funny look.
Must of been because I had on one of these semi-trans-
parrant mack's I suppose with nothing under. I got this
naturel read hair see down there as well as on my head
so it sort of shows through. He stares at me and comes
right up close so he's trying to xxxx squint down between my clevidge but this macks buttonned right up to

35

throat. Well there is limits, thats what my Kev says. But this guys so close I can feel his breath on my face so maybe thats what makes my nipples get hard so their sticking out all dark under the see through plastic. I got these big orrioles I think my Kev calls them. Anyway I feel a bit embarased with him standing so close but then a gain its usefull because these old cows in queu cant see I got nothing on under mack.

Hadnt' twigged when I put it on it was more like fully transparant than semi, when light shines straight on it from front like when I looked in mirrer you cant see-through see. Then the bloke speak to me in wisper, hop you dont mind me standing so close dear, we dont want them old cows to see as you given me this hardon. Then he gets this little box out a his pocket, its got tabs in it and before I know what hapening he pops two in me mouth, their all fizy. Then bus comes and we get on and I cant stop him sitting next to me. Must of been them tabs I feel all hot and flushed and sort of funny down their like when Kev does me know what I mean. What I done then I undone buttons down as far as waste to let air in. Then conductor comes up, indian wose usuly very frendly. Says I dont lik the cut of your ~~gibe~~ jib young lady and turns me off bus.

Well I feel so hot standing their outside public bath's I decide to go in and have a bit of swiming. Course I cant reelly swim but the way I feel from them tabs I feel like I can do any thing. So what I done I walk in and in stead of buying a tiket from shy young guy behind little window I lean forward and stick out bear tity to give him a treat. Then I march straight on into the mens changeing room, I couldnt' give a toss. I dodge into an empty cubical and slip of mack and shoes then without looking right or left and totaly ingnoring wolf wistles I run starkers through shower part and out to swiming pool.

Then I jump in with great splash, luckilly it must of been shalow end. Dont feel quite so much centre of atention no more now Im up to neck in water and just sort of flounder a round for abit enjoying feel of water on bear body. It was lovely not having ~~biokin~~ bikini interfearing with freedom to wollow and let water get at parts I usuly keep privet.

Some young girls in black one peace costumes start playing with me, they dive between my legs' and sort of brush against my tittys', I try to get a way but loose my balence and go under. They have to rescue me all gigly and the bigest one actuly puts her hand on my thing, she pulls the hairs. There teacher it must of been comes over and tells them its time to get out. Its just me and these 3 guys left in pool but lots of kid's runing round the edge.

Before I know whats hapening one of these hansom blokes dips under water and sticks his head between my legs and stands up with your's truely sitting on his shouldiers like in a piggy ~~bank~~ back but other way round so his chins sticking into my cunt. Yes I blush when I think about it now it was so rude but when it hapened I was all exited it must of been them tabs what the man give me. I heard one of the school girls scream out look she's got read hairs all over her pussy miss. Me I just stuck my tong out laughing.

Then the other 2 guys swim up to us and takle this one Im on his shouldiers so he falls under water draging me with him. I swalow lots of horid tasteing water but they all pull me out so I can breath then they fight each other just larking about reely, trying to get hold of me and press there hard dicks up against me. Im sure one of them got his dick out of his trunks and was trying to do me under the water or even bugar me like what my Kev try to do that time round the back of the boozer.

We see an attendent coming down from deep end to sort out trouble with school kids, there quareling and kicking up stink trying to push littlest girl in water and the teacher cant' do nothing with them. Well we dont want him to see me in the nude though I dont give a toss my self its my 3 escorts what dont want no agrovation so 2 of them clime out then they pull me out of

37

water with other one under me pushing me up with his hand in my xxxx croch. Then they rush me into changeing room before attendent can see whats up.

Well whats up, youve guest it 3 big fat dicks was up and before you could say fuck me they was right up my cunt one after the other in one of them ~~cubbie~~ cubicals. It seemed like the cold water made them abit narow and thin but extra hard and there nobs was dark blue. And because of cold water Im all tight and narow two though the fucking soon losen me up. How they done it in that tight place, I mean the cubical not my cunt, well one of them stick it in me standing up while I cling to his neck and rap leg's round him he got his hands under my bum like. Then number 2 come up behind me and sticks his up my bumb hole. There mate stands on bench and I turn my head side ways and take him in my mouth. So their I am with 3 cocks in me at once and whats more they all mannage to come more or less at the same time.

Well I dont know if its still the affect of them tabs or maybe Im just geting exited but any way as soon as they shoot there load's I come out of cubical and see all these men and boys gorping at me so I laid down on wet tiles and let them all do me one after an other 'till Im streaming with there cum and reely need to go in shour but in stead I grab my mack and try to cover-up because I heard police sirens out side. They put me under a rest and say I may have to be ~~repri~~manded in custardy, in next Chapter I will right a bout what they done to me in the sells.

The Captain was beginning to regret that this material was so unprintable. Before he was able to start the next chapter or to use Helen, dozing contentedly beside him, to relieve the pressure it had generated in his loins, he heard the buzzer downstairs and remembered that he had an appointment. Leaving the girl in his bed he slipped into a black dressing gown, grabbed the dog-eared manuscript and hurried down the narrow stairs to admit his visitor.

While he waited for this person to come up from the street below, he glanced at his diary to remind himself who it was. Yes, that was it – one Victoria Eisenberg, who had responded to an advertisement he had placed in a number of likely publications. The ad invited applications from graphic artists and book illustrators with a keen interest in the adult market.

'Come!' he called, reacting to a tap on the office door. It swung open and in marched a tall, efficient-looking, thirty-something lady in severe business dress and seriously sophisticated makeup. Probably what they called a power dresser, he thought. Her flaxen blonde hair was swept back into a bun on the back of her head. She carried a large portfolio. 'Ah Miz Eisenberg, I take it,' he gushed, rising to greet her and take her hand. 'Do be seated, my dear lady.'

Victoria Eisenberg evidently combined qualities of steely resolve and icy disdain. All attempts to flirt with her or to deflect the angle of her gaze towards the opening in the front of his dressing gown got the Captain precisely no-where, but once he closed the loosely hanging garment and opened a discussion of his business and her work she showed energy and enthusiasm. Her portfolio contained artwork of the highest standard; indeed, the Captain was not sure he didn't find it even more erotic than the kind of photography he was so keen on. With the possibility of line drawings like this, it would be truly difficult to decide which books should be illustrated by this talented artist and which by his own efforts behind (and sometimes in front of) the camera.

So impressed was the Captain with this applicant's work as well as with her personal attributes that he decided then and there to put her on the Honeymooners payroll. He knew better, however, than to tell her that immediately, and left her sitting opposite him at the desk while he worked his way slowly through the contents of her portfolio. Every now and then he let out a low whistle, but Ms Eisenberg sat there apparently unmoved.

Helen breezed into the room in black knickers and bra.

'Whoops! Sorry, sir,' she said, with a wriggle of her narrow hips. 'Didn't know you were engaged.'

The Captain looked up and gave her a sly wink. 'Not to worry, dear,' he replied. 'Just be a good girl, would you, and get a cup of tea for Miz Eisenberg here.'

Helen slipped into the little kitchenette and switched the kettle on. From the office she was clearly visible as she stood at the sink and washed out a couple of cups and saucers. The Eisenberg woman took a drawing pad and pencil from her large handbag and began to sketch the girl in bold sinuous lines. When she had finished the picture she tore it off the pad and placed it nonchalantly on the desk. The Captain gasped at the sensuality captured in this striking likeness.

He adopted what was meant to be a critical expression and continued to examine the portfolio. But instead of sitting meekly while her professional fate was decided, this self-assured woman strode to the kitchenette and got Helen to perch on a stool while she sketched some more studies of her.

The next time the Captain looked up from the artwork on his desk, Helen had removed her black bra.

The time after that, she was perched on the stool with her bottom bare.

The third time, the two women had moved out of sight. The kettle had switched itself off. From the kitchenette came a deep purring sound, interspersed with Helen's giggles.

THREE

NEW RECRUITS

The sounds from the kitchenette had become quieter. They had nearly stopped altogether, apart from the occasional squeal of protest or purr of pleasure. The Captain sat at his desk and tried to concentrate on Victoria Eisenberg's portfolio.

One by one he turned over the sheets of heavy cartridge paper, some quite small but most of them the size of an open atlas. What he saw almost converted him from the art of photography, so suggestive, so sensual and so *real* were these erotic drawings. Nudes and semi-nudes of both sexes, singly and in pairs and groups, followed in rapid succession as he worked through the collection. Some of the models displayed themselves in lascivious poses while others were engaged in acts of sex with themselves or their eager partners.

Three sheets were clipped together. The first showed twenty representations of a fine breast, arranged in four rows of five. In the top left hand corner it was depicted in its normal condition, pert and shining but with the nipple soft, pale and not much more than a bump in the middle of a tender-looking areola. It was then shown going through every stage of arousal until, at the bottom right of the sheet, the teat had become a long, hard stalk of toughened flesh springing from the tightly puckered darkness around it. The means of arousal were left to the imagination; it was as if, between the pictures, things were

41

being done to the owner of the breast which caused this dramatic localised reaction.

On the second sheet Ms Eisenberg had drawn twenty sets of male genitalia, or rather the same one twenty times over, the phallus growing even more dramatically from its hooded, flaccid state to full erection. Indeed, she had not just taken it to erection but to ejaculation. In the first sketch on the bottom row there was already the hint of a clear droplet welling up from the little slot on the tip. Successive pictures showed the fluid gathering until it spilt down one side of the engorged bulb and formed into a viscous rope that stretched across the down-drawn foreskin and was beginning to crawl down the stem towards the bulging, hairy ballsack below. Finally, the slot had widened as a beautifully drawn stream of white semen gushed forth. How the effect of sudden movement had been achieved was beyond the Captain's comprehension.

As he expected, the theme of the third sheet was the development of a richly haired vulva from neat, tight dryness to blatant readiness for penetration. The contrast was immense, but the intermediate stages showed slight and subtle gradations until the point, at the start of the bottom row, where the stickily engorged lips suddenly fell apart to display the gaping channel of a cunt craving to be filled with hot cock.

The sound of a dropped cup breaking on the floor of the kitchenette was followed by giggles and then by rhythmical sighs. The Captain turned the sheet and found himself examining what looked like a large comic strip. Some of the separate frames bore neatly written captions and speech and thinking balloons hovered around the characters' heads. The strip was headed 'A SCENE FROM *FANNY HILL*: A Party of Pleasure beside the Thames'.

Two pretty young ladies were depicted in the company of two gallants in the gardens of an elegant riverside mansion. Beside the water was pitched a gaily striped marquee or pavilion. Taking a turn on the wide lawn, these beaux and their belles were attired in the elegant finery of the eighteenth century. From their deportment one might suppose all four, and not just the gentlemen, to belong to the higher reaches of society. The Captain, of course, was well aware that Fanny and Emily were in fact a pair of accomplished young whores who had been hired out to these rakes for a day of debauchery.

The next frames showed the inside of the pavilion, extending right out on one side into the river. Tables were laid with sumptuous refreshments; the gay structure was richly carpeted and furnished with couches and plump cushions. Fanny and Emily were being undressed by their young men. This process was spread over several frames and it was apparent that Ms Eisenberg had taken great care in researching the costume and especially the underwear of the period.

When the girls had been reduced to nakedness, they first held their hands in mock coyness over their private parts. The caption to this frame read: 'Our hands screened all from the tufted cliff downwards, till . . .' And beneath the next picture, illustrating the words, the sentence continued: '. . . we took them away at their desire, and employed them in helping them off with their clothes . . .' This extended commentary concluded under the third frame of the sequence: '. . . in the process of which, there pass'd all the little wantonnesses and frolicks that you may easily imagine.'

In fact, not too much had been left to the imagination; or rather, the imagination was fed a diet of richly stimulating visual details on which to exercise its creativity. The 'frolicking' mentioned in the caption involved, as the archaic spelling could have suggested, a good deal of playful tongue-work administered by Emily to her handsome and virile friend, who stood before her as naked as the girl herself. This rake's member was hidden from view within her mouth but the artist had drawn the other spark holding up the front of his shirt to display his own equipment for Fanny's inspection. A thought balloon floated above Fanny's head: 'He is shewing it me at so upright a stand as prepares me for his application to me for instant ease.'

In the next picture a large balloon containing spoken words issued from her mouth: 'A little suspense will only set a keener edge on the pleasure, sir. Let us shew our friends an example of continency, which they are giving signs of losing respect to.' And, to confirm this observation, Emily's escort appeared already to have inserted a finger between the lips of her cunt.

Fanny and her partner were then shown leading Emily and her young man into the water. Caption: 'We lav'd and wanton'd, or sportively play'd with our companions.' This prepared the way for a larger picture, filling the height of two rows, in which the two young ladies stood in close contact with their gentlemen, the water reaching to just above the bases of the gentlemen's upright cocks and rather higher up the bellies of the young ladies, who stood a good head shorter than their escorts. The Captain was pleased to see that Victoria Eisenberg had drawn the parts below the surface in such a way that they were not distorted by refraction. A simple wavy line across the picture represented the water-level; what was below this could be seen as clearly as what was above it. Caption: 'Nothing hinder'd my spark from feeling and toying with that leak that distinguishes our sex, and it so wonderfully watertight: for his fingers, in vain dilating and opening it, only let more flame than water into it.' A balloon emerged from the man's mouth: 'Feel my engine, dear girl: it is well wound up' – as indeed the artist's pen had shown.

Then came another picture of similar size. It might be supposed that the size of the wound-up engine had also remained undiminished. Certainly its thickness had, if anything, increased since the previous frame. But only the last few inches of the stiff stem were to be seen, as the main part of this organ had been swallowed up in Fanny's cunt, now lifted clear of the current by a pair of powerful hands beneath her buttocks. Caption: 'He had won his way so far as to make me sensible of the pleasing stretch of those nether lips from the in-driving machine.'

In the remaining pictures the two couples had emerged from the water. Fanny and her partner, their hands toying with each other's visibly excited parts, stood watching while the other young buck sat on a couch with Emily on

44

his lap, his hands on her breasts and his rigid tool sticking up between her thighs. The couple's wetness was very convincingly suggested, and the caption read: 'Emily learns the difference between jest and earnest.'

The next picture hardly needed any commentary but was labelled: 'The champion had tied at all points the true lover's knot.'

The final sequence showed this pair, now satisfied, standing with drinks in their hands. A mass of sperm could be seen clinging to the inside of Emily's left thigh, and drops were still oozing from her partner's member, which now curved slightly downwards, having lost something of its rigidity but not much of its formidable size. They stood watching and urging on the vigorous fucking of Fanny by her gallant. Caption: 'It would have been cruel to suffer the youth to burst with straining, when the remedy was so obvious and so near at hand.'

So impressed was the Captain with the way Ms Eisenberg had wielded her fine-nibbed pen that he immediately determined to employ her. Why, he would not only use her as an illustrator for those novels where her drawings could be more suitable than photographs, but might even get her to produce some cartoon books, or graphic novels as he believed they were called, as a new line for the Honeymooners Library. Of course, there was no guarantee that she possessed the necessary narrative talents. But never mind: he could commission cheap story-lines from some of his contracted authors. Those hacks would be glad of a couple of hundred for a synopsis and could hardly insist on royalties.

To begin with, however, there was no need to go commissioning anything. Hadn't he just been reading a novel that could never hope to make it into print without the most laborious and expensive re-writing? He would get Victoria Eisenberg to do him a full-blown comic-strip version of *Fucky Days*. It might need a less tacky title, of course. Something like *Adventures of a Naked Girl* – but that had already been used in a memorable classic all Honeymooners readers would be likely to know. Still, the title could come later; he might even decide to leave it unchanged. The important thing was to get this new graphic talent working on it. In particular, he looked forward to seeing how she would handle that scene in the swimming pool. She was really good at water and wet bodies . . .

Wandering into the kitchenette to explain his ideas to her, the Captain found Victoria Eisenberg kneeling on the floor between the splayed legs of Helen, who perched on the draining board, bare from the waist down. The aroma which caught his nostrils was not that of brewing tea. Young Helen evinced some embarrassment, but not so Victoria, who continued to lick coolly while he made his proposition and stated his terms. Every now and then Victoria withdrew her tongue to ask a question or make a comment. She wanted him to give her a selection of manuscripts to take away with her and work on, but he insisted that she should install herself in the office on a full-time basis, at least until the business was in full production. She agreed on condition that full time could mean three days a week, and calmly brought Helen off by rubbing her nose against the girl's clit while working her tongue deep inside the opening to her cunt.

Two days later the Captain sat nervously at his desk. It had been agreed that Victoria need not report to the Palace of Eros on Thursdays and he had given Helen the afternoon off. The woman who had phoned the previous day saying she had a really interesting offer to make him had stipulated very emphatically that she could see him only if he promised to receive her with nobody else present on the premises.

When at last she arrived she sat down on the other side of the desk and requested him to lock the door behind her. She was a strikingly handsome woman who appeared to be in her early thirties. The Captain introduced himself but his visitor declined to give her full name, saying her business was so confidential that she would prefer it if he simply called her Sylvia. 'I call myself Cicely for professional and tax purposes,' she confided, 'but my real name's Sylvia.'

He sat back, scrutinising this Sylvia from between narrowed eyelids. Her glossy scarlet lipstick matched her nail varnish and the expensive-looking red dress, trimmed with black, that hugged her figure up to her throat, leaving her arms and shoulders bare. He had noticed, as she entered the room, that her shapely legs were also bare. Her reddish-blonde hair was combed severely back and held behind her head by a black band. Despite the tightness of this coiffure the fine hair was evidently frizzy by nature; a few strands left loose with deliberate negligence confirmed this fact. Her eyes were a cool, piercing green, set beneath the blonde but distinct arches of her eyebrows. Her complexion was pale and clear. She was definitely a stunner and with any luck a goer.

The Captain attached great importance to outward semblances in the early stages of a relationship. Building on his actual attributes, he did his best to improve on these by trying to look even more like Jack Nicholson and to sound a bit less like Arthur Daley. 'Well, er, Sylvia,' he began, concentrating on these requirements and leaning forward slightly, 'it's very nice to meet you like this. What's all the mystery about?'

Sylvia, or whatever her name was, explained that she was a successful and well-established writer of erotic fiction. Her difficulty was that she could churn out novels much faster than they could be got into print. Unfortunately, the terms of her contract with her publisher, the market leader, did not allow her to tout for business elsewhere. This was why she was obliged to approach the Captain in such a clandestine way. 'These people have their spies everywhere,' she told him. 'Sometimes you can seduce them into your confidence, but the game's risky and the stakes are too high. That's why I'd like you to take care of two or three of next month's titles and bring them out under a different *nom de plume*. Sally Casseville, I think.'

'Should be no problem,' the Captain replied. 'Just let me see a synopsis and a couple of chapters.'

'Oh, I haven't actually started yet. I came to see you now because I was hoping for an immediate contract and advance. Not always easy to make ends meet, you see.'

'Well, all I need to do is take a look at some of your published stuff. Or maybe I know it already – I've researched the field pretty thoroughly.'

Sylvia pouted. 'I'm sure you have,' she said. 'But look, I value my independence. I don't want my other publishers to know about you and I don't want you to know who they are. Well, I've told you they're the market leaders but I'd rather you didn't know the name I use writing for them.'

The Captain sat back thoughtfully and narrowed his eyes. 'You can appreciate my difficulty,' he said. 'You're asking me to take quite a gamble if I write a cheque here and now. You know as well as I do that this game's got more than its fair share of con artists. Everyone thinks they can write a dirty book. But it takes two qualities that aren't as common as most folks might think. I'm sure you'll agree, as an active porn, er, practitioner. You've got to be able to write – well, at least you mustn't be totally illiterate – and you need a fertile dirty imagination. How can I be sure you've got those qualities, Sylvia, if you don't want to show me what you can do?'

A pause followed. The woman's fingers toyed with the top button of her dress. Then she spoke, gazing at him steadily across the desk with her cool green eyes.

'Oh, I can write,' she said. 'Nobody's ever accused me of illiteracy. You can take that much on trust, surely. And as for having a – how did you put it? – a fertile dirty imagination, well, that's the other reason I asked you to make sure there was no one around. You got a bed somewhere?'

His heart knocking violently against his ribs, the Captain led Sylvia up the narrow stairs. He felt like a character in an erotic novel, and this, he realized, was precisely what he was: a puppet under the control of this woman who would use him in her fantasy and then commit the episode to paper, to be read and masturbated over by punters in their thousands. Or so he hoped. He didn't care to be conned.

He stood at the door to his living quarters but changed his mind and took her into the studio. It would be fun to watch the tape afterwards and see what the hidden cameras had picked up. He indicated a screen in the corner, behind which, he suggested, Sylvia might care to prepare herself. She declined.

'Sit on that bed,' she ordered. 'I want you to unzip yourself and take out your cock. Don't touch yourself, though – I want to watch it growing spontaneously while I undress. I need to know how much life my men have got in them before I really get going.'

Sylvia's scarlet dress buttoned down the front. She stood beside the bed with her legs apart, laid her handbag on the pillow and unfastened the top three buttons. Her hands dropped and she started working upwards from the hem, which reached to mid-thigh and stretched across the gap between her legs. As the buttons were unfastened it fell open but still covered her parted thighs. She stopped before she reached the crotch and resumed unbuttoning from the cleavage downwards.

As her fingers worked their way down, the dress was pulled open by the breasts on either side of the lengthening gap. Sylvia stopped just below her navel; at that point the long V of the material revealed the white inner surfaces and undercurves of her lovely round breasts but seemed to be catching on the prominent nipples which held it in place like little pegs.

She used one hand to hold the dress together at the level of her pelvis while with the other she unfastened the last few buttons. 'I'm not too impressed yet by what I can see,' she remarked. The Captain felt the blood draining from what he had taken for quite a reasonable erection at this early stage in the proceedings.

Letting go of the front of the red garment, Sylvia stretched up and clasped her hands behind her neck, exposing the shaven and slightly damp underarms. The dress fell open and the Captain's chastened cock immediately raised its head once more to pay its enthusiastic compliments to her beauty.

The long, slender body shone creamy white, the skin firm and unblemished. The breasts were quite large but

49

beautifully shaped. Although he judged her to be in her early to mid thirties, they seemed to be in no need of the support of a bra. A pair of dark erect nipples stood out fiercely; the areolas were small and tightly puckered. The slim waist with its dimpling belly button curved down to generous but well-proportioned hips and powerful-looking thighs. But what really caught the Captain's eye and brought his cock up to full stretch was the pinkness visible through the wispy, red-gold fleece that highlighted her pubic mound and the plump outer lips between her thightops. This pinkness began as a thin but clearly demarcated double line curve near the middle of the downy triangle. As it ran down and curved back, it became darker and redder and swelled into two engorged flaps of flesh which hung down clear of the surrounding hair.

Sylvia shrugged the dress from her shoulders, turned her back to the Captain and bent forward with her hands resting on her knees. Because her feet were planted wide apart, the cleft between the beautiful globes of her buttocks was open to his gaze. The puckered pink eye of her anus seemed to wink at him. His prick throbbed painfully. Below this small but inviting orifice pouted the much larger fruit of her sex, a wet, succulent bulge with those shameless lips gaping open in hungry readiness.

He leapt to his feet. Like some heat-seeking missile, his penis homed in on that defenceless target, dragging him with it. Nothing impeded its impetuous lunge until his wiry hair ground into her bottom.

With surprising force, Sylvia thrust back against his abdomen and upper thighs, sending him crashing backwards while still locked into her cunt. He fell on the bed behind him, the full weight of the woman landing on his belly as her legs kicked in the air. In a flash she had disengaged and was kneeling above him, pinning his wrists back above his head.

'Don't you be getting fresh with me, Jock,' she hissed. 'I call the shots when we play this game, get it?'

'What game's that, then?'

'I call it "Down on the Farm". We start by milking the cow.'

Quite ready to humour this whimsical lady who, he remembered, was trying to impress him with her lewd inventiveness, he seized her elongated nipples and began to tug rhythmically at them.

'Not so fast!' she cried. 'You don't understand.'

'What don't I understand?'

'We start off with you being the cow. Get those clothes off.'

The Captain scowled; this woman seemed to be making fun of him. Then he reconsidered and, smiling, undressed and got up on all fours on the bed. His scrotum hung down between his legs like a full udder. Sylvia knelt beside him and fingered it; for a moment he dreaded the worst, but then she moved one hand to the tip of the penis which stretched horizontally along his belly and forced it downwards. The fingers of the other hand continued to caress his balls. She began to milk him. 'Moo,' he bellowed, entering into the spirit of her game.

After half a dozen strokes she interrupted her pumping, lay on her back in front of him and slid her body down between his arms and legs until her face was under his hairy chest and his prick was level with her breasts. She took hold of it again and smeared the oily tip against her nipples, which she held up in turn to be kissed in their gleaming wetness. Then she let her tits fall to the sides and resumed the stroking of his testicles and her steady milking.

Reluctant as he was to succumb to this rather undignified hand-job, he felt fairly confident that his erection, already proud and angry, would soon be so hard that she would be pleading for him to screw her properly. So he let himself go.

As she felt his balls tighten, however, she made him use his own hand to jerk off into the valley she made by lifting her breasts until they were not quite touching each other. So copious was his emission that not all the milk landed in this creamy reservoir. The first spurts hit her frizzy tied-back hair, her nose and mouth. A large gob splashed down on her throat. But most of it pooled steaming in a wide lake between the two fleshy mounds. It began to spread at the edges, where it was less milky and more runny than in the middle. She moulded her breasts and thrust up her belly to contain the flood.

'Right,' she said, 'look lively! Didn't I tell you? In my handbag there – the syringe.'

The Captain reached over and took the bag from the pillow. Sure enough, among its contents he soon found a large calibrated syringe. Instead of the needle he had been rather wary of as he rummaged, it had a harmless-looking blunt nozzle.

'Fill it,' Sylvia commanded. 'Make sure you get all the thickest stuff from the middle of this puddle.'

Keeping the nozzle submerged in the salty-smelling ejaculate, the Captain slowly and carefully eased back the plunger. As a whitish column of spunk was sucked up the plastic cylinder, the congealed mass on Sylvia's body contracted as if the tide was going out, leaving a wide expanse of shining wet foreshore. The plunger reached the top of its run; the syringe was full to the fifteen-millilitre mark, but her heaving chest was still awash with the surplus.

Sylvia instructed him to put the syringe down carefully. 'Now you're the old tom-cat that hangs round the dairy,' she told him. 'Lap up the spilt milk and cream with your tongue.'

He made no objection. He lapped up every drop and as the spermy film was licked away he fancied he could smell and taste the sexual exudation of her skin. When he had finished, Sylvia rolled over on her belly and then got up on her knees and elbows.

'Right,' she said. 'Now it's my turn to be Daisy the cow. You're Farmer Giles. This is a modern farm – time for artificial insemination.'

The Captain had guessed that this might be the purpose of the syringe. He felt a bit cheated; after all, what was wrong with his own pizzle? But he continued to humour her. 'I'd better open the way with my fingers first,' he panted. 'We don't bother with rubber gloves on this farm – the cows are so clean and wholesome.'

When he inserted his fingers he found the passage so loose and lubricated that it hardly needed opening. Still, the vagina felt deliciously hot and silky and his deflated cock began to throb once more. He withdrew his fingers and used them to stretch the cuntlips wide apart while he ran the syringe up the channel until the flanges at the top were almost engulfed in the wet flesh. He gripped these flanges and depressed the plunger with a long, firm stroke. Daisy the cow emitted a contented moo. The syringe slipped out, sticky with her juices.

She turned her head and grinned at him. 'Can't be too sure these days,' she said. 'Farmer Giles never did trust these new-fangled scientific methods, so he's borrowed the squire's old bull to service Daisy and make doubly certain. Get on with it, then.'

The Captain's pizzle had already lengthened until it hung halfway to his knees. At these words it lifted, the weight of its purple head holding it down slightly from the vertical. He bellowed and mounted her, the shaggy front of his body covering the smooth length of her back and fitting round the curve of her rump. As he drove up her freshly inseminated vagina his prick displaced masses of spunk, which issued foaming from the slippery seal of flesh; his stout member rammed its way up through the stretched lips while the sperm leaked back to lubricate him and turn his bush into a sopping sponge. To the Captain, the operation felt like pushing a thumb into warm butter, except that what he was shoving home was longer, thicker and more sensitive than either of his thumbs and the flesh he was attacking was pulsing with life and lust. Forward he ramped until the dark sponge was squeezed between his pubis and Sylvia's bottom and the surplus spunk crept up the rift between her buttocks.

Daisy mooed with pleasure and then again with impatience. The old bull flared his nostrils and bellowed out a throaty roar. For a moment everything hung in the suspense of anticipation; the two magnificent creatures drew deep breaths and braced themselves for the storm.

It came. With lightning strokes the male whipped in and

53

out, in and out, as the female below him quivered and held her ground. In a flash it was all over. Even as the spunk of his previous climax was spreading over the curves of Sylvia's bottom and down the backs of her thighs, hot surges of fresh semen gushed into her womb. She gasped and fell flat on her stomach, the fierce pizzle still pumping its load of seed into the heart of her lust.

Exhausted, the Captain rolled off to the side. His prick remained enlarged and pulsing; its dark red head emerged from the depths and drew a trail of spendings across her flank. But Sylvia's farmyard fantasies were not yet played out.

'That's the mistake people make,' she complained. 'They forget that, with all this milk around, the poor cows feel really thirsty. But all they get's a load of old bull, for fuck's sake. Come on, now – I need a drink.'

The Captain knelt behind her and hoisted her up on all fours again. Then he lowered his face until his nose ran down the groove of her arse and his tongue found her sex. He plunged it into the creaming cunt, relished the pungent liquor for a moment and withdrew. 'Another thing people forget,' he remarked, 'is that the cows need to be milked and milked till it's all drained out of them. Otherwise they burst.'

This time he let his head hang sideways as he clamped his lips over the length of her labia. One of his hands reached up between her thighs and felt its way through the rapidly cooling semen clinging to her pubic hair until it found the nub of her clitoris. He took this between his thumb and index finger and pinched; it slipped out. He seized it again and pinched it harder and closer to the root. The projecting end of the oversized nub swelled out, giving him a firm purchase on the collar of flesh between his fingertips. The Captain had never encountered a clit like this before but it suited his purpose exactly. It was like the teat of an udder and he proceeded to milk it.

His other hand reached forward round her thigh until he was able to grasp a hanging nipple. This too he milked. His cow swayed from side to side to the rhythm of his milking and as she swayed this rhythm became the rhythm of her sexual pleasuring.

With his lips covering the edges of his teeth he squeezed and mumbled at the plump pouch of flesh between them. Thick juice was expelled into his mouth. He swallowed with relish, then stiffened his tongue and ran the point from side to side, up and down the slit. The leaves of her cuntflesh were parted and the channel of love, brimming still with his own emissions and her sweeter fluids, yawned wide within his enclosing mouth.

He milked her breast, he milked her clit and he churned his tongue within the rich dairy of her cunt. Daisy tensed and quivered. His tongue was forced back by the orgasmic contraction of her vagina. He sucked powerfully as the contents of that delicious organ flooded into his mouth.

For the second time Sylvia flopped forward, spent. The Captain rolled her over on her back, drew her legs apart and entered her frontally. He had not even realised that he was stiff once more, but as her convulsing cunt gripped him he knew he was so highly primed that no more than a couple of thrusts would be needed to get him spurting and replenishing her churn. His balls tightened and lifted.

Drops of sweat fell from his forehead to trickle down Sylvia's face. She smiled up at him and he smiled back. As the pent-up charge poured from his loins he brought his mouth down on hers. His tongue touched the seal of her lips; they opened. So did his. The muscles of his cheeks relaxed as the load of thick, foaming cream he had carried from her cunt spilt into her mouth. Sylvia came as she gulped it down and this wettest of sticky kisses continued.

At last he pulled back, several threads of persistently clinging spunk stretching from mouth to mouth as he did so. When he tried to speak he produced only a gurgle. He coughed and tried again. 'You've got the imagination all right, Sylvia,' he bubbled. 'You can fuck like an angel – I'm sure you can write like a devil. I'll make out a cheque when we go downstairs.'

'Cash, please,' she replied. 'If you haven't got enough in your safe we can meet tomorrow. There's no need for you to know my name. I'm just Sylvia, remember? Or Daisy if you prefer.'

After this new acquisition to his stable (or did he mean cowshed?) of writers had left, the Captain sat thinking for some time. The experience he had just enjoyed with Sylvia had been unforgettable, of course, but something troubled him. Unforgettable. There was something about it that set the bells of recollection jingling. Could it be that the experience seemed so memorable because it chimed with some residual memory buried deep within the collective unconscious, some archetype of human lust with origins far back in our animal past? He would have to ask Mary Muttock about this the next time he saw her – she had interesting, if crackpot, theories about the evolution of our sexuality.

And then it flashed on him. Getting up, he went to one of the shelves of paperbacks published by his various business rivals. There: *Down on the Farm*, by Ellis Vessacally. He opened the book at random and scanned a few lines.

She milked Farmer Giles [he read] until his cream welled out into the receptacle she formed for it between her generous boobs. He took the heavy-duty veterinary syringe and drew the steaming fuck up into the cylinder. As soon as he had licked up what was left on those lovely titties he hoisted her up on her knees and secured the chain attached to her collar to the wooden post.

A succession of stinging strokes from the farmer's riding crop left Daisy's buttocks striped and open. The great syringe forced its way into a cunt that at first resisted but soon widened to welcome the obscene intruder. She shuddered as the hot infusion was injected into her in one long pulse of cock-juice. The instrument was withdrawn, only to be replaced by a human ramrod that felt even larger than the artificial one . . .

What was this? Had the Captain been conned after all? Instead of displaying the fertility of her improvisatory imagination, the woman had simply been acting out this scene from an erotic novel she had read. He had given her an advance of eight hundred pounds, cash in hand, and he didn't even know her name.

All he had to hold on to was that pseudonym she had made out she would use for the Honeymooners Library. What was it, now? Sally something. Sally Casswill. No – that was it: Sally Casseville. At least that looked like a real name. The one on this *Farmyard Fun*, or whatever it was called, was so obviously made up. More like an anagram.

But that was it, surely. Ellis Vessacally was an anagram of Sally Casseville. He looked inside the cover of the paperback. This one had been given to him not so long ago as a present – he remembered now. The inscription read 'Xmas 1992, with love and kisses from Helen'.

Ellis Vessacally was an anagram of Sally Casseville, and – let's see, now – they were both anagrams of Sylvia Lascelles. Yes, this Sylvia must be Helen's mother. It was true that Helen had told him her mother wrote under the name of Lucette Arrowpoint. But perhaps she had even more pen-names. A bit of a dark horse, it would seem, this Mrs Lascelles, not just a randy cow. No wonder she had insisted on visiting him under conditions of such secrecy.

`This was a first for the Captain. Never before had he knowingly fucked both a daughter and the daughter's mother. It was hard to say which of them was the more delightfully fuckable; maybe one day he would have them both at the same time and be able to make a fair comparison.

And he had not really been conned at all. If Sylvia Lascelles had been re-enacting a scene remembered from a book, the important point was that it was a scene she had already created herself. So her imagination was fertile enough after all – and certainly dirty enough for the Honeymooners Library.

A raucous female voice floated up from the street market below. 'Get your finger out, Sharon. Gent here wants to know if you've got a nice soft juicy one.'

FOUR

TRIAL AND ERROR

When Melanie left Miss MacDonald's bed on Easter Monday, the sun was flooding through the chintz curtains of the cottage and the garden and orchard were loud with birdsong. She rubbed her eyes, went to the bathroom and, having attended to some of the less interesting needs of nature, looked at herself in the mirror.

Not bad. Not bad at all, considering how they had all spent the weekend. Melanie Winspur was twenty, still slim and cock-stiffeningly pretty. She wore her hair in a thick yellow plait which now hung forward over her right shoulder. The little rounded cones of her breasts lifted her baby doll nightie at the front so that the hem didn't quite hide a wisp of gingery hair between the pale, shapely thighs. She lifted the hem to her navel with one hand and with the other scratched lightly at the wiry bush. Then she flicked her fingers rapidly through the hair, fluffing it up and freeing a shower of powdery dried sperm. Last night she had been too tired to do anything about it and if Mac noticed she had not objected.

Melanie crept quietly into her own little room with its narrow bed and the desk under the dormer window. She rarely used the bed except when Derrick called. She preferred to sleep with her friend and protector Miss Mac-Donald, with whom she had lived in this cramped but delightful cottage just outside Upchester ever since leaving Cunlip College. Miss MacDonald still taught English and

58

Physical Development at the college but said that life there now was much duller. It had been duller ever since Mary Muttock, with whom they remained in touch, had lost her job as principal at the same time as Melanie's forced departure. And it was the same chain of events, Melanie reflected, that had cost the Captain his temporary post there as odd job man. Those had been the days!

The youngsters were tucked up snugly in Melanie's bed, looking for all the world like an innocent brother and sister for whom separate sleeping arrangements had not yet been deemed imperative. Tim and Gail were not, of course brother and sister, and this was just as well. They must both be about seventeen, Melanie calculated, but they looked several years younger. Although technically speaking Tim's voice had surely broken by now, it was still so high-pitched and fluting that she could hardly believe he had been fucking the little redhead Gail for nearly a year.

All that could be seen of the lovebirds was a pair of pretty heads on the pillow. Gail's thumb was in her mouth and her frizzy red hair straggled over her face. Lighter than the strands of hair, a constellation of freckles dappled the smooth cheek. Close behind her, breathing into the nape of her neck, slept her youthful boyfriend, cuddling up as close as he could get. Tim's fair hair was cropped short; otherwise he might have been mistaken for a girl. And yet, inhaling the air of this cosy little bedroom, Melanie was sure she could detect a whiff of freshly performed sex. Young Tim, as the events of the weekend had confirmed, was quite a budding stud.

Melanie moved stealthily over the varnished floorboards, avoiding the ones that squeaked. It was not just that she was anxious not to disturb the lovers in her bed. On the couch-bed in the room below slept Tim's elder brother Darcy and Darcy's wife Susie. They had generously let Gail and Tim have the bedroom as the younger couple still lived with their respective parents and didn't get much chance to spend the night together in a real bed. Get that lot awake and Melanie could kiss the idea of writing her diary goodbye.

She sat at her desk without scraping the chair on the floor, and took the yellow notebook from a drawer. The sun filtering through the curtains in the little dormer window was quite bright enough for her to write. She took up her pen.

Mon, April 12

Ages since I last wrote this diary. Well, not much has been happening in frantic Upchester. High-point of week ought to be Derrick's visits but they tend to be the low-point. Such a berk!

The other day, though, Mac had this letter from the Captain. Haven't seen him since last year. He's used all that money from insurance when his motel burnt down last year to set himself up as publisher somewhere in London and wants me and Mac to do some more writing for him. Like when we did it before, I would rough out the basics and Mac would tidy up grammar and so on and generally give it a bit of class. Not pseudo-Victorian porn this time, though, but straight erotica – he sent us a few books from other publishers to give us idea of sort of things punters get off on.

I was keen to get started right away but Mac had this rather brilliant idea of having the O'Flammerys over with Darcy's brother Tim and Tim's girlfriend Gail to try out a few scenarios (spelling?) and make sure we weren't describing anything physically impossible.

Well, the four of them turned up Saturday morning. Lovely to see them again. Can't get over how much this Tim's like Darcy was when he was only sixteen or seventeen, except Tim's hair very fair and Darcy's is brown – don't much go for the way Darcy has this pigtail held back with a rubber band. He must be nineteen now, same as his Susie. Quite the respectable married couple, you might take them for. His voice has gone quite deep and he's grown lots of hair on arms – he's rather thin and *narrow* but still, he's matured so much since the old days when he used to climb wall and pester Cunlip girls, but Susie with those adorable golden plaits has hardly

changed at all except she's got proper little tits. Darcy
and Susie were dressed what you might call unisexually
– both in jeans and tight-fitting black vests. Susie's tits
big enough to jiggle when she moved. I expect it was
from rubbing against vest when this happened that her
nipples had got so big and stiff. Something similar
seemed to be going on in front of Darcy's jeans, or maybe he was just pleased to see yours truly, as they say.

I love Tim's crew-cut – not *too* short, but neat and
tidy and somehow sexy too, in spite of him looking so
young. He was wearing what he always seems to have
on if there's a bit of sun (and this weekend it's been
amazingly warm) – shellsuit top in green and mauve and
a pair of cute little white shorts. They fit so snugly.
They're so brief they've hardly got anything you could
call legs but even so they've got little V-shaped nicks at
the sides. That can't be why they call them knickers,
though. What I like about them is that Tim's legs, which
have the beginnings of nice muscles but no hair on
them, just like his brother's used to be, are quite white
but these shorts are so much whiter that somehow the
legs look really lovely, almost that golden brown they
get in the summer, all the way down to those sandals he
wears. But I mustn't go on about him – he might find
this diary when he gets up and get the wrong idea from
reading it.

His Gail's a funny little thing, quite shy until she gets
going, with red hair, green eyes and all those freckles all
over her. I dare say her shyness comes from her not
having been a Cunlip girl like most of our friends but
just a town girl Tim picked up somewhere in Upchester.
They've been going together nearly a year now. She had
on one of her long flowery skirts. It hung down rather
straight as she hasn't got much of a bum on her and no
hips worth speaking of. Her feet were bare and none too
clean. I've often seen her before in this outfit on warm-
ish days. To draw attention from narrowness of hips
(though I know some guys like them that way and hate
your broad-beamed models) she rolls a flowery-pat-

61

terned scarf into a strip and ties it round her flattish chest instead of a proper top. It's sexy because you could untie it so easily – in fact, if you waited long enough it would probably just drop off.

Mac had her plum-coloured track suit on. Hardly ever takes any trouble with her personal appearance but always looks ravishing and really sophisticated whatever she wears. I'd chosen my loose red miniskirt with nothing under it and white T-shirt. We had a bite of lunch, not bothering to take our things off and actually enjoying looking at each other dressed like I've described and just imagining what was underneath. Didn't want to get too distracted, though it was hard not to make a move when I realised Tim and Gail were up to some sort of one-handed game under table while eating with other hand.

Mac packed a few items of special equipment in a bag and we all squeezed into the Morris Minor. I had Gail on my lap in front and Susie and Darcy insisted on Tim sitting between them in the back. Derrick says this sort of overloading can ruin suspension but I bet I can get him to fix it if something gets busted. Mac drove straight to college. Staff car-park was empty – hardly anyone stays at Cunlip over Easter. We got out of car and straightened ourselves out, then walked briskly down avenue of chestnut trees to stream at bottom of valley.

Really strange to be back after how many years – four, it must be. Trees looked bigger, though they can't really have grown much in that time. Mac turned left at plank bridge and led us up stream. Gail wanted to paddle and Mac promised she might get a chance to go in water later. Pool under the trees quite deserted and perfectly calm – what a change from rowdy scenes I remember there. Then out into bright sunshine and across Lower Field to old games pavilion we used to call Palace of Sweethearts. Even more rickety than it used to be and most of the windows broken and boarded up. Mac had a key, of course. Couldn't help wondering how often she's been down here those days she comes home smelling of girl.

Tim and Gail had never been in the place but for Susie and Darcy it must have brought back very special memories. This was where they'd been wedded and bedded in that mock ceremony I arranged to amuse Captain. Maybe if we hadn't married them like that they wouldn't have got married properly later – it was beginning of a good thing for those two rascals.

Mac got busy with her equipment and I helped her. We stood on chairs and fixed a couple of ropes over a beam running across from wall to wall. Then we tied Susie's wrists together with silk cords. We made her stand on a wooden box to make her about the same height as her husband, looped one of the hanging ropes between her wrists and hoisted her up till poor girl was dangling there with a slight dew of sweat filming her smooth armpits, just able to stand on her toes.

Darcy looked apprehensive – he guessed same was in store for him. The other two helped us drag him into position and soon we had him hanging there, his toes just touching floor, about four inches from Susie. When we twisted the two of them round and let them unwind they kept bumping and bouncing off each other.

Mac told Gail to undo Darcy's belt and take his jeans off. I was quite shocked to see how hairy his legs have got and how his chestnut-coloured bush runs up in a triangle to his belly button. He still had his black vest on but I guessed he must have a fair bit of fur on his chest too. And even though, when Gail got his black G-string down, his dick was hanging limp, it certainly looked bigger than last time I saw it, whenever that was. Anyway, most of my blokes are disgustingly hairy hunks (think of Derrick!!) and to me, in the mood I was in then, Darcy's shagginess made Tim's smoothness all the more appealing.

Not that young Tim's effeminate (spelling?) or anything like that. Inside those little shorts he got quite a horn up as soon as Mac made him strip off Susie's jeans

63

and G-string. I know he's seen and handled his sister-in-law's body plenty of times but I suppose having her hanging up like that at his mercy was specially exciting for the lad. Hanging beside her husband, young Susie made a pretty picture. They both wore just these black vests but colouring and build below hemline was so different. Susie used to be a bit, well, a bit girlish round the pubic region but now she's turned into a really lovely young woman – that slightly rounded tummy, those smooth white thighs and the beautiful golden thatch between them.

Then Mac started getting imaginative.

MAC: Gail, dear, let's see you take Tim's jacket off. See if you can do it so suggestively that poor old Darcy here gets stiff from just watching you.

GAIL (*standing behind Tim, slowly unfastening front of his shellsuit top and stroking his tummy as she pulled it open*): Something like this might do the trick, miss.

MAC: No need to call me 'miss', dear. What's he got under his arms?

GAIL (*slipping top back over his shoulders and down off his arms, then lifting his left arm for us to see*): In some sorts of light you have to get quite close to see it. It's not very thick and it's such a light colour.

MAC: Is it sweaty?

GAIL (*stroking armpit with fingertips of left hand*): Yes. It's starting to get a bit slimy. Ooh, it smells yummy.

TIM: I can't keep my arm up like this – my shorts are cutting into my crotch.

MAC: He's really getting his knickers in a twist, isn't he? Let his arm down and see if you can get his little nipples as excited as his hard cock.

As Gail reached round under Tim's armpits to stroke and pinch his nipples, I noticed a change in his brother's prick which, unlike Tim's, hadn't shown any signs of hardening so far. But now it seemed to be getting fuller and stretching down more, rather like when you put a condom over a tap and let the water slowly fill it. The foreskin crept back a little and we could see part of the knob, still more pink than that shiny purple they get when they're ready to burst – cocks, I mean, not condoms. Then it lifted itself a bit from his bollocks and seemed to look round sleepily. I thought it was going to loll down again but quite suddenly it grew and curved right up towards his belly button. Kind of scary. Knob completely uncovered now and really angry-looking.

What a sly devil Mac is! She'd got this all worked out, I'm sure. She told Tim to reach behind Gail and untie her scarf. When it came off I saw her chest wasn't quite as flat and boyish as you might think with the scarf tight round it. She's got these little bumps, very delicate looking, whiter than the rest of her skin and without freckles. Hard to describe shape of these tits except instead of being rounded outwards – convex I suppose you'd say – the outlines curve other way. Imagine climbing a mountain which starts with a very easy slope and then gets steeper and steeper. Like those pictures of Mount Fuji or Fiji. (Not that you could call these little cones mountains!) On the tips they've got these pink caps. The puffy outer bits (aureolas?) are bigger than you'd expect and the actual teat parts stick out quite a lot, or at least they did when Tim started touching them.

Mac made Tim and Gail rub their nipples together and Darcy looked as if he was ready to bust. I had thought Susie wasn't reacting at all but then I noticed a droplet of sticky juice had gathered at bottom of her fluffy yellow bush. When she shifted slightly on her toes it came into contact with the inside of one thigh. Droplet clung to the skin and stretched out in a thin string between thigh and damp hairs. Seeing this made same thing happen between my own legs. Hoped my nice skirt wouldn't get ruined.

Now Darcy was good and stiff, Mac got a couple of wooden rulers out of case and gave them to Tim and Gail, who had to use them on the bare bums hanging there. Tim got quite vicious, holding his ruler at one end, bending other end back and letting it go like the

65

way we used to flick paper pellets in the classroom. That treatment really made Susie's bottom pink. Mac didn't want any damage done so she took the rulers away and made them use their hands for the smacking. Of course, this made Susie and Darcy swing backwards and forwards. His stiff dong kept prodding into her, leaving wet smears but never actually touching right place.

Mac took Tim aside and started groping him through the little cotton shorts. She gave me a wink and I did same with Gail, unfastening her long skirt and sliding hands up lean freckled thighs to the bright green bikini briefs she had on. Mac and me were both kneeling and the youngsters standing. Gail's knickers felt and looked quite damp but that was nothing to the wetness when I rested finger along length of her pussy and let it push the material up between her lips. Mac wanted to change with me. I was amazed at how alive Tim's naughty bits felt through his shorts. I could feel the little bollocks moving about under my fingers, quite firm but obviously very sensitive and vulnerable, and above them the hardness of that thing of his trying to burst out of shorts.

MAC (*to Gail*): Often get to suck your boyfriend's cock, dear?

GAIL (*blushing and sort of tensing up over Mac's hand*): Well, I . . .

MAC: It's a lovely taste, you know, and they love it too.

GAIL: I know, but whenever I do it Timmy's stuff comes squirting out almost at once.

MAC: You mean as soon as your lips touch him?

GAIL: Well, no, but as soon as I start sucking. I can't keep it in my mouth. He just goes crazy and sprays it all over me.

MAC: In that case we'll get you to touch the tip with your tongue and then run your lips down the length of it and up again, but just once, mind. And positively no sucking. Where's that cocky little penis, Melanie?

Usually Mac called me Mel, so I could tell she was

having some sort of game with us. Anyway, I eased elastic of Tim's shorts down over tip of his rod and it wasn't so little at all. Inch by inch I rolled shorts down till the soft yellowish hair came into view and the pink bag with his balls. Then I eased back of waistband down over his bum. I left the shorts round tops of his thighs, keeping them together.

Mac pushed Gail down on her knees. The girl shut her eyes and reached out for the little opening on the end with tip of her tongue. Tim bucked forward like he'd had an electric shock and his thing went right into her mouth. I could tell she was just about to suck – what they call a reflex, I suppose – so I pinched her nose to make her pull back for air.

Tim's prick jumped up straight. It's nearly as long as his brother's now, though much slimmer and without that upward curve. Mac pushed the end down and let it go, and it twanged up like the rulers had done.

Then Mac made Gail bend down over it, open her mouth very wide and take a couple of inches in without actually touching it. I thought of those games where you move a ring along an electric wire and if the ring touches it a buzzer sounds. Gail concentrated. Her mouth flooded with saliva, which soon coated the prick from head to root and started soaking into the thick soft hairs round it.

Meanwhile poor Susie and Darcy were still dangling on their ropes, their arms stretched up above their heads. I knew what had to be done – Mac had explained the outline of her plan before. Mac turned Darcy and Susie to face each other, the head of his cock touching her tummy. I got Gail to stand behind Darcy and stood close behind her myself. Mac made Tim stand behind the box Susie was hanging on, his shorts still tight round the tops of his thighs. She squeezed his prick gently and pushed his head down – he had to lick between the cheeks of Susie's bottom and get as much spit as possible into the crack and especially up her arse. Susie squirmed when he did this and her front pushed against

Darcy's, making his bum bounce back into Gail's tummy as he swung on the rope.

Before the spittle on Tim's stiff cock could dry off, Mac got him up on the box, parted Susie's bottom cheeks, told him to bend his knees and stuck the knob up against her rude place. She grabbed Susie by the hips and pulled back hard so Tim was squashed in a sandwich between the two females and his prick went right up Susie's bum. At first she yelled out but then went all quiet and got this funny look in her eyes.

Gail couldn't really see what was going on so I had to control her from behind. First I forced her down and made her lick and slobber into Darcy's arse. (I nearly wrote *Arcy's darse*. Didn't Mac once tell me that old poets like Dartford – or was it Rochester – used that word to mean willy?) Then I pulled Gail up and told her to lick two of her fingers and stick them into him. She seemed very embarrassed (spelling?) and hid her face between his shoulder blades.

MAC: Tim, you've got two free hands and Gail's got one, right? Now, I want Tim to reach round the front of Susie and try to open her cunt. Think you can do that, Tim?

TIM: But how can I open her cunt? I thought I'd got my thing stuck in it.

MAC: No, Tim, that's not your sister-in-law's cunt you're buggering. That'd be a bit too much like incest. Just feel for those nice lips of hers and ease them open for me.

SUSIE: Ouch! He's pulling my hairs.

MAC: Careful now, you scamp! Feel about a bit with your fingers till you find where it's really wet, then slide your fingers along the length of it and it ought to open of its own accord. OK?

When she was satisfied that Tim had parted Susie's cuntlips properly she told Gail to reach her free hand round Darcy, bend his cock down and push the swollen end into the waiting cunt. I'd got a hand between Gail and Darcy and inside the front of her knickers, sliding it over a sparse border of hairs and wanking her hard little clit. I knew from our plan that Mac was doing the same to Tim's hard but not-so-little prick, or the part of it that wasn't sheathed in Susie's bottom, and to his tight little bag of balls. We must have looked something like a reverse tug-of-war, the three of Mac's team facing the three of mine, all six of us linked together in some kind of sexual nexus as Captain would call it.

It must have been sheer chance that Susie, Darcy, Tim and Gail all seemed to be ready to come at the same time. (Weak point of Mac's brilliant plan of action: our own climaxes had to be deferred.) Suddenly Susie's legs flashed up to wrap round her husband's bucking hips.

This was a disaster and also quite a hoot.

Until this point most of Susie's weight (apart from whatever fraction of it was supported by Tim's prick) had been shared between the wooden box as she stood on her toes and the rope tied to the beam. But when she threw herself at him like that, the rope Darcy was hanging from had to take the weight of both of them. It was too much. Darcy's rope broke, and so did Susie's as the double weight was transferred to hers.

Six astonished bodies, still sexually linked in various ways at the moment of falling, tumbled on the floor. Nobody was hurt but the fingers and pricks got dislodged at the crucial moment. Considering there were only two of the latter I was amazed at the amount of hot spunk that went flying everywhere. As we lay there cooling off it was lovely to run hands over all that panting flesh and smear the juice in wherever it had landed.

Well, after that we all wanted a splash in the pool. I pulled Gail's knickers off, getting my first view of her funny scrub of bright red hair. Mac did the same with Tim's shorts and she and me both got naked ourselves. Susie and Darcy stripped off their black vests and I caught my breath at sight of Susie's lovely round breasts which look more perfect every time I see them. Then, bold as brass, we stepped out into dazzling sunlight and romped down Lower Field to stream.

We hurried along bank and felt a bit more secure when we got into cover of trees and bushes where stream opened out into pool. Mac was leading way and motioned us to be quiet. Someone up ahead laughing and splashing about.

Crawled through undergrowth, scratching ourselves a bit, till we came to edge of water. Two young girls, as nude as us, larking about and squealing with fun – water still pretty cold as it's only April. Must have had parents abroad, so staying on over hols. Mac whispered to me – said they were a couple of sixteen-year-olds, a bit slow on the uptake but speedy enough on the playing field. And they didn't seem to be at all behindhand with what they were up to in the water.

The six of us lurked there in the bushes, wondering when to make our move. But we weren't the only ones spying on these pretty but rather naughty water nymphs. Suddenly two skinheads stepped out of shadows on other side of pool. Had their cocks out and stood there on bank frigging themselves and chewing till girls noticed them. Nymphs pretended to be horrified and splashed squawking to our side of water. The two guys jumped straight in, fully dressed, and grabbed both of them from behind. One of them lifted his prisoner right up out of water. I saw her pussy for first time, almost hairless, but only for a moment – he clenched his great ham of a hand down over it and she yelped as he squeezed it. Then they spun the girls round and seemed to be getting to work on them in earnest with their underwater hard-ons.

Mac gave us a whispered instruction. On a signal from her we all started yelling, especially Darcy. Skinheads looked up, terrified. They couldn't see anyone but didn't hang around to find out who had caught them at it. In a flash they were pulling themselves out of pool, their cocks still big and swollen but beginning to droop and flop about like distressed balloons. I hoped their denims would shrink on them before they got somewhere to take them off. We yelled again and they broke into a swift trot towards fence on main Upchester road.

The young girls looked even more distressed than the yobbos' (spelling?) dicks, so we all took the plunge and did our best to comfort them and cheer them up.

MAC: This one's OK, Mel. I can feel she's still intact. Like to check the other one? Your name's Jill, isn't it, dear?

MY GIRL: That's right, miss. Ow! What's this lady doing?

MAC: Remember that last Physical Development class we had, girls?

MAC'S GIRL: About virginals, wasn't it, miss?

MAC: Virginity. The hymen. Melanie there's just going to have a feel to see if those bad town boys did any damage to Jilly with that over-excited equipment of theirs.

ME: Seems to be fine, but I reckon this one would be tight anyway, even if he'd had her.

It's a funny thing, but cunts often feel drier and tighter in water than on dry land. They sort of close up to keep their juices from getting diluted, I suppose. But when I was fingering her, this Jill really started flooding. If she hadn't been so dry at first I'd have thought the yob had spunked in her after all. She went all quivery and rubbed herself against my tits.

Well, we mucked about with these girls and with each other for a bit, but Mac thought it unwise to take things too far with them as Jill's grandfather was a governor. Darcy and Tim seemed disappointed. Me and Mac helped girls to dry off and slip into their pale blue Cunlip dresses, then sent them packing. Jill gave me a little kiss and said she was sorry she couldn't stay and play with me.

After this bit of fun the six of us ran back to Palace of Sweethearts, feeling slightly chilly. Mac got blanket from bag and spread it out in sun on part of veranda where floorboards hadn't given way. Not having towels we stretched out on blanket to dry in warm sunshine.

Me and Mac looked at each other and knew each other's thoughts. After all this excitement we both needed to be fucked.

71

MAC: Susie, Gail – you don't mind if we borrow your blokes for a bit, do you?

SUSIE: You're welcome to my Darce, Miss Mac-Donald. He's always going on about you at home. See if you can't drain it out of his system so he can concentrate more on his poor little wife and her needs.

MAC: Thanks, darling. What about you, Gail?

GAIL: You can have a try. But I don't think Timmy's very good with older women.

ME: Oh, come on. I'm only a couple of years older. You make me feel like an old hag.

TIM: I think she's OK for me, Gail. Got that girlish look about her. Pretty. Sort of playful, too. Ooh, yes! Get an eyeful of that – I'm getting big just thinking about doing her. Anyway, you can help, just to be on the safe side.

MAC: Good idea. And Susie, I'd like you to help Darcy and me, then nobody will be left out.

Mac lay on her back and opened her legs to Darcy. She opened them really wide. Susie knelt beside her and pulled Mac's cunt open with one hand while she used the other one to guide her husband's huge curving prick up into it. He shoved hard and lay on top of Mac, drilling her. Just as well she's so athletic and has these strong muscles in her tummy, because Susie stretched herself face downwards, pointing towards his feet, along length of Darcy's back while he was humping. Put her hands on cheeks of his bum and pulled them apart so she could lick down the groove, right down over his bollocks to where the fucking was happening. I brought a bundle of our clothes from pavilion and stuffed them under Mac's head so she could get decent (or indecent!) view of Susie's fanny. Every now and then she strained upwards and ran her tongue between the dripping lips. Darcy was a bit left out of this part of operation, his face buried between Mac's left ear and inside of Susie's left thigh.

Now it came to crunch, I didn't so much fancy having young Tim face to smooth-skinned face after all. Well, he's very pretty to look at but maybe that's more an aesthetic (spelling?) thing than a sexual one. So I lay down on my side with my upper leg cocked up and got him to lie behind me. Gail paddled about a bit in my cunny with her slim, delicate fingers, then guided her boyfriend's rod between the lips. It was slim like the fingers but maybe not so delicate – a powerful, efficient tool with one heck of a lot of life in it. I pushed my bottom back against his tummy as he thrust forward. Because his thing was so slim it slid up me like a tongue into a bowl of cream. And because it was so stiff he was able to wiggle his hips and stir it about like a spoon in my honeypot.

Lying like this, the whole of my front was uncovered and available to Gail. She got down on her side facing me in a sixty-nine position and started tonguing my clit. I pulled her legs open and used her lower thigh as a slightly hard pillow while I licked over her dark red hairs and nuzzled deep into the pink cunt.

So Tim was fucking me and Darcy was fucking Mac. That seemed fair because we two older ones had gone unfucked earlier. Gail couldn't complain about the mutual tonguing she was getting with me but I thought of way we could do a bit more for Susie. She was, of course, already getting a bit of licking from Mac but she seemed really pleased when I reached across Gail's body and stuck my fingers into her blonde pussy, which was dribbling into Mac's mouth.

Darcy started moaning and trembling first, then

At this point Melanie snapped her diary shut. Tim and Gail were awake and grinning at her from the bed; suddenly Gail twitched the sheet off their nude bodies and revealed the tall, pink-tipped column standing up from the base of Tim's belly. The boy blushed as his mischievous girlfriend seized the cock and wagged it towards Melanie. 'Look,' she giggled. 'He wants to poke it in you, Mel – from the front this time.'

* * *

73

Eight days later the Captain sat at his desk studying the drafts he had just received from his friends in Upchester. In the covering note, Miss MacDonald explained that this was only their first shot at a bit of contemporary porn. It could be regarded as a dry run, or maybe a wet one. They had been strongly influenced by the specimens of high-class erotica he had sent them and could easily modify the style or subject-matter of the two samples she and Melanie had decided to send in for his comments.

He flicked through the typewritten pages, pausing at random to get the flavour of the writing.

Her body was overheating inside the shiny black rubber. Beads of sweat gathered at the open zips until the openings became salty lakes that drowned her armpits, nipples, navel and buttocks.

The subtle smell of L'Elegance was quite obliterated. But within the open zip over her mouth, her tongue and throat felt as dry as dust. Nor had the sweat formed a lake in the opening between her thighs but the pad of flesh and hair that pushed down through the unzipped opening was heavy and sodden. Patience trembled as she swung from the pulley above her.

She swung forwards.

The masked and collared man beside her swung too.

In their swinging they touched each other. They touched each other, bounced back and touched again. At the first contact the man's penis lengthened and the foreskin drew back, unhooding the mauve glans. When they touched again the penis had attained full rigidity.

The blunt end pulsed and strained but the man's chain held him too high for the penis to lodge in her unzipped cunt. Instead, the tip wandered over the shiny covering of her belly, smearing a trail of sexual fluid across the surface.

Dr Birch adjusted the pulley supporting Patience. She knew that her vagina was now at the level of the man's penis. But their swinging had stopped. Even with the penis standing out in horizontal erection, their bodies still hung a good six inches apart.

74

'Use your tongue on him, Komiko,' ordered Dr Birch.

The Japanese girl, who had opened her riding habit to expose her small breasts with their hardened teats, moved behind the hanging man.

She knelt and placed her hands upon his flanks. Patience saw a small hand reach between the thighs to cradle the hairy testicles. She could not see Komiko's face but had no doubt about what she was doing.

She was using the tip of her tongue to titillate the man's anus.

Patience found her voice. 'What now?' she asked.

Dr Birch said nothing. He removed his dark glasses. He took one of the riding crops from where it hung on the stable wall. He felt with his free hand between Patience's legs from behind until he found the tag of the zip which had released her bulging sex. He tugged on the tag, extending the opening until the rubber was unzipped all the way from her clitoris to the base of her spine.

He peeled the skin of rubber back on both sides of the divide. Her steaming buttocks rejoiced at the touch of cool air. The small diamond branded on her left cheek was exposed.

He stood back and raised the crop.

She closed her eyes, frozen with fear.

'Unfreeze, slave,' said Dr Birch.

'Yes, master,' she replied, but her attempt to relax the clenched buttocks was pathetic. Instead of opening out for the master's inspection they merely quivered.

The crop swished down and stung her across both buttocks.

Patience swung forward on her chain. The bulbous head of the masked and collared man's cock nudged against the lips of her cunt. Her cunt refused to open. She went swinging back while the man was held firmly in place by Komiko's hands and tongue.

At the limit of her backswing the crop snapped down again, sending her forward once more. This time the tip

75

of the cock pierced her. She gasped as the slick plum slithered in and moaned as it slithered out and she swung back once more to receive a third lash across her smarting buttocks.

This one was a real stinger.

Patience squealed.

She swung towards the man with more force than before. As she did so, a hot stream of semen shot from the slot in the head of his cock. It soaked her sweat-damp hairs.

The cock impaled her. This time it went in all the way. Patience squeezed on it with her vaginal muscles and held herself there, hanging forward on her chain.

The cock pulsed inside her, emptying itself in the hot depths of her cunt.

The Captain sighed and turned his attention to the other draft on his desk. After skimming few pages of the manuscript he paused to read properly.

At her lord's bidding, Ulva crawled across the wet flagstones. Dragged down by the two golden eggs the lustful Lady Mamilla had clipped to her nipples, her heavy breasts almost brushed that slimy floor. She crawled right up to the lord's feet and licked them.

Lord Kriproq placed his bony fingers beneath Ulva's armpits and teased the damp blue curls. He ran his hands down her slim arms and tied them behind her back with a silken band by which he hoisted her to her feet. 'Now, what is your pleasure, my precious?' he croaked. 'Your lord will be pleased to deliver it – in the fullness of time.'

Ulva was too frightened to reply. Without waiting for her response the cruel lord passed the hook through her tied wrists. The paunchy dungeon-master pulled at the chain and hoisted Ulva up until her toes just touched the cold floor and she hung dangling beside the male bondslave. Lord Kriproq stood behind her; she felt the heat of his breath on the nape of her neck. He reached round and laid a hand on her belly, then let it slide down over the cloud of vivid blue fur that covered her fleshpot. For a brief moment it hovered over her sensitive nubbin. Ulva's wanting was aroused and she could feel the weepings beginning to well out around the plug between her leaves of flesh.

Her lord twisted that wicked plug and worked it from side to side. It felt like a cockstem pleasuring her. But Kriproq was intent on denying the girl's pleasure. He tugged at the plug. Suckered around it, Ulva's flesh leaves were dragged forwards and down, reluctant to relinquish the plug's hard thickness. Slowly her lord peeled back those leaves of flesh until all they had to suck upon was the oiled thong of plaited leather attached to the plug. As Kriproq's ancient fingers pulled at that thong, she felt its supple length uncoiling within her and slowly easing out between those sucking lips. The golden egg, similar to those clipped to her nipples, dropped to the flagstones, followed by a flood of honeyed seepage that puddled around her toes. Lord Kriproq brushed her blue curls upwards, lifted the hood of flesh and with a finger of his other hand tapped firmly against the extruded nubbin.

He withdrew both hands and turned to the dungeonmaster. 'She is not ready,' he said. 'Before her pleasure can be drawn down she must be smacked. Yes, she must taste the triple tongue.'

Ulva was very frightened. How could this lord, to whom she had entrusted her safety in that terrible slavemarket, treat her with such cruelty? She felt his bony fingers walking over her bottom like spiders. The fingers were removed and the palm of her lord's hand descended on those soft buttocks in a stinging slap.

The slap caused Ulva to swing forward on her chain. She swung towards the male bondslave and her belly butted against the long fleshcock that had lifted from his hairy bumps and pointed at her when the oiled thong was removed. Already that fleshcock was weeping its milt.

The slave swung away from her on his chain and then, like the great pendulum in the palace clock-tower, swung back. Ulva tried to lift on her toes, hoping that the step would spear her or at least ram her hardened nubbin. But it caught her at the base of her belly and sent her swinging back. And as she swung back, the dungeon-master lifted his arm and brought down the triple tongue with a stinging thwack across the soft cheeks of her bottom . . .

Once more the Captain sighed. 'You've looked at these, haven't you, Helen?' he called. 'What do you think of them?'

'Yes, I glanced through them on the tube last night. They made me come in my knickers.'

'Well, let me tell you something. They're pretty hot stuff, considering they're from beginners. But these two ladies in Upchester have still got to find a voice of their own. They do fine as long as they're imitating other writers – after all, their obscene versions of Victorian novelists fooled the scholars and Melanie's reworking of *Romeo and Juliet* looked pretty good on video. But if Honeymooners published these two pieces as they stand the punters would laugh at us and we'd end up in court. Anyone who knows his way around in the literature of pleasure, and the literature of pain for that matter, would recognise the influences at once. These are cheap imitations of two of the opposition's best novelists. Far too derivative.'

Helen grinned, left her desk and walked over to him. 'But this is the real thing,' she giggled, unzipping his flies and seizing his massive hard-on, evidence of the power of their writing, however derivative. 'At least we can give them the credit for that.'

'And another thing that disqualifies them,' he said, as Helen straddled his thighs and pulled aside her knickers. 'Honeymooners is going to break new ground by publishing a cruelty-free product. Well, more or less.'

Helen slid down on him and shut him up by clamping her mouth over his. The drone of the Captain's critical

discourse gave way to Sharon's raucous cries drifting up
from the market below.

FIVE

BLACK LACE AND BLUE MOVIES

The following morning Helen discovered they had run out of coffee, so the Captain slipped out of the Palace of Eros to fetch a jar of instant from the nearby supermarket. On his way back he elbowed a passage impatiently through the crowds, whose numbers had not been reduced by the unpleasantly wet and blustery April weather.

This part of Fulham depressed him. Street markets were usually places of cheerful bustle and uninhibited bottom-pinching but here, to his jaded eyes at least, the people looked as mean and narrow as the slippery, litter-strewn strip of pavement between the stalls and the shopfronts. As the national economy made its alleged recovery, more and more of these shops, like the one above which his business and living premises were located, closed down.

Most crowds the Captain could handle. Down in the Underground, for example, the commuters formed a disciplined mass through which he could scythe a pathway by staring straight ahead and marching purposefully forward. Things were different here in the North End Road. Nobody looked at you, so it was impossible to daunt them with your impassive stare. The spokes of an inconsiderately wielded umbrella drove him sideways into the bosom of the well-grown stallholder Sharon.

'Handle the merchandise and you fucking got to buy it,' she laughed. 'Fancy somefing soft and juicy, love?'

'Not today, thanks,' he replied sourly. 'I prefer them

firm and not too ripe. And as far as I'm concerned, madam, your greengrocer's apostrophes are a definite turn-off.'

Sharon contemplated her pair of ripest endowments with an expression of bewilderment, being unused to anything but vulgar admiration out here on the street. 'You what?' she muttered.

The Captain, too, was momentarily troubled. Even as he made his remark about the apostrophes, he had caught himself wondering whether *greengrocer's* ought to have its apostrophe before or after the *s*. After all, it was not just one greengrocer who was guilty but the whole bloody tribe of them, together with the whole worshipful company of fruiterers. He felt even more perplexed as he turned away from Sharon to the narrow door with the small brass plate screwed to the jamb bearing the inscription 'First Floor: HONEYMOONERS LIBRARY'. The honeymooners, he hoped, would be plural, very much so, but it had never occurred to him that they might require an apostrophe. Now he was not so sure.

When he entered the office Helen and Victoria came scurrying out of the kitchenette. Whatever they had been up to in there, they had not been making coffee. He opened the new jar and proceeded to do that himself. While the kettle was heating he picked up a pair of black lace panties from the floor.

Well, they couldn't be Victoria Eisenberg's. Today she was sporting a snug pair of black velvet hotpants over sheer black tights, the clinging blackness below her waist contrasting with the frilly whiteness of her blouse above it. Yet Helen was wearing jeans with her red T-shirt. Maybe the knickers had been left there overnight. He slipped them into his pocket and took the coffee out to the ladies.

Ever hopeful, he drew a chair up to Victoria's desk and sat down beside her. She was certainly making rapid and impressive progress with her comic-book version of *Fucky Days*, which the Captain had provisionally and rather unimaginatively renamed *Girlie Delights*. Perhaps, though, he would stick with the original title after all. Victoria seemed to be working on the very sequence he had read the day he took her on, almost a month ago now. He watched her using a shiny but antique-looking dip pen that reminded him of his early schooldays to copy out some lettering between faintly ruled lines of pencil. He leaned forward to read the stylish capital letters: 'WAARGH! YOU'RE TICKLING ME DOWN THERE! LEAVE IT OUT, BIG BOY!!' Some inches away from this, Victoria inked the words 'LEAVE IT OUT? WHAT A WASTE, BABY – YOU KNOW YOU CAN'T WAIT TO HAVE IT IN YOU.' Taking a sharply pointed pencil, she drew the outlines of speech balloons round these utterances and cut them out with scissors.

The Captain looked at the page she had already drawn. At first his attention was drawn to a frame showing an underwater view of a handsome, square-jawed young man sticking his head, face upwards, between the heroine's thighs and extending his tongue towards her vulva. Victoria had drawn this part to look like some kind of sea anemone, with the fronds of pubic hair swirling around the fleshy opening in a way that could only happen in water. Then his eye wandered to the next picture, in which the guy had stood up with the girl perched on his shoulders. The girl was Helen. The Captain watched, fascinated, as Victoria positioned the adhesive balloons on this frame and pressed them down carefully.

There, in the frames that followed, was the girl splashing about in the water of the public baths and getting up to all sorts of tricks never seen in the fondly remembered comics of his youth. There could be no doubt. Wherever her face was depicted, it was Helen's face with its dark eyes and long thin lips. The Captain was delighted to think that his versatile editorial assistant's talents were being put to such good use.

He reached his hand behind the artist's back and squeezed her velvet-covered haunch. Victoria sipped her coffee and failed to respond. He felt in his pocket and produced the knickers, which he then dangled in front of her face. 'These yours, my dear?' he enquired.

'Not any more. They're a present for Helen.'

Helen smiled rather bashfully, the Captain thought. 'Why don't you try them on for us, Helen,' he suggested.

He was charmed but puzzled by her new-found modesty when she took the tiny black garment into the tea-kitchen to change in private. Helen's body, after all, was offered to him on a regular and uninhibited basis. And he had caught Victoria at the girl's cunt in that same kitchenette on the day he had employed the artist. It was as if Helen felt a certain uneasiness at the thought of bringing the two relationships together. Yes, this was quite charming.

While Helen was getting herself ready, Victoria continued to work on her speech balloons as if unaware of the hand around her waist which was now gently stroking the inside of her thigh through the black nylon of her tights. Coolly, she asked the Captain what had given him the idea of naming his business the Honeymooners Library.

'Oh,' he said, 'I jotted down a whole list of possibilities: Annexe, Headlamp, Masthead, Hardline, Bodyline, Crimson Lace, Collop and Cundew, Dick Head and Lipcraft, Pluckett and Baldrop – to name but a few, as they say. But then I realised some of the sexiest things I'd read had been about couples on honeymoon. Call me old-fashioned if you like, but I reckon that's a real turn-on. And before I came here I'd been running a motel specially for honeymooners and people who liked watching them getting to know each other. So Honeymooners Library seemed the obvious thing to call it.'

At this point Helen returned from the kitchenette. She had rolled the T-shirt up above her rather large navel, so that the tiny black knickers formed a downward-curving triangle framed by the smooth skin of her belly and thighs, their whiteness set off by the occasional mole. As she stepped towards them, wiggling her narrow hips provocatively, the Captain observed little wisps of her silvery-gold fur poking out through the interstices of the lace. 'Delightful,' he remarked to Victoria. 'I must compliment you on your taste.'

'My taste in underwear or my taste in friends?'

The Captain paused for a moment to consider his response. 'Oh, I knew your taste in friends must be impeccable when you consented to join our little operation here at Honeymooners.'

'You mean no one in their right mind would do it for the money?' Victoria laughed. 'Still, it's true that the companionship here in the office goes some way to make up for the sweated labour.'

'And you can always get naked if you sweat too much,' the Captain quipped.

Helen blushed under Victoria's cool gaze. Unperturbed by the restless prodding of her boss's fingers at her hips and thighs, Victoria had already nearly completed a lightning sketch of the editorial assistant in her scant panties. The Captain noticed that she had not omitted the saucily extruding pubic hair.

He was very surprised when Victoria, whose interest in men had so far proved non-existent, reached into his lap to confirm the state of his erection, which seemed to satisfy her. He squeezed harder at her thigh but she brushed his fingers away and stood up. With an arm thrown casually round Helen's shoulders, she whispered something in the girl's ear.

Both of them then gathered armfuls of shabby cushions from the two or three easy chairs in the office and laid them on the floor to form what the Captain rightly assumed to be a little love-nest. Helen lay down on her right side and the Captain prepared to witness a scene of matutinal sapphism or pre-lunch lesbianism, as he described it to himself.

But such a scene was not to be presented to his boggling eyes. Neither was he to be disappointed, however. Victoria explained that she wished to sketch him, or part of him, in action with Helen as part of her *Fucky Days* project. His trousers were off in a flash and he got down, also on his right side, behind the girl.

He was already easing the new (or second-hand) panties down over her bottom when Victoria stopped him. She used one hand to lift Helen's slim left leg and hooked the

84

fingers of her other hand into the gusset of the knickers, which she pulled upwards until the fluffy sex-mound sprang out of its lacy confinement. Then, still supporting the leg in an almost upright position, she seized the Captain's prick (somewhat gingerly, he thought) and stretched it to the point where the bulb bedded between the lips of Helen's cunt.

The Captain clenched his buttocks and shoved forward. His whole length slid up into the silky sheath. Helen now kept her leg sticking up without assistance from Victoria, using her own left hand to caress the whole area of contact between the two sets of genitals and at the same time to discourage the leg from collapsing inwards. Victoria, meanwhile, pulled the red T-shirt up over Helen's left breast and applied her lips to the nipple until it was hard, dark red and shining with saliva. For a moment the two women kissed mouth to mouth. Then Victoria knelt beside the copulating couple very close to the point of juicy conjunction and began to make rapid sketches as they fucked.

As he felt the pressure mounting in his loins, the Captain reached across with his left hand and began to play with his partner's exposed tit. He delighted in the contrast between the pebbly hardness of the nipple and the soft whiteness around it. Helen responded by contracting the muscles of her vagina so that his throbbing prick was sleeved even more tightly as it drove in and out.

Victoria gave a sigh of satisfaction and laid her sketch pad aside. She fingered the lace of Helen's knickers where it was gathered into the stretched space between her left thigh and her vulva. She smoothed the damp material over the swollen lips so that the girl's pubis was now fully covered except where the thick, slippery tube of male flesh held the elastic aside. And then, using the heel of her left hand, she began to masturbate the hidden clitoris through the knickers while with the index and middle fingers of her right hand she lightly squeezed the root of the Captain's member.

His loins quivered and heaved, and with a series of grunts he came. Stream after stream of foaming fuck-juice jetted through the constriction of Victoria's fingers, up through the length of his tightly clasped rod and out into the ecstatic depths and narrows of Helen's cunt. Worked just to the right pitch at just the right moment by Victoria's skilful frigging, the girl moaned her appreciation and brought her raised leg down to increase the pressure and coax the last drop of fluid from the spurting cock.

But the artist in Victoria Eisenberg was not yet satisfied; she was determined that her graphic version of *Fucky Days* would depict sights rarely attempted by erotic draftsmen. Helen, limp and exhausted, was made to sit on a straight-backed wooden chair with her thighs parted. She was allowed to remove her T-shirt and clasp her hands behind her neck so that the pert conical breasts with their dark tips pointed up cheekily and the hint of fine but luxuriant blonde hair in her armpits was ventilated, releasing a sexual fragrance into the room.

Victoria got the Captain to stand behind the chair and lean forward. Helen let her head flop back. His eyes tracked down over the fringe of her light brown hair, past the dark eyes shining up at him and past the wide, wet smile. His lips and tongue followed his eyes in their downward progress, dragging a moist trail across her forehead and nose until mouth found mouth. This inverted kissing gave his hands plenty of scope to wander over the mole-freckled whiteness of Helen's chest and belly, lavishing attention on those underarms and nipples and just teasing the little hairs escaping from the upper edge of her knickers – to describe it as a waistband would make the garment sound too decent.

While he occupied himself in this way until Helen began to squirm and slide her bottom forward on the wooden seat, Victoria squatted between her legs expectantly, her sketching materials on her lap. Soon her patience was rewarded. Helen writhed in the chair and the muscles of her narrow belly shuddered into tautness. She tried to control herself by bringing her legs together but Victoria leaned forward so that her shoulders were clamped between the girl's thighs and her face some six inches from the triangle of black lace. In this position it was still possible for her to draw on her pad down on the floor, sketching the arousing phenomenon that now developed before her eyes.

And before the Captain's eyes. He withdrew his tongue from Helen's mouth and licked down wetly across her chin, neck and chest until, by leaning sideways and letting her head loll free, he was able to hang right down over her belly-button, which was now forced out into even greater prominence by her orgasmic straining. From here he had a clear though inverted view of what Victoria was attempting to capture with her pencil. And as he leaned over her trembling abdomen, Helen twisted her upper body and head to take his cock, still thick and gleaming with sexual fluids, into the side of the mouth.

With each spasm of the girl's cunt more and more of his recently ejaculated sperm was forced out through the lace of her knickers. At first it appeared as a galaxy of tiny stars oozing through the network between the major features of the design. Soon it had formed a wet, whitish background to the floral whorls and curlicues of the lace. Finally, as the Captain reached into the creases of Helen's thighs and gently pinched her pussy between his middle finger and thumb, a thick, steaming flood was expelled, spreading over the surface of the knickers to drown the pattern completely and sluice down over her bottom until she was sitting in a pool of spunk.

Having finished the last of her sketches, Victoria inhaled deeply. 'I don't mind the smell of a man so much when it's spiked with girl-juice,' she remarked, looking up to give the Captain a cool wink. 'And maybe the taste won't be so bad when it's been strained through black lace.'

She buried her face in the sopping mass between Helen's thighs and slurped, tentatively at first but then greedily. When she withdrew her mouth she looked up. 'Not so bad at all,' she said. 'Sometime I must try it neat – straight from the tap.'

But that was an experiment Victoria would have to defer. Even as she spoke, it was Helen's throat that received the Captain's hot effusion and Helen's lips from which the

87

bubbling spunk overflowed in a thick cascade, coating her chin and falling in viscous stalactites to cover her right breast.

Meanwhile, a series of events had been initiated which would eventually impinge dramatically on the Captain's affairs.

A pretty young woman sat forward nervously on the seat of a minicab, her ripples of golden hair veiling the sides of her oval, innocent-looking face with its fresh complexion. She had taken the tube from East Acton, changed at Notting Hill Gate and boarded an Amersham-bound train at Baker Street. Alighting at Rickmansworth, she made for the waiting cab and had given an address somewhere out on the way to Harefield.

The middle-aged driver showed an inclination to be chatty and nosy, which was the last thing she wanted. 'Which one are you, then?' he demanded.

'What do you mean?'

'You know. I can never remember which one's which. What's their names – Annie something and Agnesthesia, is it? Which one's the blonde one? Don't tell me you're not even Swedish. Give us a song, love – you're looking like a number one all right. A regular dancing queen, if you ask me.'

'Just leave me alone, mister,' she replied, wishing this vulgar slob of a number two would mind his own business. 'I need space.'

They were now negotiating winding, leafy lanes. The morning's blustery rain had given way to sharp sunshine. She suspected that the few houses visible from the road must belong to people with more money than was good for anybody, probably obtained in ways that would make you blush.

But Sally Nugent blushed herself at the thought of what she was contemplating in her own quest for ready money. Mrs Nugent had not yet been married a year. Only eighteen and here she was taking this horrendous step without her husband's knowledge, let alone his blessing. Rod would hardly have given her his blessing if he had known what she had in mind, of course.

The truth was that the Nugents were badly strapped for cash. The nation's much-publicised emergence from recession, even the recovery – the repeated recoveries – of the housing market, had done nothing for Rod's business interests. How could a freelance estate agent and property developer survive in this climate? Sally didn't understand much about these matters but she couldn't see a secure future in Rod's scheme to build a colony of sheltered units for senior citizens on an eroding south-coast clifftop. At this rate all the land would be lost to the sea before the first bungalow was built, and she and Rod would still be living in her mum's semi.

The cab swung off the lane into a driveway blocked by a white-painted gate. A uniformed security man stepped forward to ask for ID. Sally cleared her throat and leaned forward to speak over the driver's shoulder. 'My name's Sally Nugent,' she said. 'I think Mr Yglesias won't mind seeing me – he said I could drop in any time.'

The guard stood back and spoke into his mobile phone. He frowned. 'Who did you say, madam?' he asked. 'Mr Yglesias can't remember anyone called Nugent.'

'Tell him it's Rod's Sally. Say he got to know us on honeymoon.'

'Where was that, then, madam? You'd better give a bit more detail if you haven't got an appointment or any documentary evidence.'

'Tell him the Honeymoon Palace Motel. Last July, it was. Remind him that he and Mrs Yglesias were in the room next to ours.' Sally couldn't help blushing as she said this. She was still very sensitive about these things. In fact, she blushed whenever Rod's business plans were mentioned, as he was planning to erect his senior citizens' units on the site of the burnt-out motel where she had become in some ways more intimate with the Yglesiases than with her own husband.

After a crackling outburst from the mobile phone the security man's manner changed. He opened the gate and waved the car on. It pulled up in front of a handsome, modern residence. The house was large, but dwarfed by the building beside it, an ugly barn or hangar on the side of which was painted 'YGLESIAS ENTERPRISES (VIDEO) LTD'. Sally paid off the driver and timidly approached the front door of the house.

In no time at all, an elegant and apparently delighted Yvonne Yglesias was embracing Sally and leading her through the house to a swimming pool at the back. This extension to the building had many characteristics of a middle-sized outdoor pool but was enclosed in an airy conservatory-like structure which retained and seemed to magnify the warmth of the sun's rays. Stretched on a lounger by the edge of the water, Talbot Yglesias waited to greet his unexpected guest. He did so without rising. Instead, he extended both arms and drew Sally down to receive his kiss. Her shoulder-length, straw-coloured hair fell in sparkling waves about his neck and cascaded down into the dark fuzz showing in the V at the front of his white silk gown.

The two women joined Talbot on adjacent loungers. Sally, as usual, felt a little out of place, not just because of the opulence of her surroundings but on account of her clothes. Yvonne and Talbot were classily rigged out in matching gowns, which set off their deep tans and dark hair. Sally had turned up in damson-coloured cords and a pink angora sweater which was beginning to feel uncomfortable in this greenhouse-like atmosphere. She envied the Yglesiases their cool sophistication and thirty-something good looks, and shuddered at the memory of how Rod's presence had sometimes embarrassed her in their company during that otherwise lovely honeymoon. It had been so good to spend time with a more experienced couple. Yvonne and Talbot had had plenty of time for the Nugents, as this was not their first honeymoon. They had been married before – to each other.

Talbot tinkled a little bell and asked a maid who glided in from the house to fetch drinks for the three of them. 'Great to see you again, Sal,' he said. 'You still with your Rod? Did he get over that hair-trigger problem of his?

90

Why didn't you bring him over with you – we could have had ourselves a ball.'

Sally explained with some embarrassment that she had come to discuss a matter she did not want her husband to know about, a business matter. Yvonne stood up and shrugged off her silk robe. Her long, dark body shimmered, naked, in the sunlight reflected from the surface of the water. Sally noticed that the little patch of black hair at the base of her belly had been trimmed into a perfect triangle. Discreetly, Yvonne slid into the pool and swam away from her husband and their visitor.

Talbot notched the back of his lounger up and leaned forward, allowing the front of his robe to fall open and reveal the winking gold medallion dangling in front of its bed of tight black curls. He rested a hand on Sally's knee and brought his face close to hers. 'What can I do for you, then, kitten?' he asked.

Shyly, the young woman laid her cards on the table. Rod would be furious, she reflected, if he got to know she'd been telling other people about his dodgy financial position. After the initial restoration of his sexual staying-power following their return from honeymoon it had been Rod's money worries, of course, that had brought on his pathetic state of near impotence. A sensitive issue, but Sally divulged everything, glad of an older person to confide in. Talbot sipped his drink and listened sympathetically. 'No problem,' he smiled. 'You know I said there'd always be a part for a girl with your looks and talent. Just a little matter of the so-called casting couch formalities and a quick screen test and there you go. Yglesias Enterprises can sign you up today, darling.'

It was obvious from her trembling that Sally was apprehensive, so Talbot made her finish her drink and told her to relax. 'Look,' he said, 'before we go over to the studio why don't you join Yvonne and I in the water? I've got something to do anyway before we get down to business – otherwise I'll be having your Rod's old trouble. Here!' He tossed a fluffy towel at her, disrobed his muscular hairiness and plunged cleanly into the pool. As he did so, Sally caught a glimpse of the magnificent equipment between his thighs. Her impression was that it was as impressive as ever and in a state of semi-arousal.

Withdrawing as far back as possible from the edge of the pool and trying to hide behind a small tree growing in a tub, she took off her sweater and trousers. But when she stood on the edge wondering how to get in, Yvonne waved her back. 'Get those knickers off,' she shouted. 'They're much too pretty to get wet.'

Sally found it hard to imagine what harm the water could do to the little white garment spotted with rosebuds and secured at the sides with pink bows. Still, what did it matter? She was being ridiculously coy really, considering what she and Rod had got up to with this couple on their honeymoon. Stepping out of the knickers, she sat on the edge of the pool, unclipped her white cotton bra and tossed it on the lounger behind her. The water was beautifully warm. Talbot had swum over towards her and was now splashing her, aiming at the pussy she had for a moment forgotten as she sat there with open legs. She brought her knees together and slipped down into the relative privacy of the water.

To her relief, Talbot was swimming away from her in the direction of the deep end, where his wife was floating on her back. Being a good six feet tall, he was able to stand on the bottom when he reached her. As if knowing what he had in mind, Yvonne let her legs drift apart and manoeuvred her floating body forward until her thighs had slid over his shoulders and his tongue was lapping at her waterlogged cunt.

Talbot began to wade backwards into shallower waters, towing Yvonne with him. With her legs hooked over his shoulders and the sopping sponge of her quim spread round his mouth, it became increasingly difficult for her to hold her back-tilted head above the steadily falling surface. Her husband brought his hands up between her thighs, which he then eased down until they were gripped lightly between his arms and his sides. Now she could drift behind him in a comfortably flat position as he moved backwards,

92

the lips of her sex slowly sliding down the front of his body as the water level dropped away.

Sally Nugent had anticipated his next move. As soon as the depth was just right and the blunt purple head of his prick bobbed up between the two bodies right on the plimsoll line, he used one hand to divide Yvonne's flesh while with the other he guided the dolphin-like member into her. Yvonne sighed in this weightless embrace in which the only point of contact between their two bodies was the carnal link that joined them as man and wife.

But Talbot was not yet ready to fuck. He eased himself a few feet further into the shallows, this time pushing Yvonne ahead of him on his spike instead of towing her. Her floating body subsided some six inches but by gripping her buttocks firmly in his hands he was able to keep his cock firmly seated in her vulva. Yvonne's pubic mound was now the highest point of her body. It shone in the sunlight as water streamed from its closely trimmed thatch.

Talbot beckoned Sally to move closer. He took her elbow and moved her into position so that she stood facing him with Yvonne's head floating between her open legs.

Yvonne grasped Sally's creamy hips and hauled herself up a fraction until the tip of her stiffened tongue rasped against the young woman's cunt. Sally shivered and opened her legs wider as she adopted a slightly crouching posture. This made things easier for Yvonne by allowing the water once more to support most of her weight. The busy tongue began to flick up and down between Sally's clitoris and the entrance to her vagina. Exciting memories of her seaside honeymoon came flooding back as Talbot now leaned forward to cup her firm, round breasts and plant a clinging kiss on her mouth. She remembered it had been in the moonlit sea that Talbot had first had her – he had taken her in the same way that he was now fucking Yvonne, his huge rod rummaging about inside her like a corkscrew. And at the same time Rod, her Rod, who couldn't swim, had been doing it with Yvonne up on the water's edge.

So now, as this handsome couple's tongues penetrated

her mouth and pussy with the insistence of penises and Talbot's penis screwed around in his wife's cunt with the agility, Sally recalled, of a glib tongue, she almost expected to feel her absent Rod doing something rude to her bottom. All such fantasies, however, were suddenly banished in an onrush of sexual tremors as the handsome man embracing Sally began to roger his wife convulsively. His movements drove Yvonne's tongue into a mad dance against the cunt it was licking and stretching. As the three of them fell apart in blissful satisfaction, Sally noticed that the water was tainted with a whitish cloud of spermatic jelly which formed a loose connection between Talbot's still-throbbing manhood and Yvonne's glutted slit.

They emerged from the water panting and helped to dry each other off. Talbot looked at his watch and declared that they ought to hurry over to the studio at once. It was now the lunch break and they would have the facilities to themselves for a bit. He and Yvonne put their silk robes on; Sally, the ends of her long ringlets still darkly wet and dripping, was about to get dressed when Yvonne told her to forget that and simply wrap the white towel round her. Yvonne opened a little canvas bag and with practised hands applied make-up to Sally's cheeks, lips and eyes. Then the three of them left the pool by a side door and hurried along a glass-walled passageway connecting the house to the barn-like studio. During this brief walk Sally was aware of her own juices trickling down her thighs and could not help wondering how wet the older woman must be so soon after intercourse with her husband.

There were cables all over the floor and lights everywhere. The lights, though, had been switched off and it was some moments before Sally was able to make anything out. It seemed that parts of the large floor space had been randomly allocated to a number of mini-sets. The bits of scenery looked surprisingly flimsy and ramshackle – unsafe, even. Sally commented on this and Talbot explained that work on these sets was still in progress. In any case, he said, a lot of the shooting was done outside on location. And the distributors of the kind of movie produced by

94

Yglesias Enterprises were looking for rapid throughput rather than high production values.

Sally was very struck by a superficially sumptuous interior with lots of pillars and artificial vines that looked like one of those displays she had seen in Harrods or somewhere. 'For a script called *Rogue Roman*, by the author of *Adventures of a Naked Girl*,' Yvonne told her. 'It's supposed to be the atrium of a villa where all these orgies are held. But the writer seems to have dried up on us, so we're having to sort of feel our way through by instinct and improvisation.'

To keep the conversation going and to try to conceal her nervousness, Sally asked what other projects were in the pipeline.

'Well,' said Talbot, 'there's a hot little musical number known to connoisseurs of the bizarre as *The Miracle at Kahburg*. Got to change the title, of course, or it might attract the wrong sort of punter – all those holier-than-thous. Probably best to avoid that by calling it something like *Buttered Bums*, unless our hired hacks can come up with something more appetising. Can't tell you about the other sets. They're for our next release, due out in a couple of weeks if we can sort out this glitsch in the casting. It's still under wraps, you see. You'd be surprised at the amount of industrial espionage in this game.'

They hurried past a little ticket office where Sally half expected to be asked to pay for admission. Just beyond a London bus stop beside a shelter screaming with obscene graffiti they came to a small room, or rather the corner of a room with no ceiling and with two of its walls missing. The only purpose of this apology for scenery seemed to be to provide a backdrop for a piece of furniture Sally identified as a chaise longue or chaise lounge – she had never been quite sure which, but had often thought one might look right in her mum's longish lounge in East Acton.

'Is this the famous casting couch?' she asked. 'Or do we go straight into the screen test?'

Talbot grinned. 'We're short of time, so it can be both. You can have your screen test on the casting couch.'

Still wrapped in her towel, the budding starlet was asked to recline on the couch. Yvonne made sure Sally's head was supported comfortably on cushions and draped one of her legs over the low back of the couch. As she did so, the towel fell away from the lower part of the girl's body.

Sally flinched as Yvonne switched on a cluster of powerful lights. When she got used to their dazzle, though not to the heat they generated, it registered with her that this place was not quite like the film studios of her glamorous fantasies. Something was missing. Not, of course, the sexy male lead – Talbot stood there, incredibly sophisticated and mature in that silk dressing gown. Why, he looked as if he ought to be called Raoul or Rudy or something. Come to think of it, Rudy would sound one hell of a lot more romantic than Roddy, and more appropriate as well, considering some of the things her husband got up to with her to make up for his lack of stiffness . . . No, she could see her leading man for the duration, the lights and other paraphernalia – but where were those big black cameras with their round things like Mickey Mouse ears turned sideways?

'Where are the cameras?' she asked.

'Ours is a strictly VT operation,' Talbot replied.

'VT?'

'Video. Everything's taped. I told you, it's all about low budgets and quick turnovers. Get it rolling, Yvonne. We'll do without the clapper board for this one.'

Sally saw Yvonne raise an efficient-looking piece of technology to her shoulder. It was larger than those camcorders people had used on the beach at the Honeymoon Palace Motel, but still compact and light enough to be portable. Before Sally could comment on it, however, Talbot's lips were fluttering over her eyelashes, brushing against her cheek and mumbling into her mouth. She yielded to the probing tongue which snaked between her teeth.

Out of the corner of her eye she saw Yvonne shifting about with the camera. Sally trembled, knowing she had to keep her leg up on the back of the couch so that some shots could be taken down there between her legs. She wished she'd had a chance to wipe that wet stuff off her thighs, though usually it was quite clear and colourless. But what if there were globs of it trapped in her yellow hairs? That could look as rude as Rod's stuff did when he used to squirt it out while trying to stick his thing in her.

These embarrassing thoughts were overtaken by electrifying sensations as Talbot's hand pulled away her towel and palmed one of her breasts. The tip of his tongue traced a wet trail down over her chin, neck and chest before flickering at the tip of her other nipple. Oh no! The teat was standing up so stiff and wet that it reminded her of a little prick – and now Yvonne was crouching beside them filming it.

Talbot had discarded his robe and she could feel the cool gold of his medallion resting on her tummy. Best just to relax. After all, it had been really nice when he'd done it to her on their honeymoon and she'd got used to being watched on those occasions, mostly by the Captain. Let yourself go, girl, she urged herself.

The tongue, predictably, had now moved down to the open flesh between her thighs. Even worse, a licked finger was abusing her bottom. In spite of her resolution Sally couldn't help feeling a bit ashamed at being penetrated in this way on camera. And yet, however guilty she felt about it, she knew those waves of lewdness were soon going to wash through her tummy and her naughtiness was going to burst uncontrollably.

Without removing his face and hands from her quivering flesh Talbot had swung himself round, straddling her body with his knees. His behind stuck up in the air. Sally could see his balls dangling above her, swaying in time with his licking and probing, and his long prick curving against the thicket of hairs on his belly. She stroked up the insides of her screen lover's muscular, hairy thighs; he responded by bringing his haunches down and using his free hand to force the knob of his penis into her mouth.

Loosely gripping the veined shaft between her lips, Sally ran the tip of her tongue over the contours of the wicked intruder. The actual head felt as smooth as satin and it seemed to be especially hard and firm at the rim, beyond which the surface texture changed as she explored the drawn-back skin. Still further down it was more like velvet, a velvet sheath clinging to a gnarled rod of iron.

No, she thought. I mustn't think of anything that reminds me of my Rod. Let me concentrate on tall Talbot. After all, this is supposed to be some sort of a test. She reversed the direction of her exploring tongue, dragging it up the seamed underside of Talbot's cock and lingering at the place where that little piece of skin connected the foreskin to the plum. And then, with a little gesture of daring, she licked right into the slot that was going to spit all that white stuff out.

It would flood her mouth. Even if she swallowed down as much as she could, lots of the sticky liquid would be bound to dribble out between her lips and she always felt embarrassed when that happened, even with Rod – somehow it seemed so rude and degrading. And yet she couldn't resist pressing the tip of her tongue really hard into Talbot's slot, making it gape open in her mouth as his own tongue sliced between the soft layers of her girlflesh. She was getting carried away.

There, it must be starting. She recognised that salty taste. She had noticed it as soon as the head pushed in past her teeth but now it had suddenly got so much stronger. The head was all slippery now, and Sally knew it wasn't the slipperiness of her own saliva but that clear stuff that came welling out when a man got excited and was going to come. The whole prick had swelled out even more and was twitching and throbbing in her mouth.

The funny thing was, she was so excited herself that it felt as if the prick was ramping about down there in her cunt.

With reptilian swiftness Talbot slipped his dick out of her mouth and his finger out of her bottom, relinquished his tonguing of her pussy and completely reversed his position. Rod could never move with that sort of agility. Nor, for all his skill at getting her worked up, could the Captain, who had given her such wonderful morning workouts after the Yglesiases had finished their own honeymoon. But he was older, of course, the Captain.

Already Talbot had hooked his stiff corkscrew up into her and then drawn it right back to diddle about at her squelchy opening for the benefit of the camera. Yvonne, she realised, had grasped the leg that rested on the back of the couch and forced it up further to get a better view for her hungry lens. Sally didn't care. She had lost all sense of shame as she thrilled to this glorious lovemaking. Talbot's hands were working at her tits and his tongue, coated with her sweet and sour juices, was sliding against her own as his prick had been doing a moment before.

His whole body stiffened. Sally thought his mouth would suffocate her as the great tube of pulsing flesh thrust deep, deep into her belly and discharged burst after burst, wave after wave of his boiling virility into a cunt which was now convulsing with a gulping, orgasmic life of its own. Sally shouted out loud and thrashed about. When at last her tremors began to subside she lay back gasping in Talbot's firm embrace. She became aware of the faint murmur of the camera as Yvonne filmed the rivers of spunk that ran down into the recently fingered mouth of her bottom and on down to gather in a slippery lake on the couch between her buttocks. But Sally was not ashamed of herself. She was proud. She knew she had passed her screen test and was going to be a starlet. She might one day appear on TV. She might even go to Hollywood.

'Come on, you lovebirds,' Yvonne was saying. 'Let's go sign that contact. There's caviare and champagne waiting over in the house and we can watch this tape while we celebrate. No, Sally dear, don't bother to wipe your cunt. Talbot and I like our caviare served in a rather special way.'

SIX

LOOPHOLES AND PEEPHOLES

The Captain looked forward to Thursdays. It was not that Victoria Eisenberg's presence on the other days failed to stimulate him – on the contrary. But it made a change to have young Helen all to himself, just as he had done when he first set up shop with her. Since the talented illustrator had joined Honeymooners a month ago his quality time with his editorial assistant had been encroached on to such an extent that he was often reduced to the role of a drooling spectator of displays of affection indulged in by the two girls. This, to be sure, was a role he relished and was well fitted to play. But from time to time he craved more active involvement.

In what was becoming an established Thursday morning routine, he had got Helen to clear his desk and remove her lower garments. Two flat cushions protected the girl's pointed hips from bruising and made the compression of her small breasts more comfortable as she stretched out on her stomach. Helen's height was only a few inches more than the length of the desk; with her feet and ankles sticking out over the right-hand end it was possible for her to cradle her face in her arms over to the left. When the Captain drew up his chair his own face was immediately above her neat white bottom. He loved to rest a notepad on the small of her back and scribble little memos to Victoria and himself. From time to time he would interrupt this work to dip a finger or his nose into the tempting and fragrant flesh before him, much as an old-fashioned clerk would have dipped his pen into an inkwell.

This morning, in spite of the coffee they had been drinking since eleven-thirty, he felt drowsy. He had dispensed with the notepad and was running his fingertips lightly up the back of Helen's right thigh, over the soft hillock above it, across the small of her back with its scarcely perceptible dusting of fine, downy hair, then down again over the left buttock and on down the nearer thigh. Up the left leg, across and down the right one; up the right one, across and down the left one. Sometimes, for the sake of variety, he crossed directly from the back of one knee to the other, to repeat the circuit he had just completed instead of retracing it in reverse.

On each circuit he took a different route. Instead of sticking to the central high-road along the thighs and over the swelling curves of her buttocks, he would deviate widely between the limits set by her prone position. When he chose the outer pathway, pressing the tips of his fingers between the front of a warm thigh and the cushion beneath it, he paused for a while at the top of the run, gently probing under the girl's lean but slightly yielding flank and stretching the middle finger inwards as if reaching for her sex. The inner route offered more temptation. Stroking up between the insides of her two thighs introduced a note of uncertainty to the exercise – Helen could not be sure whether, at the top of his run, he was going to stroke up over her left buttock or her right one.

She couldn't even be sure he would swerve one way or the other at all. The Captain's hand hovered deliciously, just touching the damp hairs of her fanny. She was aware of his breath in the groove of her bottom and thought she could feel a dribble of saliva irrigating the groove.

The phone rang.

Instead of removing his right hand from its warm nesting place the Captain twisted his wrist so that the fleshy web between his index finger and thumb fitted snugly against Helen's perineum. Quite suddenly his thumb was pressing into her tight little anus, his index finger slipped up into her vagina and the nail of his middle finger was lightly scratching at her clitoris. Helen gasped at the blissful and unexpected invasion.

Resting his stubbly chin on her right buttock, the Captain reached across her with his left hand and lifted the receiver of the phone to his ear. He spoke between clenched teeth.

'Honeymooners Library,' he said. 'Thank you for your call. At this time there is nobody in the office. Please give your name and telephone number after the tone and state your business as clearly and briefly as possible. Thank you once more – *bleeeep.*'

This practised bullshitting was followed by a muffled burst of female chatter from the earpiece. 'Oh, Captain,' the familiar voice began, 'I was really hoping to speak to you in person. I hate these answering machines, don't you? I'm phoning from California, so if you could just call me back on . . .'

Foreseeing cashflow problems if he got into habits like that, the Captain abandoned the pretence, unclenched his teeth and interrupted the caller in his normal voice.

'So glad to hear from you, my dear Miss Muttock. Not in trouble with the authorities, I trust?'

The Captain knew that his old friend had opted for an extended visit to the States to avoid interrogation on the matter of procuring a forged British passport. Just as well she had decided to do a runner, as any investigation would have been likely to uncover the identity of the main culprit, the Captain himself. He also knew that the choice of America for her temporary exile was not without its dangers. Although Mary Muttock had many friends and former satisfied clients out there, dating back to her Arizona days when she had turned tricks at that notorious Raunch Ranch, the Californian heavens would fall on her if ever the lid blew off the Banesville University Library scam. Her role, secondary though that had been, would not be easy to conceal.

'Any doubts being cast on the new Banesville acquisitions?' he asked.

'Captain, I'm in Banesville right now. If anyone suspects this material's not kosher, they're certainly not letting on. No, the library's mounted a big exhibit, as they call it. *Shameful Secrets: the Sordid Flipside of Nineteenth-Century British Literary Classics*. It's really pulling the crowds. At this rate old Frolander – he's putting me up for a couple of nights – old Frolander reckons they'll recover what they paid for our stuff by Thanksgiving at the latest.'

'Three fucking million?'

'Well, they've also done a deal for the film rights. Some obscure British studio, he said. An unknown independent producer out near Rickmansworth, I think. Hollywood won't touch anything as strong as this.'

'Been to Hollywood yourself yet?'

'You bet. Spent a few weeks in Beverly Hills before I came down here. Did the tour of the stars' bedrooms, you might say. I'm passing myself off as a Hollywood call-girl now – most of them are Brits, you know. I'm really in demand, partying every night. Oh, Captain, life's just great right now. Like the old days at the Ranch, but without the barbed wire. Whoops – someone's just come in. No more talk about nineteenth-century classics. Hallo, there. Ouch! Yes, Captain, life out here's one long party.'

As Mary Muttock enthused about life in the New World, the Captain worked patiently at Helen's private parts. The girl was beginning to quiver and the cushion beneath her sex was damp with her seepage. It amused and excited him to recollect that in her Cunlip College days his caller had entertained lustful yearnings for Helen, who had been one of her wilder students.

He placed the telephone receiver in the hollow of Helen's back and rested his right cheek on her nearer buttock. In this position he could still hear the Muttock's outpourings loud and clear from across the Atlantic and could also mumble into the mouthpiece from his warm cushion of quaking flesh.

Miss Muttock asked him what he was doing. First he answered the question in general terms, outlining the Honeymooners Library project and inviting her to write down and submit one of the erotic fantasies she had so often related to him. After this, he told her what he was doing there and then.

'I'm sitting here in my office. I don't think of it as my office though. It's my Palace of Eros.'

'Because of all the erotica, no doubt.'

'That too. But mainly because of what I get up to with my staff.'

'Got it up now, have you, that staff of yours?'

'You're a wit, Muttock. I'm referring to my employees. Remember your little friend Helen Lascelles? I've got her right here on the desk in front of me and I'm in the middle of giving her a three-finger fuck. Well, strictly speaking two fingers and only one of them up her cunt. The other one's teasing her clit and you can guess where my thumb is.'

'Oh, I can guess, Captain,' came the reply, a strangely vibrant tone distorting the Muttock's voice. 'You've got your thumb in her just where your ex-colleague Professor Wayne Packard's got his big bully of a willie in me right now. He's shagging my bum like one of those pioneers opening up the West. Ouch! I tell you, it's a magnificent piece of meat he's got between those beefy thighs of his, but I sometimes wish he'd put it where I imagine your first finger is. This man's a cowboy, I tell you. Wow! He's a frigging animal. Oooh! No, Professor, I can't take any more. Not another inch. Sorry, Captain, I'm getting carried away. Yes, I'll see if I can write something for your bored honeymooners to read. Plenty of inspiration out here. Must go now. No, not go – I must COME!'

The conversation was abruptly terminated. At last the Captain was able to devote his full attention to his assistant's needs. Very little further attention was required to bring her to the brink; in fact, she had already been hovering there for some minutes, the flesh of her inflamed womanhood twitching around his fingers. To trigger her release he rolled her over so that she was lying on her back. Then he pulled up the loose sweater which was all she was wearing, reached over to her further breast with his left hand and twisted the nipple. At the same time he stooped his head to the left and closed his teeth lightly but definitely on the stiff, dark stalk of the right teat. Helen rent the air with a shriek of ecstasy which provoked exclamations of surprise from the market down below.

All this time the Captain had been exercising a high degree of self-command. He had not even opened his zip, in spite of the painful constriction of his erection. For him, the game had only just begun.

He instructed Helen to remain where she was and made his way rather awkwardly down the stairs, taking care not to let his gonads get pinched in his trousers as he negotiated the steep steps. Something struck him as odd. As always on a Thursday, the North End Road market would be closing down for the afternoon. The stallholders were packing up their barrows, he realised, but even so the hubbub of voices out on the streets seemed unusually subdued. He heard busty Sharon wondering if they ought to get the Bill round to see if any damage had been done. 'I always thought that old geezer had a funny look in his eyes,' she was saying. Helen's shriek must have been clearly audible down at street level, then. But Sharon's Sid told her to stop worrying – he reckoned it was 'just a bit of domestic'.

Only one fat letter lay on the floor. The Captain picked it up but the typed label on the large brown envelope told him nothing about the sender. He returned to the office with it and found Helen breathing rather more calmly but still very deeply.

Removing one of the cushions from under the girl, he turned the one on which her bottom rested through a right angle with her on it so that her slender white thighs projected over the front edge while her feet dangled down. He parted her knees and drew up his chair between them. Immediately before his eyes Helen presented the ultimate erotic feast: fringed with pale, silky fur and oozing with the juices recently released, that pretty little fuck-hole he was growing so fond of pouted and twitched expectantly.

The Captain leaned forward. But instead of burying his face in the moist flesh that gave off such a heady fragrance he reached right up to her bare tits and squeezed them

105

while lightly licking the skin of her belly right at the edge of her pubic fluff. Then he sat up, opened the letter and asked Helen to read it to him in her supine position while he devoted himself in earnest to her pleasuring.

At first, with the tip of his nose lodged against her clitoris, he simply pressed the flat of his tongue over the engorged labia. Next he curled the tip into a point which just tickled her anus, at the same time using his hands to fondle the undercurves of her buttocks, the soft outsides of her thighs, the velvet points of her little hip-bones and the sensitive creases dividing the inner thighs from the outer lips of her sex. As he fondled and teased, the layers of flesh fell apart and the whole width of his tongue luxuriated against the tender slickness of her opened inner petals.

The girl started to read. Only a slight tremor in her voice betrayed the arousal of her loins as she began to move towards a second climax.

'*Dear sir-stroke-madam,*' she began. '*As you will be aware, I am an established author of erotic novels and wish to stress that I am writing to you in confidence on the advice of my friend Mrs Sylvia Lascelles.*'

Helen gasped in surprise at this mention of her mother's name. The Captain, too, was puzzled. Strange, he thought. If this person was put on to me by Helen's mum, how come the uncertainty about my gender? He told the girl to continue, then tightened his tongue into something like a fleshy tube and thrust it into the syrup of her tight vagina.

'*I am growing somewhat disillusioned with my publisher, who until now has held a dominant position in the field and has been able to set the going rate for royalties at a disgracefully low percentage. The Chancellor's recent budget has spared us the ultimate squeeze of a tax on knowledge in the form of newspapers and books but his fiscal if not his personal reputation seems insecure and the threat remains. I am obliged to look around for more generous terms and understand that your new enterprise is one which seeks to slough off the old stereotype of the polished mahogany, leather-upholstered, horsehair-stuffed publishing house with rambling consultations over sherry and vague promises over lunch at*' *the Athenaeum. My informant tells me that the Honey-mooners Library is a cut-throat, cost- and corner-cutting, up-to-the-minute outfit anxious to engage writers of quality and to undercut your rivals in this highly competitive field.* Yes,' panted Helen, 'I suppose I would have given Mummy that sort of impression of the business. But I didn't think she'd be chatting to other writers.'

'Don't worry, dear,' the Captain reassured her, with-drawing his tongue for a moment to do so. 'At this stage of our operation any publicity's good publicity. How does this greedy pornographer go on? We don't even know yet if it's a sir or a madam addressing me as "dear sir-stroke-madam".' He returned to his licking and thrusting and Helen, her articulation increasingly disrupted by the invol-untary heaving of her loins, continued.

'*In line with pernicious standard practice, the contract for my last novel stipulates that my next work of erotic fiction must also be submitted to the same publisher for first refusal. I would seem to be trapped in a cycle of deprivation and depravity: the harder I work, the more I have to sweat for an ever-dwindling pittance. I have thought with envy of the lot of those writers who have signed up with you, for every-thing tells me you are set to sweep away the stigma of pov-erty to which we hacks in the service of Venus have too long been condemned.* Believe me, Captain, I never told Mummy anything like that. Oh yes – slip your finger up there and rub your nose up and down while I clench my cunt muscles as hard as I can on your tongue. Oh yes! Mmmm! ... Where was I?

'*But perhaps there is no need for me to languish in a state of impotent envy. Although I have no stomach for litigation and do not propose to follow the dangerous example of a lady whose interests are dear to my heart –* who can that be? *– I believe I might gain admittance to your stable of mettle-some thoroughbreds without violating the terms of my con-tract.* Go on – put your hands on my tits and twist the nipples the way you do. *There is an obvious legal loophole through which I propose to slip.* Oh no – you've slipped right inside again! *I am required to submit the manuscript of*

107

my next work for first refusal, but the publisher is under no obligation to accept it. My plan, then, is this. I have deliberately lowered my standards to a level that guarantees rejection. Aaah! What are you doing to my cunt, you wicked man? *I have, in short, produced what is known in the trade as a turkey. As soon as I receive your assent I will deliver this piece of poultry to my current exploiters, get it rejected, pluck it and gut it and generally spruce it up. Then it will be yours. As you will see from the enclosed synopsis and specimen chapter, "The Palace of Peepholes" in its polished version promises to be – o-o-o-ooooh! – a minor erotic masterpiece. Yours in confidence, Delver Maddingley.'*

Unlike Helen, the Captain had managed to contain himself until the end of this curious letter. But now his urgings could be denied no longer. Rising to his feet, he unzipped his trousers to let his swollen staff leap out. He forced his hands, palms upward, under Helen's bottom and lifted her open girlhood so that its petals clung to the knob. Then he shoved, cramming the length and thickness of the pulsing cock right up into her cunt. By leaning forward he was able to batten on a hard nipple with his lips and teeth. The girl tightened on his bursting flesh, kicking her legs up behind him.

Half a dozen thrusts and the pent-up spunk was racing along the tormented penis to gush into a cunt which had been thirsting for it all the morning. He raised his head from her nipple and found her gazing up at him in mute adoration.

He had hardly zipped his prick back in his trousers, got Helen settled down to work at her word-processor and wiped the musky spillage from the top of his desk when the door buzzer sounded. Although he had meant to devote himself for the next hour or so to this Maddingley manuscript, he was happy enough to admit Anne Amory and Carla Merryweather. Today they were dressed in expectation of rain. Carla had let her dark curls down to rest on the shoulders of a shiny red plastic mackintosh. Except that Anne's hair was blonde and cut in a fringe at the

108

front, it struck the Captain for the first time that she rather resembled her friend now that Carla had adopted this shoulder-length hairdo. Anne's raincoat was of black gaberdine. Somewhat incongruously, they both wore white socks – Anne's pulled up to her knees and Carla's rolled down round her ankles – and black shoes. Neither of their pretty faces was made up.

The girls said they had come over from Earl's Court on the off-chance of a bit more modelling work. 'Didn't I tell you?' he queried. 'We may be having a bit of an outdoor shoot in about a month's time – I'll let you know.'

'Pity,' said Carla. 'We thought you might like to take us the way we are now.'

Turning their backs on him so that they stood facing Helen, they unbuttoned their coats. Helen giggled. The Captain quite expected them to be naked underneath but when they turned round and removed the outer garments he realised what Helen was finding so amusing: they had put on their old Cunlip uniforms.

With her darker colouring Carla looked splendid in the crisp white shirt, striped tie and short grey pleated skirt he remembered so well. The effect was enhanced by the fact that her bosom had filled out a little since the days when she wore these clothes daily. He could tell from the slight bouncing when she walked that she had no bra under it.

Anne had chosen the alternative gear, the pale blue dress, buttoning down the front, that the girls had worn in the summer. Her knees peeped out cheekily between the hem of this dress and the tops of her white socks. She too had grown a bit since those glorious days at Cunlip College and the buttons over her chest were straining at their buttonholes.

'That would seem to be quite correct, girls,' the Captain remarked, eyeing them up and down. 'All shipshape and Bristol fashion, wouldn't you say, Helen?'

Helen grinned. 'They can't be shipshape without the regulation navy knickers. Show the Captain what you've got on.'

Anne and Carla needed no prompting, although Anne

was blushing deeply. They raised their skirts to their waists, revealing a pair of pussies bare except for the young-womanly growths of pubic hair – a little blonde triangle in Anne's case and a rather more luxuriant delta of black fur on her chum. After posing for a moment with their thighs crossed and their fingers toying with the curls at the base of their bellies, they turned, parted their legs and bent right down to display their bottoms and the tempting cunt-mounds pushing out as if asking to be fucked.

Carla's hand reached up through her legs and cupped the pursed flesh. The tip of a finger flicked up and down the damp lips and plunged in until it was completely swallowed. 'Don't you want to get out your camera or something after all and zoom in on us?' she asked. 'Don't we look naughty enough for you and your honeymooners?'

'They look naughty enough for a good spanking,' Helen observed. 'Remember that time when the Muttock caught you frigging yourself behind the bike sheds, Anne?'

The Captain considered for a moment. 'Come round to-morrow morning, my dears,' he said. 'Wear the same clothes. We'll save the spanking till then – I'd like our bright new illustrator to make a sketch of you in that atti-tude. We don't need any more photos for a while, not indoor ones, anyway. But let's go upstairs. It's not all lights and cameras up there, you know. Get back to work now, Helen, and take any phone calls, will you?'

He took Anne and Carla up to the bedroom and began to undress. Seeing this, the girls sniggered and did the same, leaving their white socks on at his request.

'I feel a bit funny about going on this bed,' said Anne. 'I mean, it's where you and Helen sleep, isn't it?'

'You silly goose,' mocked her bolder chum. 'They're not married, are they? We've got as much right as her.'

The Captain put Anne right about his domestic arrange-ments. 'We're not even living together,' he explained. 'Helen comes in every day. She commutes.'

The three of them got on the bed, the Captain lying on his back between the two girls. 'Make love to each other, you two,' he ordered, 'but see if you can do it reaching across me. I've just had a bonk with young Helen and it may be a while before the old Adam's restored. *Non sum qualis eram*, as the Roman poet complains.'

Anne smiled at him. 'We did a bit of Latin with Miss Muttock on Tuesday afternoons but each new lesson we started we all seemed to have forgotten the last one. I think we only got as far as that thing called the Absolute Absolute and Questions Expecting the Answer No.'

'Most of my questions these days are like that,' the Captain replied. 'But I never take "no" for an answer. Get on with it, girls. Let's see how well you know your principal parts. Come on – *amo, amatis, amamus*. Go for her *anus mirabilis*, Carla.'

Carla began to quake with laughter, setting her breasts a-quiver. 'I've just remembered what we used to chant in the dorm,' she said. ' "*Hunc hanc hoc*, a lovely big fat cock; *horum harum horum*, he stuck it in and tore 'em." How witty that used to seem.'

Anne, too, was becoming hysterical. 'Oh, look,' she hooted, 'I think his old Adam's apple's on the move again!'

Both girls fell about, pawing each other and rubbing their bodies all over the Captain's coarse-haired trunk and limbs. Although they were more or less following his instructions, devoting themselves to the arousal and satisfaction of their mutual needs, it was obvious that his restored virility was acting as a powerful catalyst and the focal centre of their activities.

Still with a clear memory of those Latin lessons twenty or thirty years ago (well, it must be more like forty really, he admitted to himself), the Captain pictured himself sitting in the back row beside Hardwicke Minor. In those days of county scholarships you didn't need to be posh to get yourself a decent education, just a bit cunning – what you might call scholastically streetwise. Hardwicke Minor used to lift the lid of his desk and jerk off over black-and-white photos of big-titted, bald-twatted tarts. As well as recalling those illicit thrills in the back row, the Captain also remembered old Scrotebag clutching the tatters of his gown round his narrow shoulders and rambling on about the *meta*, the pillar, at the end of the arena, round which the charioteers had to race. Carla and Anne were reining themselves in pretty tightly as they cavorted round the Captain's pillar of flesh and brushed over his bollocks. His male scent, laced with the recent spendings of Helen's cunt, seemed to be driving them wild as their laughter died away and they got really serious in their headlong race to orgasm.

For him this was sheer enjoyment. His hands wandered loosely over the squirming bodies of his companions but, although they had started with Anne on his left and Carla on his right, they were so active that he soon had no sense of who was who. There were breasts everywhere, firm but bouncing, their nipples as hard as bullets. His genitals were swathed in silky hair, soft and voluptuous, and a curtain of silky tresses trailed over the ticklishness of his belly. Tongues aimed at girlish flesh lapped against him on the way to their goals. Moony bottoms filled his field of vision and youthful thighs parted to disclose the downy fruits of sex, vulvas wet already and dripping with lust.

And now his hands ceased their random wandering. They homed in on the sexual parts of the two girls to caress them internally and externally at the same time. His fingers were quite firm in their manipulation but he let his arms hang loosely so that the friends, who were getting more and more worked up, could still move about as they wished or as their lewdness impelled them. Without giving the matter much thought, the Captain supposed they must be manoeuvring themselves into some kind of sixty-nine position above him.

His manhood was totally enclosed in their embrace. Both cunts were held in and on his fingers. Both mouths were working wetly around those fingers and cunts, and yet it felt as if his prick was fucking its way into a third vagina, tight, pulsing and slippery. Before he could fathom what was happening, his balls clenched themselves, the sensation along the length of his stem grew unbearable and he released a jetting fountain of sperm up through the writhing, sliding bodies that sleeved it so lasciviously.

* * *

As promised, Anne and Carla returned the next morning, again wearing their Cunlip uniforms, to act as models for Victoria Eisenberg. Victoria was delighted to meet them. She began with a few quick sketches showing them looking quite demure but plainly bent on mischief. Soon they were holding up their skirts to display their bare bottoms and fannies. Helen had to stand between Anne and Carla as they bent over with their backs to Victoria. The Captain's editorial assistant placed her hands on the buttocks as if administering a sound smacking; Victoria used clever cross-hatching to suggest the marks already inflicted on the soft flesh.

Helen seemed eager to go further, but Victoria shooed her away and arranged the girls in a suggestive posture on the couch. To distract his frustrated assistant, the Captain called her over to sit on his lap while he fondled her privates through her yellow silk knickers and dictated a letter to her. Her tapping on the computer keyboard became somewhat irregular as his fingers made their presence felt.

'*Dear Delver Maddingley,*' he began. 'Well, I don't know if it's mister or miz, do I, Helen? *I have read your synopsis and specimen chapter with interest and with some surprise and I must tell you at once that I doubt whether your "Palace of Peepholes" is suitable material for the Honeymooners Library. Indeed, although you seem to imply that you have sent me what you call the polished version, I cannot help wondering if you have erroneously enclosed what bibliographers would call your foul papers.* Spell that "F-O-W-L", pet. I think our Delver's smart enough to get the allusion to turkeys.

'New paragraph, dear.

'*Although we make exceptions for established erotic classics and for writing of really high quality, this company specialises in commercial fiction tailor-made for the mass market. We have to be confident of substantial sales quantities before taking a project on. Frankly, I believe most of our potential readers would find it hard to cope with your laboured syntax, exotic vocabulary and over-adjectival, poncy style.* Remember to check whether "poncy" has a "Y" or

113

"EY", Helen. No, don't go grabbing for the dictionary now – just concentrate on your typing and let me soothe you through your knickers like this so the juices trickle through on to my fingers. How far had we got?'

'You were just starting to make my clitty push out under its little hood.'

'No, I mean how far had we got with the letter?'

'*Laboured syntax, exotic vocabulary and over-adjectival, poncy style.* You were wondering how to spell "poncy".'

'Right. Let's go on. Same paragraph. *We don't actually split the syllables up with hyphens, but if we could afford the paper we would like to use jumbo-sized print with lots of space between the words. Moreover, we are breaking new ground by using photographs and drawings to illustrate our novels; this will obviate the need for convoluted descriptions of acrobatic group activities such as I find on page thirty-six of your manuscript.*

'New paragraph, Helen. No, sit still – I'll keep it just inside the lips, like this. Let's try to keep you simmering away nicely for the time being. It can all boil over when we've finished this letter.

'*Another thing. We are publishing what has been described as one-handed reading matter. We aim to give our readers the sort of thrill experienced by voyeurs. They will be able to get off on imagining they are watching beautiful people fucking. Your book is evidently about –* underline "about" *– about a voyeur; it is hard to believe that the punters would derive much pleasure from imagining themselves watching the rather unattractive hero masturbate while he hangs around peepholes watching other people doing sex.*

'That's right, just relax those thighs and we'll toss off our last couple of paragraphs.

'*Finally, in spite of its veneer of sophistication, I find the taste of your erotic fantasy somewhat questionable. And when I say "taste", let me be more precise: the action is pervaded by bad smells.* Underline "smells". *While these might inflame the lust of the perverted and dirty-minded, I do not think they would appeal to a mass readership. There are, after all, certain standards to be upheld.*

'Paragraph.

'Please feel free to submit other work you think we might be able to use. And in appreciation of the interest you have shown in Honeymooners by availing yourself of this legal loophole to solicit our support, you are cordially invited to attend a masked reception we are giving at 7 p.m. on Friday, May 7th, for our authors, most of whom are understandably jealous of their reputations and reluctant to disclose their identities even to their fellow toilers in the vineyard. I remain, etcetera.

'By the way, Anne and Carla, I'd like to hire you for that evening. I want you to take part in a little entertainment we're laying on for our distinguished and talented guests.'

Helen gasped with undisguised relief that this session of dictation was over. 'I'll check the letter through and correct it later,' she said. 'But first you've just got to bring me off. The things you've been doing to me, Captain – I can't bear it any longer.'

She clamped her own right hand over the Captain's, which was resting on the crotch of her yellow knickers as he probed and tickled through the thin silk. Frenziedly she ground his palm all over her pubic region and then pressed three of his fingers so hard into the central cleft that the sodden material was forced deep into her cunt. Her head fell back on the Captain's right shoulder and she screamed so loudly that he hoped all the market stalls had been cleared away by now. He could do without the reputation of a suspected serial killer.

This little scene had distracted Victoria and her two models from their work. The youngsters were sitting side by side on the couch. Both still wore their black shoes and white socks. Just as they had been yesterday, Anne's socks were pulled up to her knees while Carla's were rolled down to her ankles. Carla had shed her skirt, loosened her tie and unbuttoned her white shirt, opening it so that one of her breasts was completely uncovered and the dark areola of the other one just visible at the edge of the garment. Anne retained her blue dress. She had undone the buttons from the mid-thigh hem up to just below her bosom and pulled the lightweight cotton fabric to the sides, tucking it

115

under her so that the points of her little hip bones were exposed. The girls' arms rested lightly on each other's shoulders; they gazed dreamily into each other's eyes. Carla's leg was lying across Anne's thigh, not high enough to conceal the blonde hairs that fringed her cunt and offered such a soft contrast to her friend's black ones.

'I'm just making pencil sketches now,' Victoria explained. 'Later I want to do some really classy airbrush work based on them. These little dears are screaming out for acrylic treatment. And I want to use you two as well.'

She finished her latest sketch with a few deft strokes of her pencil and asked Helen to take everything off. But when she saw the girl pushing her yellow knickers down her thighs Victoria told her to pull them up again and leave them on. The Captain could tell that she was fascinated by Helen's rather large belly-button. He supposed she was probably reluctant to let the eye be distracted from this feature by a wet cunt.

Victoria's intention was to begin with a picture of Helen alone. Anne and Carla moved to the ends of the couch to make room for her. At first she was told to cross her legs and clasp her hands behind her neck. This exposed the damp underarm fuzz, slightly fairer than the straight, light brown hair of her head. It also lifted the small breasts. Although the other two girls were not going to be in this picture, the artist instructed them to lean across and lick and suck the dark little nipples into arousal so that they stood up like shining snouts.

A quick sketch in this posture, the curves of Helen's crossed thighs emphasising the narrowness of the waist with its saucily pouting navel, was followed by another. This was identical except that her legs were uncrossed and parted, revealing the dark stain that soaked the yellow silk and the straggling light brown hairs poking out round the sides and top of the skimpy garment.

'Fine,' purred Victoria. 'You're looking really sultry, dear.'

'That's how she always looks,' Carla volunteered, whereupon Helen's glower became even more sultry.

A third picture followed, similar to this last one but with

one of Helen's hands inside the knickers and her bottom thrust forward to the edge of the couch.

By this time the Captain was feeling uncomfortably hard and he was pleased when Victoria asked him to get undressed for one last sketch in which he would appear with the three girls. Helen was told to get up and he sat down between Anne and Carla, who were still dressed as in their previous pictures. The outsides of their smooth thighs pressed against his hairy ones. At the touch, he stiffened up even tighter.

Victoria placed his arms round the girls' necks and made him reach down to cup their outer breasts while they slumped against him and gazed up rapturously into his face. At first his hands completely covered the soft tits but Victoria was a perfectionist and insisted that although he could pinch the nipples he must leave the engorged tips showing for the picture.

She encouraged Anne and Carla to fondle his genitals for a while, just to give the final touch to his towering erection, which was soon fully primed. 'Helen, darling,' she said, 'slip out of those cute little knickers, will you, and sit on his lap, astride his legs. No, not facing him. I want a full frontal view of his rod standing up stiff between your pretty pussy lips. That's right – it looks just as if it belongs to you, poking out like that. What do you want to do with your hands? Good. Just lift those little titties of yours so I can get some nice highlights on them, but don't hide them.'

The picture was rapidly executed and a slight adjustment called for in preparation for the final sketch of what promised to be a really hot sequence. Helen had to lean well forward with her breasts right down on her knees so that Carla could guide the Captain's cock into her tight cunt. Then she leaned back into her previous position against the hairy chest. The Captain gasped as he felt his stiffness being bent right back into a steep curve. Victoria made Helen move up and down on him for a few thrusts until the thick stem was thoroughly lubricated, wet and shining with her juices. Then she got the girl to rest back against him once

117

more and told him to use his hands on her tits, moulding and tickling them. Although his swollen glans was firmly lodged inside her, most of the glistening cock was now visible. The Captain was well aware of this and his mouth watered as he imagined what it would look like with the airbrush treatment.

Now that Helen's hands were no longer needed on her chest, they were directed to the pubic areas of the half-naked girls on either side of her. The thumb and forefinger of one hand served as an intrusive frame for Carla's wetly spread vulva while the middle finger of the other probed Anne's blonde-furred slit to the knuckle. As a final touch, the two flatmates had to use their outer hands to tease their own tits and their inner ones to hold Helen's cuntlips wide open. They did this with the palms turned to face each other so that their thumbs could titillate and gently lift the bollocks that hung over the forward edge of the couch.

When, after what seemed an hour of exquisite agony, Victoria laid aside her sketchpad, the Captain asked her to run upstairs to fetch a camera. It would be interesting, he thought, to compare the products of lens and airbrush, and in any case he didn't know how long it would take Victoria to come up with the finished article. He couldn't wait.

As for his present predicament, he found he was able to wait just long enough for a couple of photos to be taken by Victoria. By this time Helen, too, had reached the limits of endurance with his bent stiffness forced so tightly against the front wall of her vagina. It was unnecessary as well as impossible for the Captain to move beneath her, restrained as she was by the hands of the other two girls in her crotch. Starting with a violent twitch, Helen's cunt began to convulse in a series of rippling contractions which became faster and stronger until they induced precisely corresponding ripples along the length of his cock. Each of these ripples propelled a heavy charge of spunk which rounded the upward bend in his urethra to burst gloriously out into the tightness of her belly until she was flowing with milk and honey.

'Oh Helen!' he cried. 'Did anyone ever compliment you on your fuckability?'

Miss MacDonald awoke from a heavy sleep and reached across the bed for her lover. Melanie seemed to be up already but her side of the bed was still slightly warm and sweet-smelling. Mac snuggled into it and clasped the girl's pillow to her face. Then she forced herself to look at her watch.

Already twenty to ten – she would never make it to the college in time for that Monday morning physical development class. And she had been looking forward so much to using young Alison Jinks, a strikingly pretty late developer, for demonstration purposes in her talk on puberty.

Just as her foot touched the soft bedside rug, Mac remembered. Of course – she had allowed herself to sleep late because she had cancelled her classes in expectation of an exhausting weekend. It had indeed been exhausting; when Melanie left the party on Friday night Mac had stayed on and let herself in for a load of hassle with that fascinating man disguised as the Devil and his sinister mate. She had only returned to Upchester late on Sunday. But now she could relax. What bliss! The sun was shining on the drawn curtains and her ears were full of the mating songs of birds.

Mating songs and, if she was not mistaken, girlish laughter. Yes, it must have been Melanie's high-spirited giggles and squeals that had awoken her. Mac crossed the narrow space between the bed and the cottage window and pulled aside the chintz curtain.

For once she regretted the flourishing condition of the little orchard with its blossoming fruit trees. Very pretty, to be sure, but the fresh young foliage and foamy sprays of blossom were obscuring her view of an even prettier, fresher sight.

Flitting about in the long grass and darting between the mossy trunks of the trees, from sun into shade and out again into sunlight, danced a fairy vision, gold, pale blue and creamy white. More prosaically, it was the figure of Melanie, Mac's darling, wearing nothing but the top of the

119

blue play-suit in which she often slept. Her golden tresses streamed out behind her.

Considerably less pretty, at least in Mac's eyes, was the swarthy form pursuing the girl with clumsy determination. Derrick, of course. He too was naked from the waist down. His upper parts were encased in his black leather motorcycling jacket. His stubby legs looked hideous in their shaggy covering of hairs; between the hairs and the leather his buttocks winked with an obscenely smooth whiteness. As he swerved round one of the apple trees, the purple head of his cock wagged like an overripe plum. Mac found the spectacle both distasteful and thrilling. Ugly this Derrick might be, and his frequent calls on Melanie's company were far from welcome to the younger girl's handsome thirty-something lover. Yet imagine a pair of cheeky horns hidden in that sticking-up hair and you would have a satyr, a real Pan, chasing the most delicious of nymphs through this Arcadian grove. Mac pinched herself, fearful of following her former boss Mary Muttock into a paranoid world of fantasy in which humans were transmogrified into ramping animals. Yet she admitted to herself that she had always enjoyed the Muttock's accounts of those fantasies.

Melanie stumbled, falling on her belly in a patch of sunlight. Her hair fanned out, golden, between her white, outstretched arms. Pale blue, the little top she wore made her look even more vulnerable. Above the top the bare shoulders shone in the early May sun. Below it, the white softness of her bottom quivered with life.

Goat-legged Derrick threw himself down on her. But even as he dived, Melanie willed herself to her feet again and hurled herself forward. She fell, one of her ankles ensnared by her pursuer's hand. This time, though, a blossom-laden branch concealed all except her legs as far as her mid-thighs at one end and her head and shoulders at the other. And then Derrick was at her.

Miss MacDonald turned away in disgust and frustration. She had no objection to the girl going with Derrick – in moderation – when she herself was involved. It was just that she didn't like being left out. She slipped into a scarlet

120

silk dressing gown and crossed the narrow landing to Melanie's little room, the one where Melanie went to be private and to entertain Derrick when the weather was unsuitable for outdoor activities.

As she expected, the bed was undisturbed; the lovebirds must have made straight for the garden and orchard. There on the little desk lay the discarded blue panties with their trimming of white lace. Mac picked them up for a sniff. Beneath them on the desk she found Melanie's diary, open at the page she must have been writing when Derrick interrupted her.

Mac sat at the desk for a sly read. She could easily slip the yellow notebook back under the panties if she heard footsteps on the stairs. It would be interesting to look at the girl's account of the party the two of them had attended on Saturday. In particular, she wanted to know if that tall, severe-looking woman who had been introduced as the Captain's designer had made out with Melanie. This cool blonde had taken Mac aside and asked her quite openly if her young friend was available for sex.

With one hand softly stroking the full, brown bush that flourished between her thightops, she turned the pages back until she found the beginning of the current entry.

SEVEN

PIRATES AHOY

Captain invited us to this party Friday night, the one he
threw for his authors and staff. Me and Mac went as
authors. Felt a bit awkward at thought of having to
mingle with professional pornographers, especially seeing as we haven't actually written any books. What
made it a bit easier was that invitation said masks would
be provided for authors – seems some of them are quite
respectable citizens who don't want to be recognised.
Legit, Booker-aspiring novelists, clergymen, TV pres-
enters, a couple of judges, even a member of the cabinet,
Captain says, along with the regular sleazebags you'd
expect. Of course, they probably wouldn't all be there.
I thought it might be kind of interesting to try and guess
who the famous ones were. Imagine getting to lay a
judge! I was rather letting my fantasies run away with
me, I supposed, as Mac drove us up to London.

Quite hard to park the Morris Minor in those Fulham
back streets. And all the mess on pavement where Captain has his premises! Newspapers, cabbages, banana
skins – must be some sort of market there in day-time.
Thought the place was supposed to be gentrified.

Cardboard box in sleazy passageway inside front
door contained large collection of masks for us to
choose from. I found an ordinary black one, just to
cover eyes – no one important was going to recognise

me anyway. Admired effect in spotty mirror. I was wearing a sleek little short dress in black velvet with long sleeves and a square neck cut not too low. A string of black beads round neck, dangly black earrings and a black bow to hold my hair back. Very restrained. Just the thing for a young lady using her brains to make a living, Mac said. Stockings and shoes black too, as well as tiny suspender belt – only touches of colour my yellow hair, blue eyes and pink lips.

Mac chose a mask in shape of a cat's face. Or maybe a panther. Her dress, though, was a complete contrast to mine. She'd got some of the girls at Cunlip, where they have metalwork classes now, to make it for her as a special project. Just brill. Basically it was a network of really fine silver chains covering her from just above her nipples to just below her crotch in a mesh of vertical and horizontal lines about an inch apart. Well, the vertical chains were an inch apart, I'd say, and the horizontal ones more like two inches. Threaded on the vertical ones she'd got hundreds of these oval silver plates – each of them just overlapped its neighbour on the next chain, but there was all this white skin showing in between. Says she wants another one made with glass plates instead of silver ones. She sort of tinkled as she moved about. Maybe about half the area of each one-by-two rectangle enclosed by the chains was filled with the silver plates and the other half with Mac's bareness. She wore this literally dazzling creation with self-supporting red stockings ending at exactly the level of her hem when she stood up straight, and a tiny red G-string, really conspicuous through the silver web encasing her. You could see she didn't have a bra on, though two of the oval plates were positioned over her nipples and seemed to be held fairly firmly in place there, maybe by some kind of adhesive.

Lots of noise coming from upstairs so we went up to the first floor and into smoky room full of flashing strobes. Office furniture had been pushed back against walls. Music quite quiet and old-fashioned, though.

123

That cool jazz or something. Captain can't stand what he calls kids' racket – seriously sad.

Anyway, the Captain himself spotted us and came over to give both of us kisses. Dressed like a sort of swashbuckling Errol Flynn lookalike with this great loose-fitting satin shirt open down to navel. Said he'd know us anywhere, masks or no masks, dressed or nude. Quite unfazed (spelling?) by Mac's outrageous get-up. Told us to grab drinks and mingle with crowd.

CAPTAIN: I'm telling people they can overflow upstairs if they feel too crushed.

MAC: Our Mel's always overflowing everywhere, aren't you, dear? If it's not that Derrick's spendings it's her own juice, you know. No crushing needed. Just brush the back of your hand over her knickers and the floodgates open. Install a hydro-electric generator and you could light up the bedroom from her gushes.

CAPTAIN: I'd just love to brush the back of my hand over her knickers. Maybe I'll get a chance a bit later, when all the guests have arrived. Would you like that, dear?

ME: Strictly between ourselves, Captain, I forgot to put them on. Thought this was going to be a party for old fuddy-duddies, not the kind of joyriders who'd be ram-raiding up my skirt.

CAPTAIN: Think you'll find we've got all sorts.

MAC: And sizes too, I hope. Come on, Mel, let's circulate and dip our toes in the water – see if we can catch some big fat fish.

I didn't quite know what she meant by that – whether she was hoping to hook a well-heeled sugar-daddy or just wanted some jumbo-sized cocks up her. Anyway, we picked up drinks from desk under window – plenty of booze but not much to eat – and went our own ways.

The room was crowded and I kept getting groped and goosed. Tightness of dress saved me from too much indignity at this stage. Mainly I had to put up with scratchy kisses from masked faces. Not everyone had masks, of course – only the writers, men most of them, but a few women who might have been quite attractive for all you could see. I recognised most of the unmasked ones. That Anne Amory and Carla Merryweather were there, blonde Anne in a dark blue silk bikini and dark-haired, suntanned Carla in a white cotton one. They fancy their luck, those two. Not surprised to see Helen Lascelles, as she's Captain's editorial assistant or some-thing. Helen wearing black, like me, but her outfit was just a long strip of black satin about a foot wide with opening for head and little bows holding back and front halves loosely together at waist. Came down to just above her knees. Lots of white flesh showing, all the whiter because of the black wrapping. Then, believe it or not, the last people you'd expect to see at a literary gathering like this, Susie and Darcy O'Flammery with Darcy's kid brother Tim and Tim's girlfriend Gail, the petite, fragile-looking redhead. They must have come by train – we could have given them lift if we'd known. I love it when we all squeeze into car but I think Mac gets a bit nervous. All four were in jeans and sweaters, not quite the gear for this kind of party. But when I asked Susie how they'd got invited she said they were there to perform in some kind of entertainment the Captain was laying on. Well, I knew what kind that was going to be.

The other unmasked face was one I didn't know. A tall, severe-looking, steely blonde woman in a sleek black leotard (black seems to be flavour of the month) and pink woollen legwarmers. Gave me a really piercing stare when she noticed me looking at her, then ran tip of tongue over shiny red lips. Helen told me she was doing art-work for the books. Victoria Iceberg or some-thing I think she said her name was. More about her later.

Well, I sort of danced about a bit as well as I could to that music, but really it was only good for smooch-ing. Found myself cheek to cheek with an exotically per-fumed woman with well developed but neat figure. Instead of ordinary mask her face was painted with wild designs that completely distorted it – an extra eye, nose and mouth in funny places made her look like a living Picasso (spelling?).

WOMAN (*in deep, velvety voice*): My own daughter hasn't recognised me, I'm glad to say. These affairs can be embarrassing.

ME: Your own daughter?

WOMAN: Helen Lascelles – know her? I'm her mother, but I don't want her to know I'm here. I'd feel inhibited.

ME: So would she, I should imagine. Yes, I know Helen. I was at Cunlip College with her.

WOMAN: Not an intellectual, our Helen. Not the academic type at all. (*She slipped a hand between our chests at this point and worked her fingers down into bosom of my dress.*) But I think she's starting to find her way around in the world. The Cunlip regime seemed to do that for girls, if nothing else.

ME: Did it for me, that's for sure. Now, if you don't mind, Mrs Lascelles, I'll just go and find my way around to the drinkies.

What a nerve, I thought. Kind of like incest for a middle-aged woman to be trying to get off with one of her daughter's friends. Got another glass of fizzy and circulated a bit. The Iceberg woman seemed to be trying to shark in on me so I dodged across to a tall guy in a devil's mask and a pointed beard that looked real. He patted my bottom in a friendly sort of way and asked me what I was writing. That rather took wind out of my sails so I pressed up against him and rubbed hand over bulge in front of his trousers. Pretended I hadn't heard him and asked if he knew anything about a tall person I'd noticed in long black hooded cloak and death's-head mask like that creepy figure playing chess with knight in an old Swedish movie I watched with Mac.

MAN: Nobody's sure really, but they say it may be Delver Maddingley.

ME: He looks horrible. Who's Delver Maddingley when he's at home?

MAN: Nobody seems to know who he is when he's

at home – we don't even know if it's a he or a she. But when he or she gets into the Maddingley role it's to write rather facetious books about the kind of fuck scenes I – and probably you – like to do a bit more seriously. You do take fucking seriously, I hope, my dear young lady?

At this point Captain banged a gong and asked everyone to go upstairs for the entertainment he was laying on for us. Well, not him personally but the Iceberg or whatever she's called. My masked devil said she was very artistic and had done some really filthy illustrations for book he was writing – *Behind the Bike Sheds*, I think. I ran on ahead of him and caught hold of Mac's hand on stairs but Devil was right there behind me.

Everyone crowded into room with lots of photographic equipment that had been moved to sides. Studio lights had been arranged to shine on area in middle of floor with bed, settee and a garden bench. Audience stood, sat and sprawled on odd chairs, sofas, rugs and cushions all around this lighted area. Devil bagged a rather scruffy sofa in second row and sat down with me on his right and Mac on his left.

As soon as we were settled he started groping. Well, he was certainly doing his best to grope me and I'm pretty sure he was groping her too – heard metallic tinkling as he wormed in through her chain mail. As for me, he pinched outsides of my thighs and rubbed pussy mound through dress, reached right round under armpit to squeeze my right boob then shifted so he was attacking tit from over right shoulder, reaching fingers down inside dress to tease nipple like Helen's mum had done when we were dancing. Not wanting to be a killjoy I rested left hand on his crotch and found Mac's hand there already. What was more, the hand was clenched round Devil's hard, fleshy horn, which she'd pulled out of his trousers. OK, so I dipped into his underwear and fondled his balls.

Captain stepped into lit-up area to introduce show.

CAPTAIN: Lovely to have you all here, ladies and

gents, boys and girls. As you all know, the Honey-mooners project is absolutely ready for take-off. This week we hit the bookstores, stations and airports with our first three titles. Our get-together tonight is in the nature of what I believe they call a wrap party and I'm glad to see the more laid-back of you are already well on the way to getting unwrapped. Enjoy! But first of all, let's all get in the mood by watching a modest entertainment – well, maybe *modest* isn't quite the word – specially tailored to my favourite theme and yours: Honey-mooners. (*I think he's got some sort of obsession with that idea!*) Our talented young performers are presenting a spicy study of courtship and married love. If I say we're going to begin with a scene of puppy love I don't want any of you to get the wrong idea and send for the RSPCA – nor the NSPCC for that matter. No, folks – this is strictly boy meets girl, the most natural thing in the world. Know the way it goes? You show me yours and I'll show you mine but I mustn't get big and you mustn't get wet.

He stepped back into shadows. Stage went dark and a screen lit up just above it. Actually four large TV screens facing the four walls of room so everyone could see. They were showing a caption, beautifully lettered in pretty rococo (spelling?) frame of cupids and pierced hearts. Caption: *PUPPY LOVE*.

Screen darkened and stage lights came on again. As I expected, it was little Gail (Devil said he was glad to see she was quite free of puppy fat) and her Timmy who picked way through spectators and entered stage area. They both blushed and bowed when everyone clapped and whistled. Then they stood up straight, put arms very lightly round each other's backs and kissed, not passionately but quite shyly, lips pursed and pushed forward so we could all see as they touched.

Tim wore yellow vest and skimpy yellow shorts. This yellow was quite bold and bright, setting off his golden suntan and making his short fair hair look even lighter. Legs all smooth and shining and feet bare, like Gail's.

128

Gail has to be careful what she wears with that frizzy red hair of hers and her green eyes and pale freckled skin. I thought her choice was quite sensible from that point of view, though I found out later it was the artistic Iceberg woman who'd organised all that side of things. Anyway, Gail's outfit was a white fluffy cardigan over some sort of black top, with a long loose skirt, black with little white spots. White trainers on her feet, with no socks. Not terribly sexy or glam, but sensible, I thought.

But even as I had that thought Timmy lowered his hands and started, ever so slyly, to lift the back of the skirt really slowly. Hem crept up her legs while she went on kissing as if she hadn't noticed. I'd more or less forgotten Devil sitting next to me, but his fingers pinched my nipple a bit harder as backs of her knees came into sight, followed by slim thighs. Very cleverly, the boy lifted skirt at sides nearly as high as hips, showing lots of lovely bare flesh but not her actual bum – we weren't going to see what knickers (if any) she had on, not just yet.

While he did this, Gail was just stroking Tim's bum in a vague sort of way, playing coy as his kissing got a bit heavier. Then he spun her round and hugged her to him from behind. Hitched her skirt up to waist at back but because it still hung down at front we weren't any wiser as to the knicker question though we could see plenty of long leg.

He pulled her cardigan off and tossed it away. Her arms and shoulders were bare and covered in freckles. Now he grabbed her little tits through the black vest she was wearing under it and gave them a bit of a squeeze while butting his crotch against her behind. Gail struggled and dragged his hands away – he caught hold of the bottom of her vest and rolled it up to just below the undersized bust. She relaxed and reached her arms up and back to pull his head forward till his cheek was nuzzled against hers. Straggly red hair, not much of it, under arms. They looked very delicate – her arms, that is – in that lifted-up position.

Tim was gently stroking her tummy, all over at first but gradually letting his hands move in different directions. One of them concentrated on belly-button and below, the tips of his fingers just dipping into waistband of skirt as if by accident. Other hand played same game higher up. Suddenly he lifted vest up clear of titties and closed hands over nipples before we got a chance to see them. Devil was tugging at my own right one and sort of twisting it round quite painfully, so I dug my nails into his hard dick and he eased off a bit. Could hear Mac moaning and wondered what he was getting up to with her – her hand below mine on his cock was pretty limp, unlike the cock.

Well, Gail pulled Timmy's hands away again and everyone who hadn't seen them before – most of audience, that is – gasped and hooted with delight to see those nipples. The little breasts themselves, as I've mentioned before in this diary, are rather like curving cones that get steeper towards the points and the points are really pink and puffy. Almost as if they belonged to an older, bigger woman.

Tim wasn't going to be put off like that. He dropped his hands now and hitched front of her skirt right up. I was pretty sure she'd turn out to be knickerless, but no – as he gripped her by the hips and she squirmed her bottom against his crotch, we had lovely view of tiny black silk panties with the odd curl of red hair she hadn't tucked in round edges.

She tore herself away from him. As she did so, skirt fell to floor – Tim must have undone fastening. Crowd roared approval, wanting more. She huddled in corner of stage area with her back to Tim and her top pulled down again, pretending to sulk. Quietly, he slipped off his yellow vest and eased down the matching shorts. Under them he had briefest of tight black bikini briefs. Contents looked swollen, hard and firm but briefs were too tight for hard-on to stick out much which is why he'd looked pretty innocent till he took shorts off.

Now he sidled up to his girlfriend, stroked the outside

of her thigh and hip and whispered something in her ear. Rather reluctantly Gail turned to face him. To everyone's relief, I think, she smiled when she saw him so scantily clad. He made a move towards her but she made a sign for him to keep his distance.

But she was still smiling. A round of applause went up when she took her vest right off and posed shyly in front of Tim. She was staring straight at that straining bulge in the front of his briefs. He turned his back on her, quickly eased them down and stepped out of them.

Those of us on our side of stage had clear view of the straight, thin, pink-tipped prick springing up from the cushion of soft yellowish hair and the pink bag with his balls hanging snugly between his thighs. Then he turned to face Gail and we were able to enjoy sight of the small white bottom, looking all the smaller and whiter for the surrounding golden tan. He wagged his hips in her direction and did a little dance.

He swooped in on her and I felt sure he was going to take her. So did Devil, I think. He'd got his hand between my two tits under the dress and had spread out fingers to touch both nipples – now he started scratching them. Anyway, Gail wasn't having any and waved Tim away so he backed off a couple of feet and stroked his dick while keeping it pointed at her.

Gail winked at him. Then she slipped knickers down, revealing triangle of sparse, damp-looking hair. Applause. She took Tim's hand. I thought she was going to put it on her twat, but no – she led him to bed and made him sit down next to her. They both opened their thighs. Lights dimmed and screens lit up. Caption: *TOO BAD! I GOT ALL BIG AND YOU GOT ALL WET. JUST LOOK AT US!*

The lights came on again and for a moment I got glimpse of a leering skeleton on other side of stage. It was that awful Delver Maddingley person. He moved sideways into shadow. In lighted area those two rascals were still sitting on edge of bed. Although I knew Gail gets it from Timmy at least twice a week, on Wednesdays and Saturdays, hard not to believe they were a couple of naughty teenagers just getting to know each other on first date.

Captain was kneeling in front of them. He had a camcorder aimed at them. On screens, instead of caption, we now saw close-up shot of the two open crotches. Camera zoomed in first on Tim's. The little pink bag between his thighs was tight and shiny and his thin prick was so long it nearly reached up to top of picture. Bulb at end of it was darker now and bead of clear juice had gathered at opening. As we watched, Gail's hand closed over the stem but camera switched to her cunt. She's got these puffy inner lips that hang down between the outer ones as if she's just had a really fat cock pulled out of her. Well, now they were curled outwards and we could see the inner surfaces coated with lovejuice which was trickling down towards her arse. Tim's hand came into picture, hovered above her mound and landed on the juicy pussy.

Everything went dark and we could hear sounds of shuffling about on stage. Devil seemed to have got fed up with tightness of my dress and was concentrating on penetrating Mac's metallic defences. I worked his balls and as he was leaning sideways I reached right round till my finger was teasing his bumhole.

Another caption appeared on screens: *NOW WE'RE DATING IN THE PARK, YOU CAN HAVE A QUICK FEEL.* (Whoever thought this lot up had some pretty old-fashioned ideas about what kids get up to these days!)

When lights came on Tim and Gail had disappeared. Two new couples stood and bowed to us. It was Anne and Carla, and they had these two blokes with them I found out later share their flat in Earl's Court. Blonde Anne with her cute fringe and her partner were got up as bikers in black leather minus the helmets, which might have got in way I suppose. I'm used to Derrick in biker's gear but this guy looked much more impressive – really huge, with long, greasy hair and blue stubble all over his chops.

132

Carla and friend made what Captain would call a striking contrast. She looked all smooth and shiny in her skimpy white bikini. Her man was tall and thin and was carrying his doings in a black posing pouch that didn't leave much to the imagination. It struck me that Anne was blonde with a black-haired guy and Carla dark with fair-haired one. Wondered if they paired off like this in real life, or just for the show. Maybe they go any which way, or for all I know the guys could be gay in real life.

These two couples went straight to bench and sat down side by side: Anne's guy, Anne, Carla's guy, Carla. Almost at once Carla was having her tits nuzzled through the bikini top and her pussy fondled through the white cotton of the bottom. Just threw her head back and let him get on with it. Her hand was resting on his thigh and her fingers moving very slowly on the black pouch.

I'd assumed Anne was less accessible but her bloke got to work on the zips and in no time at all Carla was looking quite decent in comparison. Without actually peeling the leathers off her this biker had brought both of Anne's breasts out into view and managed to get her middle all bare – somehow the part that covered her bum and crotch had vanished and it was as if she just had leather leggings up to tops of thighs. What a pretty triangle of fluffy yellow hair! It's surprisingly small still but doesn't look as if she trims it. And I'd forgotten Anne's got such a lovely little slit between those slim but nicely shaped white thighs – the hair doesn't hide it at all, of course.

A leather-clad arm reached round over Anne's left shoulder and tugged one nipple while the guy's prickly face buried itself in the right tit. So she pushed him off? No way – her hand tugged the crucial zip down and out jumped his big end. *Feeling* would be a bit of an understatement for the way she exercised it. I was surprised he didn't come in her hand but when she didn't let him I guessed they were saving themselves for a later stage in the show.

133

Lights out – caption on screens: *JUST A FEEL, WE SAID. BUT LOOK AT THE DAMAGE THAT CAN DO!*

Lights on again, and there was Captain kneeling in front of them with camera. Everything shown in vivid detail on screens. Started with Carla's crotch, still tightly secured in white bikini. Her partner's finger was pushing right in, forcing material into her opening. Colour being white we could easily see dark stain seeping through all round the poking finger, which had sunk in right up to second joint.

Focus switched to her man's G-string, really close up. It looked very stretched and lumpy. Camera pulled back just a little and we realised that was partly because Carl's hand was pushed down into it. The guy was squirming about desperately on his bottom, jerking up to fuck the hand that was frigging him. Suddenly Carla's other hand, with its pointed red nails, grabbed top of pouch and ripped it down so the lovely big dong was exposed. Released from its prison it grew like a magic beanstalk so that Carla's hand gripping it round the base looked quite small. You could see from way tip went an angry purple and his balls tightened that he was ready to burst.

Then Captain shifted along on knees and we had similar view on screen of other guy being felt up by Anne's little hand. Difference here was all the black leather with cock sticking out of it like veiny white marble.

This time Captain didn't hang around but went straight for Anne's tit being abused by her biker's stubby, grubby fingers. Nipple quite enormous – almost cock-sized. Then camera swooped down to the lovely pink twat, framed first with her fluffy yellow fur, then with shiny white skin – you could tell the shine was from sweat – and then with her black leathers. The dark hand came down, its back covered with black hairs. Biker opened thumb and forefinger as wide as he could with such stubby ones, applied fingertip to little pink arsehole

134

and thumb to top of slit so that web of skin between finger and thumb pressed into slit. On screen we actually saw the wet lips stretch up to take it in. Then he put fingers of other hand on her mound and sort of smoothed it back to let clitty pop out of its hood. We saw it, pink and shiny, before thumb squashed it and everything went dark.

Caption: *ENGAGED – HEAVY PETTING ON SOFA ALLOWED NOW THE FAMILY'S IN BED.*

Again it was a different couple – Susie and Darcy. They act so well that in no time at all it was as if I'd forgotten they were married. Darce was obviously mad keen to get at her and she was playing hard to get, at first anyway. He was in denim suit like the one Captain usually wears, though because of difference in ages it looks much better on Darce. I've never gone for that pigtail he has or the gold ring he's just had put in his ear, but he's certainly got quite tall and manly lately.

Fair-haired Susie was got up to look demure, I suppose. She had a frilly, long-sleeved white blouse with one of those cameo brooches (spelling?) at the throat. Her knee-length skirt was beige and fairly tight and she wore black stockings. Like Tim and Gail in first scene, they started by embracing lightly and kissing.

But things were speeding up, it seemed. Soon Susie was sprawled on sofa with Darce drooling all over her. She'd undone her own buttons and he'd pulled white lace bra up to free her pretty breasts. Somehow skirt had got kind of rolled right up to her waist. Yes, as I'd guessed, she was wearing stockings, not tights, so we saw this gorgeous white flesh above them and a little triangle of dark blue silk nicely filled out with her plump pussy. While Darcy buried his nose down there, Susie made herself busy easing his jeans down to his knees. He was primed and ready to go. Down with her knickers and he held those white thighs open for Captain's camera to give us all a glorious view of her gaping, pulpy-looking cunt before going right down on her to spike her with his tongue. At same time Susie had her hus-

135

band's stiff prick in her mouth and was squeezing his balls. All of a sudden she tensed and threw her bottom up in air with Darcy's head clamped between her thighs. Her head went back as she screamed out – what about folks supposed to be upstairs in bed, I wondered – and audience cheered as screen showed a big wet cock spurting gushes of thick come in space between her tits. Even while it was splashing out Susie was tossing and turning and spreading the spunk all over her breasts and rubbing it into her nipples. Then it all went dark once more.

Caption: *AT LAST – WEDDING BELLES (AND BEAUX)*.

Obviously Susie and Darce were not ready to appear in this one – not Darce, anyway. The belles in question were Anne and Carla and little Gail and they were being married to Timmy and the guys from Earl's Court. I've seen a few mock-weddings on occasions like this (Susie's was the most elaborate) but what I liked about this one was its almost breakneck speed. It was really lewd and lively. Guys and gals all wore white G-strings. The grooms wore white top hats and their brides had flowery head-dresses with little veils, very transparent. Easy to see their eager faces through them. What a picture! I would have wet my knickers if I'd had any on and Devil's hand hadn't already got me flowing. The three couples stood at some distance from each other so they could all be seen, the brides and grooms side by side with hands on each other's bottoms.

Caption: *FITTING THE RINGS*.

Brides moved in front of grooms and got down on knees, hands resting on the lads' hips. Grooms lifted veils from the pretty faces. It was Gail's that was shown on screen but the others were easy enough to see in the flesh. I concentrated on Gail. Her eyes were closed as her mouth opened to form a tight, round 'O'. At same time she pulled Tim's G-string halfway down his smooth thighs. His rod, thin but bone-hard, flipped up and its weeping eye was staring her in the face. The ring of her lips stretched tightly over the swollen head and

136

slipped down the stem. Gail opened her eyes, glanced sideways at camera and winked. Anne and Carla were in same position with their blokes when next caption came up: *CONSUMMATION!*

The grooms swept their brides up in their arms and tossed them side by side across bed. (Well, Timmy wasn't quite up to that strong-man stuff but Gail let him get her there without actually lifting her off ground.) First, guys swooped down on brides, who threw up legs and wrapped them round backs and bums while their veils were pulled back and their mouths and tits were kissed. Looked like they were fucking in missionary position except girls still had G-strings on so maybe they weren't being penetrated – blokes had lost theirs completely somewhere in mad rush to bed. After a few hard thrusts the grooms pulled back, rolled their brides over and yanked them up on all fours. Without being told – well, I suppose they'd been well rehearsed – girls slewed round so they were kneeling one behind the other with gaps between them. Carla was up front, then Anne, then Gail. Their guys got behind them and with what you might call military precision pulled aside the white bands running down between their buttocks and freed their pussies from the white pouches. Then they spat on their hands, rubbed spittle on cocks and in they went, smooth and easy, like they were the Queen's Own Lancers, Mac said. As Timmy screwed her, that Gail stuck out tongue and started licking balls and arse of Anne's bloke – Anne did same to Carla's. A few more couples and they could have made complete circle but as it was, all Carla could do was lick her own lips and drool and, to quote Mac again, Tim's bottom and bollocks had to waste their sweetness on the desert air. They weren't really wasted, though, because those of us on our side of stage got such a lovely view of his tight white bum wagging away as he fucked. After a bit all three couples collapsed flat on bed but I think they were only acting orgasm as there was still a bit more to come. More to come that would need more come.

Lights out. Caption: *HAPPY HONEYMOONS*.

Over in a flash, this one, though it took a few minutes before actors were ready to appear and get started. All eight of them, including Susie and Darcy, romped on to stage area in little bikinis and bathing trunks stretched out by hard-ons, bouncing a big ball and tossing it over each other's heads as if on beach. All at once they stopped playing and paired off. Men's trunks and girl's bottoms came off and they were all shagging like monkeys in different positions while Captain darted about with camera, showing us all these shots of cocks fucking cunts up there on screens. I know the Earl's Courters actually came this time – as they pulled out of Anne and Carla they were still spouting and you could see the spunk sliding down girls' legs. But when Timmy and Darce drew out it was pretty obvious they were still saving their pricks for some other coming event, *coming* being the operative word again.

Darkness again and another caption: *BORED HOUSEWIVES*.

A pause for changing, then the four young ladies stepped out wearing tired-looking housecoats and dusters tied round heads. They carried pails and scrubbing brushes and got down on knees to clean floor. Getting down like that made fronts of housecoats fall open to show dangling tits, except for Gail whose tits are too small to dangle though they did look all puffed up and excited. A doorbell rang. Susie got up and went to edge of stage as if opening door. In comes not Darcy but young Tim, carrying a crate of milk. Susie drags down his jeans, pushes him back across bed, strips bare except for duster on head and straddles his chest. We can see his stiff prick sticking up against her back. Just then bell rings again and Gail goes to 'door'. It's Darce as milkman. He gets same treatment as his brother. The two girls lift up, squat right down on the hard pricks and ride them to orgasm – the real thing this time, with loads of creamy milk overflowing from seal that cuntlips make round the male flesh. But instead of repeat performances for the other girls, Anne and Carla strip off, get on bed between the two adulterous couples and start loving each other up.

Caption: *THESE CHICKS DESPERATELY NEED MALE COMPANY. HOW ABOUT IT, BOYS?*

That's a bit sexist, I thought, but with Devil's hand right up tight skirt of my dress I sat back to enjoy watching guys from audience queue (spelling?) to fuck Anne and Carla. Some women in queue as well, I noticed. Practically everyone wanted to have a go, so Captain pulled Tim and Darcy off their temporary partners to make another pair of juicy cunts available, the operative word here being *juicy*.

What happened next was a real giggle. Devil suggested tha

Here the diary broke off, no doubt at the point when Derrick had interrupted Melanie's writing. Mac, however, hardly needed to be reminded what the Devil had suggested and what had then occurred. To her it had not been a giggle. His idea was that the three of them should join what was rapidly degenerating into a free-for-all on the stage. But as well as having his right hand up Melanie's skirt, as she now discovered from the diary, he had also had his left one up Mac's. As the three of them stood up, this awkwardly trapped hand had strained the weakest link of that glittering metallic dress beyond its tensile tolerance. Everyone had looked round hopefully at what they took for the sound of hundreds of jangling coins cascading to the floor. Mac had stood there, an object of embarrassed wonder, her bronzed figure naked except for a torn and distressed network of fine silver chains on which no more than half a dozen oval plates remained threaded like the last leaves of autumn. The bright red G-string which had snugly packaged her sex now clung damply halfway down her thighs; the Devil's bony hand still rested on her mound, one long finger probing deep into her cunt.

This memory of her humiliation now brought the athletic woman to the brink of spontaneous orgasm. She dashed down to the orchard, urgently needing to join the lovers in the unmown grass.

At about the same time on this Monday morning the bleary-eyed Captain sat hunched over a video recorder in his studio. All around him was strewn the wreckage of Friday night's party, which had raged on until well into Sunday afternoon.

The screens which had displayed close-up views of the performers in that dramatic representation of courtship and married love now flickered with images from the tape the Captain was playing and replaying, searching for a clue. It was one of number of uncertificated tapes Helen had picked up for him in Soho. At intervals in the latter stages of the party these had been exhibited to guests requiring a fresh stimulus to their jaded appetites.

The Captain had led Victoria Eisenberg upstairs hoping she would succumb at last to his advances. But she refused to be steered towards his bedroom, so he had followed her into the studio. Most of the seats were already occupied by snogging couples. Victoria had sat on a heap of cushions on the floor and he had thrown himself on top of her.

Her cries of protest had threatened to disturb the genial tone of the party, so he cradled her gently but firmly in his arms and assured her that he had no intention of forcing penetrative sex upon her against her will. To his surprise, this assurance had calmed her down immediately and although maintaining a certain emotional detachment from him she had participated with some energy in the sixty-nine he had initiated as soon as he was free of his lower garments and had prised open the fastening in the crotch of her leotard. The tightly stretched garment snapped up to her waist as the coveted vulva was liberated.

Victoria's thighs were slim and white, her bush was sparse and very fair and the lips of her cunt were pink and narrow. When he parted them with his fingers and slipped the tip of his tongue between them, the lips had closed with an elastic grip that astonished him.

Buried like this in the woman's intimate flesh, he had

been scarcely aware at first of the movie being shown on the screens above them. Vaguely the corner of his eye took in a scene at a bus stop. A man in a raincoat was offering something to a young lady. When the Captain next glanced up from his pleasant occupation, something was happening inside a bus. It occurred to him that you didn't often get shots like that in this sort of film. His curiosity was marginally aroused but Victoria's arousal was well beyond the marginal state. Still hopeful of a fuck, he plunged his tongue back between the now more relaxed sex-lips and ran the tip up to her clitoris.

Echoing sounds of laughter and splashing water caused him to snatch another glance at the screen. It showed a rather small but luxuriously appointed indoor swimming pool. A party of schoolgirls appeared to be splashing about and chasing each other over the slippery tiles. In contrast to their undeveloped figures sheathed in black one-piece bathing costumes, the long-haired blonde girl of the earlier sequences stood stark naked on the edge and threw herself into the water.

Victoria, who had stopped sucking him and was now wanking him in a rather half-hearted way with one hand, was using her other one to force his head back down into her crotch. 'Hold on,' he had gasped. 'Let's watch this video while we do it. Shift round a bit, then I'll be able to peep up between your bum-cheeks while I go on licking.'

Yet it had almost been as if the cool artist was trying to prevent him from looking at the screen. Maybe she had felt jealous. No, that was an absurd and self-congratulatory explanation, he reflected with rare insight. More likely, she just wanted him to devote himself without distraction to the task in hand. In mouth, rather.

Even so, he had managed to get a few more glimpses of the taped action as the naked girl was tackled by a couple of men in an underwater sequence and later gang-raped on the wet tiles of the changing room. He knew her, he felt sure. And what was even more annoying, he had kept snatching glimpses of other faces that looked familiar. So tantalising was this sense of being acquainted with the actors that it was only when he was on the point of climaxing in Victoria's mouth, which he had contrived to re-enter, that he was struck by the full outrage of what he was witnessing. The Honeymooners Library had fallen prey to pirates – porno-pirates. Even before Victoria's graphic version hit the station bookstalls (and it was clearly her version that had been pirated), the story of *Fucky Days* was being commercially exploited in this video version. There had been a leak. The thought of such a blatant infringement of copyright caused him to lose his erection.

Victoria, who seemed remarkably unaware of the violation considering her own involvement and input into the book, had insisted on being taken all the way. The journey was long and arduous; by the time it was over, so too was the film. At least the Captain had hoped he might now get to shaft her properly, so he said nothing about *Fucky Days*. But no – she had hurried off downstairs looking for some girl she said she was interested in.

So now, alone and sober at last, he was checking through the tape at his leisure. The opening sequence was unhelpful; *BIG BANG PRODUCTIONS* did not appear in the phone book and was unlikely to be a genuine trading name. The title was his own *GIRLIE DELIGHTS*. According to the credits, the film starred 'Jenny Taylor and Big Dick Sylvester' – not the subtlest of pseudonyms but pseudonyms none the less. However, this was no longer a problem. He had, of course, realised the identity of the blonde, wavy-haired star as soon as Victoria had sloped off: she was that pretty youngster Sally Nugent, who had let him fuck her every morning at the motel in return for an extension to her honeymoon. And as he ran the tape he soon recognised the other faces that had seemed only half familiar on Saturday night.

How could he not have remembered the sweet smile of his old flame Gina Wootton, especially as he already knew she had broken into this branch of the entertainment industry? Well, he had probably failed to recognise Gina because her magnificent auburn hair had been straightened out and dyed blue-black for her role as the randy schoolmistress who encouraged her young charges to misbehave themselves in the pool. And Gina's rough diamond of a boyfriend, Joker Jennings, the Captain knew as soon as the youth opened his cockney mouth. He played the part of the pool attendant. A weighty, impressive part it was, the Captain had to admit, especially in its girth.

Now, if he could trace Gina, she ought to be able to point him in the right direction. Or would she? She would have nothing to gain and everything to lose by the enforcement of the Honeymooners copyright.

Once more he fast-forwarded his way through the tape. Most of the scenes seemed to have been shot in a studio and betrayed no tell-tale signs of location. But the swimming pool – wasn't there something a bit peculiar about that? Here was the scene in question. The Captain noticed that the camera was hardly ever allowed to stray above the tiled surround, with occasional shots of an end wall which was bedecked with thriving indoor plants. It looked nothing like the interior of your average municipal baths, most of which were much more antiquated and harshly institutional than the Fulham pool he sometimes patronised with its water-slides and artificial waves.

He froze the picture and advanced through the sequence frame by frame. And there, quite suddenly, he had it. So briefly that he had not noticed it at all when the tape was run at normal speed, the camera had panned round from that end wall to Sally Nugent standing naked on the edge of the pool. In doing so it had taken in a fleeting shot of the side wall opposite her. It was a wall of glass, with greenery and buildings visible beyond.

Most of the frames were blurred by the speed of the panning camera. But as he scanned through them the Captain found just one in sharp focus; the cameraperson must have hesitated momentarily while looking for Sally. And there, on the otherwise blank side of a barn-like building he was able to make out the words 'YGLESIAS ENTERPRISES (VIDEO) LTD'.

So it must have been that smooth-talking Talbot Yglesias, who had been honeymooning at the motel at the same time as the Nugents. That made sense. And Talbot had boasted that he ran his own production company, hadn't he? The Captain remembered another thing he was crazy to have overlooked – his suppliers had actually sent him an Yglesias movie last year to show at the motel. It had starred Gina. But how the fuck had this Talbot got his thieving paws on *Fucky Days*?

EIGHT

GOING PUBLIC

Miss MacDonald got up and went to work the next morning still feeling a bit disorientated by her long weekend. The things she had let Derrick do to her for the sake of keeping Melanie sweet! And the more she thought about the Captain's shocking party, the less she remembered about it for certain. She knew she had been unable to shake that bearded Devil off – or perhaps the truth was that he had not been able to shake her off. Yes, that must have been more like it, otherwise she would have made some excuse when Melanie came up to her and said she was leaving with some friends and would make her own way home to Upchester. She herself had stayed on at the party for ages. She seemed to recall a bustling market out there in the street as she eventually left escorted by the Devil and that friend of his, the skeletal figure conjectured to be Delver What-was-it? Delver Maddingley. Funny, that. In her diary, hadn't Melanie made it seem it was the Devil who had offered this conjecture but had been very unsure about Maddingley's identity? Yet the Grim Reaper-like figure had got in the cab and gone along with them to the Devil's flat in St John's Wood or wherever it was just as if they were old buddies. Or man and wife? All through that long, dope-sodden orgy Mac had gleaned no further clues as to the sex of this ghoul who had frigged her so freely at one end while his or her diabolical chum worked away with unambiguous masculinity at the other. No, it

145

was all a haze. How she had got home she had no idea, but the Morris Minor seemed to be intact.

Alone at long last, Melanie took her diary and a couple of cushions down into the sunny orchard. Weather permitting, she and Mac nearly always sunned themselves naked in this secluded spot and today was no exception. Arranging the cushions comfortably on one of the cast-iron garden chairs, she addressed herself to the business of bringing her journal a bit more up to date. She took up the narrative from the point where she had broken off on Derrick's arrival the previous morning.

. . . What happened next was a giggle. Devil suggested that we should get up and have a go on stage but Mac's dress got ripped and all those silver bits showered on floor. I slipped away and went downstairs for another drink and a bit of a dance.

I'd been shaking myself about for half an hour or so and getting myself felt up by all these famous or not so famous bods when up comes this Iceberg woman and starts dancing about right in front of me, sticking out her crotch till it touched my tummy and really making like she was going for the old bump and grind. Very supple and sleek she looked in that black leotard.

Music went swoony and she sort of leaned against me, her cheek against my cheek and breathing into my ear.

ICEBERG: Your name's Melanie, isn't it?

ME: Well . . .

ICEBERG: Mine's Victoria. I've read the work you sent in.

ME: It wasn't actually . . .

ICEBERG: I spoke to the woman who keeps you. Asked her if you were available for sex.

ME (*indignant*): I really don't think . . .

ICEBERG: Look, it's hot in here and I keep getting mauled by men. Why don't you let me drive you home?

ME: Oh, no – we live right out in Upchester.

ICEBERG: I know. Your friend told me. Let's hit the road.

Well, with Mac being taken over by those horrible people in their grotesque masks I wasn't too keen to hang around at party, especially if she'd given this Iceberg woman the green light to do it with me. Mac takes too much for granted sometimes – thought I'd show her I'm not just her toy-girl. So I told the Iceberg I'd go with her if we could give the O'Flammery crowd a lift.

She made out she didn't want to squeeze so many in her car but when I explained who they were she agreed to take Gail and Tim or preferably Gail and Susie. Well, I knew Darce wouldn't want to let Susie go so I rounded up the young couple and told Mac, who was having her silver-chained boobs handled and licked by that guy got up like Old Nick and his friend the sexless skeleton. She didn't seem to mind too much, though I doubt if she took in what I was saying.

I sat in front of Iceberg's nimble silver Capri with Tim and Gail in back. They'd had a bit more to drink than they were used to and I could hear them at it like a pair of randy rabbits. Iceberg kept peeping at them in driving mirror but didn't say anything. I kept having to take her hand off my knee – didn't want her to think I was easy or anything.

When we got to Upchester, Tim started giving slurred directions for getting to Gail's place but Iceberg wasn't having any of that and said they were both coming with us. She can be really insistent. In the cottage I explained it would be best for the two young ones to sleep on couch downstairs. Iceberg could have my bed and I'd sleep in Mac's as per usual. But she got mad. Said we were all going to share one bed, and if there was only one big enough for all four then that one it had to be even if it belonged to my 'keeper' as she kept calling her. We all stripped off. The Iceberg's long white body superb – yes, that's the word – with those slim thighs and narrow pussy without much hair on it.

ICEBERG (*looking at Tim*): The boy's getting swol-

147

len. (*Or maybe she said* 'turgid' – *that's the sort of thing she would say*.) We're not going to get any sleep till he's proberly fucked out. Get him ready as quick as you can, Melanie, and I'll see to the girl.

ME: You want us to frig them?

ICEBERG: Just to get them going. Then he can fuck with her. You'd like that, wouldn't you, young man?

TIM: Yes, I quite like people watching us. Get all hard just thinking about it. Come on, Mel.

So into action I went, using fingers and mouth all over him, not just between his legs, while Iceberg was licking Gail's cunt and making the vivid red curls darker and less curly with her saliva. Soon Gail's thighs were trembling and Timmy's long thin prick was rock-hard.

He knelt between Gail's legs while the Iceberg held them open for him. I got hold of his prick and steered it into her moist opening with one hand while I used the other hand to push his bottom down on her. While they were going at it I was a bit surprised to see the Iceberg stroking his back and buttocks. Said she thought he was quite girlish really – pretty, even. She's weird.

Anyway, he soon spouted into his girlfriend like a man. Iceberg finished her off with a quick kiss on the clit, then the two youngsters dozed off in each other's arms and I was quite glad it was my turn to be done. She really made a meal of it and I must say I did too. It was probably because of her name and that flaxen hair and light blue eyes that I'd been thinking of her as sort of cold and steely but actually she's got fire in her belly, as they say. Made a meal of it? That lady was some hot lunch! Or do I mean naked lunch?

The Iceberg had wanted to sleep between me and Gail but somehow she ended up on outside, nearest the door, in my usual position. Maybe that's why I woke up on Saturday morning to sounds of 'Help!' and 'Rape!' – Derrick had let himself in with key, had let his dick spring free of leathers and was worrying Iceberg like a rottweiler with a rag doll.

He tugged a zip and the leather trousers peeled right

148

off. Don't mind it so much when he's giving it to me because I can't see so much, but I hate sight of his short, thick legs covered with that tight black scrub. Anyway, he was getting ready to stab his hot rod into the Iceberg, who was going frantic and hammering on Derrick's chest with her fists. She wasn't to know that's just the sort of treatment that gets him going.

All I had to do was stick a finger up his bum and give his balls a bit of a squeeze. Derrick yelped, bucked like he'd been electrocuted and spurted his sticky come all over Iceberg's belly. Then I gave him a great wallop and sent him packing with what Mac would call a flea in his ear.

Iceberg a bit subdued after that. But I brought some breakfast upstairs for all of us and after we'd got Gail to jerk Timmy off so we three girls could romp about for a short time without distractions, we lay back in bed to plan our day.

Iceberg keen to go swimming. Told her Upchester municipal baths were rather old-fashioned and institutional but she said that was fine. She'd been doing this comic-book version of some story with lots of goings-on in a place like that and was keen to try out some of the things she'd put into it. Then she stroked Tim's bottom and smiled.

ICEBERG: We don't want to be separated in the changing rooms, do we? What do you think, Melanie? Can we pass him off as a girl?

Well, that was quite a challenge but it appealed to me, and Gail thought it would be fun too. We didn't bother to ask Timmy himself. I fetched a shortish blonde wig from Mac's play-cupboard – as soon as that was on he looked even cuter than usual. The Iceberg was afraid it might come off in pool so she tried to fix it to his own short hair with pins. He kept protesting when she pricked him so she told him he'd just have to keep his head out of the water. We dressed him in my little black bikini. Of course, there was nothing at all to fill out the top, which is just a sort of band round the chest, but then there's not much in it when I wear it, is there? At least I've got these little points on me, which is more than he had. Still, we thought he'd just about do. People would think he was either a very backward sixteen-year-old or a rather tall twelve-year-old. All of us except Tim thought it was quite a hoot. From the back he really did look like a girl. The bikini bottom wasn't too much of a problem. It's tight, so he was squashed into it quite neatly. And because it's black you had to look pretty closely to notice anything odd. As long as he didn't get a hard-on . . .

We girls chose suitable costumes. I had my red silk bikini with bows at the sides. Gail put on that dark green one-piece swimsuit I've grown out of, cut very low at the back and high at hips. For Iceberg it had to be another bikini as she's taller than me and Mac. When she chose a little white one from Mac's drawer I didn't tell her it's only suitable for sunbathing and goes all transparent in water.

We put our ordinary clothes on over bathing things. Leotard and leg-warmers only clothes Iceberg had with her, so I gave her one of Mac's tracksuits. Just for fun I got out my old Cunlip summer dress and we tried to squeeze Tim into it but it was too tight. So I got him to put on some red tights, my knee-length grey skirt and a baggy jumper. We grabbed towels then all piled into the Capri and headed for Market Street. What a laugh!

No sweat getting Tim in. Hadn't been to Upchester baths for a long time – it felt funny to smell that smell of sour bodies and chlorine and feel the rather slimy dampness on changing room floor. We slipped out of clothes and went through to pool, all loud and echoey (spelling?) though there weren't many people in water or round the sides – mainly these hunks from the town who kept diving and jumping in, deliberately splashing us.

As soon as we took the plunge Iceberg's bikini went critical. Completely see-through. I don't think she realised. When I ducked under water and opened eyes I had clear view of her long cuntlips with the thin material sort of sucked into slit. And up above surface you could actually see the nipples, not just the hard teats sticking out but all the darkness round them. Didn't look at her too long in case it was obvious but even if she'd cottoned on there wasn't much she could do about it.

She floundered over to me and had to shout to make herself heard.

ICEBERG: In my comic book this girl's nude in the public baths. Take your bikini off, Melanie, and let's see if anyone notices or cares.

Well, I thought, if those blokes didn't notice Iceberg's tits through transparent top they weren't likely to be put off their stroke by sight of me in the altogether. I waded down to five foot mark so only my head was out of water and took off first top then bottom. Held bikini up to prove I'd done it. She snatched it from me and tucked it into her own top between the two breasts. It looked like a red flag drawing attention to her hardened nipples.

I swam about a bit but knew my bottom must be showing when those yobs started whistling and pointing. Best to tread water, I decided, then I could stay upright. Although they were making so much racket, the yobs seemed a bit timid and kept their distance.

Tim and Gail were having fun chasing each other in and out of pool. He was doing all he could to stop his wig getting a wetting and she was doing her best to duck him under. They wrestled quite fiercely. Tim broke away and climbed up steps out of water. As he stood on the wet tiles dripping and giggling like a real girl (call me sexist if you like but I remember that crowd at Cunlip) I saw that it had happened. His cock had gone hard and was forcing the bikini bottom out in front. Either he didn't realise what was up or he'd forgotten he was supposed to be a cunty girl, not a cocky boy.

OK, so I heaved myself up on bar at edge and leaned over on tiles, not caring if everyone got view of tits and bum. I grabbed Tim by the ankle and pulled him back into water with a great splash. His wig slipped down

151

over his face but I quickly pushed it back up and hoped people had been too interested in me to notice what had happened.

When I swam across to Iceberg and whispered, or shouted, that he'd gone hard, she took instant action, almost as if pre-planned. Idea was that I had to hold Gail steady in water with her legs apart and pull green material of her swimsuit to one side so Timmy could screw her and get his rocks off. Well, I held her and got my fingers inside crotch of her costume while Iceberg grabbed Tim's bikini bottom and dragged it down his thighs. I felt his hard thing jabbing into my hip as I tugged the material to give him access to his girlfriend.

The tight costume ripped, giving him much more access than I'd reckoned with. From the waist down it was just a wet rag, a piece of green seaweed. Nothing we could do about it, though, so we just laughed and egged Timmy on while he fucked into her. All the hunks had gathered round by now and were watching from edge. They must have known what was going on even though we deliberately splashed so much they couldn't have seen underwater action very clearly. I could see hunks, of course. They seemed to be sort of awe-struck, but not enough to stop them getting the horn quite visibly.

His efforts only half hidden by the blue water, Tim pumped into Gail's tight young twat. After a dozen lusty strokes he shut his eyes, went all tense and shivered as Iceberg held him in her arms. Then he pulled out of Gail or, as she told us afterwards, her tightness down there in the pool forced him out of her like a champagne cork. (That's how Captain says it can be when he fucks Helen – she's got such tight muscles down in her cunt. But that's different. Captain's cork's nearly as thick as a bottle, and I don't mean the open end of it.) I checked state of Tim's dick, which is thinner than average – it had gone all small, shrivelled up by the water, I suppose. Iceberg pulled his bikini up and I tucked the little tiddler snugly in, taking care not to tickle him in case he got horny again.

152

When I ducked my head under to inspect damage to Gail's swimsuit, water was quite thick with these clouds of spunk, rather like frog spawn (frogs' spawn?) but without the black specks in it, thank goodness. One frond was coming out of Gail's cunt, so I wiped hand over lips waving under water and tried to detach it from her. It kept sticking to her and to me, the way cobwebs do when you try to brush them off. And when I came up to breathe I could feel some of it was stuck to my face and sliding into my mouth, all salty. Funny thing – I didn't really mind if people knew it was sperm as long as they didn't think it was snot. I did get a rather dirty look, though, from this middle-aged woman with anonymous bathing cap who'd been swimming very slowly up and down all the time we were there.

At that moment the hunks – seven of them – jumped into pool and went for us. Hard to see anything for the foam flying everywhere as they thrashed about and battled with us, but I could tell I wasn't the only one who'd had her bikini torn off. All of us were nude as we gurgled, struggled and gasped for breath. All of us, that is, except Darcy, who'd done a clever thing by getting rid of wig and bikini top and hoisting himself up on to tiled surround, where he stood shouting and urging us on. Now his prick could grow as big as it wanted to under stimulation of exciting game he was watching.

Myself, I was really getting worked up as this bloke pulled his dong out of trunks and started forcing it between my legs. Another two of them were playing with my boobs and arse. Caught a glimpse of Gail, a bit neglected with just one youth hanging on to her from behind, his hands on her little tits. But Iceberg wasn't having any fun at all, screaming and shouting '*RAPE!*' for second time that day and trying to punch the four who were attacking her and to knee them in groin, which wasn't easy up to her neck in water.

Like I said, there were only a few people about apart from these guys. But one of them – maybe pool attendant – must have raised alarm. In no time at all, place was swarming with uniformed police officers, yelling into crackling radios, blowing whistles, sliding on tiles, falling into water and generally trying to impose a bit of law and order. Well, believe it or not, they succeeded. The young yobs laid off, leapt out of pool like trained dolphins or porpoises (spelling – am I thinking of tortoises?) and simply disappeared. Maybe there was a getaway car waiting outside.

We were all given VIP treatment, including hot sweet tea in manager's office. Only problem was getting Timmy dressed now he'd 'come out' as a boy. Iceberg got us out of that one. Somehow, in all the confusion, she managed to smuggle Gail's jeans into men's changing room for him. Gail put on the skirt he'd worn on outward journey. Then the Iceberg drove us back to cottage. On way I asked if experience had been useful for her comic book. She said it was too late to change anything now but yes, she could see she'd done everything just right. I mentioned that all the underwater sex had reminded me of one of those movies I'd glimpsed a few minutes of when they'd shown it at the party – *Delicious Girls* I think someone said it was called. Iceberg said she hadn't seen it, which was odd because I was sure she'd been having some sort of oral sex with Captain when I'd wandered into upstairs room where they were showing it. Anyway, the Iceberg kissed me when she dropped us off. Said she couldn't stay as she had to get back to London. She may be weird but she's quite a sport!

Melanie closed the yellow notebook with a sigh of satisfaction. One day she might let dear old Mac read her version of the adventures in most of which Mac herself had played such a major role. Meanwhile, the diary would remain Melanie's own private world, a world over which she felt she exercised complete control, subject to the constraints of truthfulness. And as a diarist she was indeed truthful, perhaps more so than in the real life she recorded faithfully within its covers.

She rose from the garden chair, stretched her naked limbs and arranged the cushions to make herself a little bed in a sunny patch between two apple trees. Then she lay down, closed her eyes and masturbated lazily as she relived the events she had just been writing up.

By that same Tuesday afternoon, the Captain had got Helen, and to a lesser extent Victoria, to clear away most of the mess from the party. If he ever gave another one he would ask Sharon and her mates out there in the market whether they'd care to make the odd bob doing a bit of charring. He had been too busy to lend much of a hand himself, having been engaged in a quest for the location of Yglesias Enterprises (Video) Ltd. He had no recollection of Talbot Yglesias's home address, which would have been lost with all the records and other rubbish when the Honeymoon Palace Motel went up in flames; it was not just his own tracks he had covered on that occasion. In mid-morning he nipped out to spend half an hour in the upstairs reference room of the Fulham Road public library. Phone-wise, Yglesias was ex-directory, and his professional activities appeared to be strictly off the record. Now the cheated publisher sat at his desk feeling frustrated in more ways than one.

Helen came down from the studio, hot, dusty and pissed off. Having spent most of the last two days in the arms of her voluptuous mother, the Captain realised that Helen's more slender charms were just what he could do with to help clear his mind. He invited her to accompany him upstairs, where he placed his private bathroom at her disposal and suggested they should take a refreshing shower together.

Although not exactly enthusiastic, his editorial assistant raised no objection and was soon standing naked with him in the little shower cubicle. The short, straight hair on her head and the short curly hair on her pubic mound were darkened by the streaming water and the small brown nipples stiffened up gamely. When the Captain stooped to touch one of them with the tip of his tongue, Helen's wide

155

lips widened still further in a smile that raised the usually drooping corners of her mouth.

'*O matre pulchra filia pulchrior*,' he mused aloud, inwardly congratulating himself on the felicity of this classical allusion. Immediately he winced at his tactlessness. Helen, after all, was not supposed to know that he knew Sylvia Lascelles. He hoped any scraps of Latinity the girl might have picked up at Cunlip were insufficient for her to realise he was addressing her as a daughter more beautiful than her beautiful mother.

The moment of danger passed. Kids these days no longer had this sort of stuff beaten into them the way it was when he was at school. The world was a greyer, graver place as result, not least for the people who used to make a living teaching it. He wondered how that wild pedagogue Mary Muttock was making out in America. Now, there was a wasted talent, and very sexy with it ... Anyway, Helen's wits were as sharp as her pointy little elbows but she was clearly no more capable of construing Horace than the Captain was of sucking his own cock.

At this moment his cock was not being sucked at all. Its shining, empurpled knob was nudging into Helen's wet belly button as if looking for an alternative entrance to her interior wetness. If it stretched up much further and Helen dipped her head down a bit ... But no, she was reaching her wide lips up to meet his in a doubly wet kiss, wet from her saliva and wet from the water streaming from the shower.

Clinging round his neck with her left hand, Helen lifted her right knee and used her right hand to hold it so that it stuck out sideways from her body and the sodden vulva gaped open. The Captain bent his knees and stooped sufficiently to hook the tip of his upright tool into the soft folds of flesh, then straightened up in a powerful thrust that lifted Helen from the floor of the shower. Both her legs were now wrapped round his hips and his tongue was sucked deep into her throat.

Her cunt contracted on him and he came.

Quite unexpectedly and with no preliminary pumping,

he spilt himself in one steady outpouring. The orgasm was like a simple, frank, spontaneous declaration of love, with no words wasted. The intense feeling of relief brought home to him how keyed up he had been. It was only fair now, he reflected with a not entirely characteristic chivalry, that Helen should be pampered and cosseted and eventually granted her own release. By which time . . .

As his softening penis slipped out of the tight embrace of Helen's cunt he turned off the water and reached for a pair of warm, fluffy towels. The lovers patted each other dry, still standing under the shower; warm droplets continued to leak from the shower-head and tickle their shoulders and backs.

As soon as the Captain had dealt with the girl's delicious underarms, fluffed with fine but luxuriant blonde hair, and her pert little boobs, he sank to his knees. Gently clutching the narrow hips he rested a cheek against the damp pubic triangle. He ran a hand up the inside of her right thigh.

The wet skin was firm over the well-toned muscle beneath. But as he approached her groin and felt a point of dripping hair touch the edge of his hand, his palm encountered the slippery spendings sliding down from her tight vagina.

`Without hesitation he forced her feet further apart and made her flex her knees. For a moment he gazed at the pink petals of her sex as they oozed spunk and girljuice. Then, seizing her small buttocks in both hands, he curled his tongue into a long, hard cylinder and plunged it deep into the love hole. The tip of his nose nuzzled her clitoris, causing the spasms of Helen's lust to shiver their tightness over the probing tongue.

Her fluids, mingled with his sperm, flooded back along the tube of his tongue, obliging him to swallow. But still the juices flowed. Reluctant to back away from this delightful vulva but concerned about the possibility of literally drowning in love, the Captain tightened his lips around the vaginal opening, withdrew the tip of his tongue to the entrance and sucked.

Surprisingly, Helen's cunt still seemed to be full of his

semen. Tight she might be, but she must have hidden depths, he thought, as he sucked and sucked again, his palate luxuriating in the combined savours of cunt and cock.

There was no way of sucking her dry, but at last the thick, creamy efflux gave way to the clear oiliness of female secretions unmixed with the offering he had pumped into her. He stood up, bundled her in a warm towel and carried her, flushed and panting, into his bedroom. He dropped her, face down, on the bed, got between her legs, pulled her bottom up and drove the length of his rejuvenated maleness into the receptacle he had just cleansed so thoroughly.

The Captain was determined to make this round last longer than the first one, when he had been 'surprised by joy' in a way not envisaged by the poet who coined the expression. Once he was securely lodged, he eased Helen down again until she lay on her stomach with her legs apart and his hands under her small, squashed breasts. Instead of bucking in and out like an adolescent, he just relaxed on her back and let himself grow and grow inside her, occasionally moving from side to side to make sure she could feel who was her master. And to delay the moment of climax further, he engaged her in conversation as he fucked.

'Get to watch any of the videos the other night?' he asked.

'One or two,' she replied. 'The best one was that one based on our *Fucky Days*, I reckon, with our friend Sally Nugent doing her thing with all and sundry. Ooh, yes, you're making me go all quivery again. How much did Big Bang Productions pay for the rights, then?'

'That's just it – they didn't. Not a penny. They're fucking pirates.'

'Can't you take them to court? Yes, that's lovely, the way you're doing it now. Even better, why not a spot of blackmail? It's not just violation of copyright – they're issuing uncertificated tapes, aren't they?'

As he slowly threaded her and felt his charge of sperm replenishing and building up towards another explosion,

he explained that although he had identified Big Bang Productions as Yglesias Enterprises, he had been unable to
locate this dodgy firm. Helen hit on the answer in one.

'Easy. We've got a leak. There's got to be some link
between this office and your Talbot Yglesias. Well, it's not
me so it can only be . . .

'Victoria.'

'That's right, Victoria. You've got to challenge her.'

'Better still, I'll watch her. That's it – I'll follow her and
see if she leads me to the pirates' cave. I'll worm myself
into her con . . .'

At this point, just as the Captain had wormed himself
right up to the mouth of Helen's womb and was about to
spout his second outpouring of seed into her, the bedroom
door opened. Victoria Eisenberg, cool and unflustered,
strode across to the bed and sat down beside the lovers.
She was holding her large sketch pad.

If she had overheard any of the foregoing dialogue she
kept it to herself. On the whole, the Captain doubted
whether even the sounds of lovemaking had penetrated the
closed door; but then he had been going slow.

Lovemaking. His lovemaking had been interrupted. Although still embedded in Helen's tightness, his member
had lost some of its substance. He wriggled his pelvis over
the firm, resilient bottom with the intention of generating
enough friction to get him going again. And coming – he
needed that.

Victoria now declared her business. She had sought out
the Captain to show him some of the sketches she had
made for their projected graphic novel version of that
arousing old classic *The Lifted Curtain*. She wished to consult him about certain details of the scene in which the
servant girl Lucette adorns young Laura with crimson ribbons knotted in her loose hair and above her elbows and
waist before assisting at her ceremonial deflowering.

The succession of lubricious drawings, lightly sketched
in as they were, perked up the Captain's lust like magic.
First, Laura's step-father was shown admiring and hand-
ling the girl's naked attractions. Then Lucette stripped off

his skilfully drawn eighteenth-century costume. Laura waited, her thighs spread, on the cushions that were to serve as the altar of her sacrificed virginity after all those years in which her guardian had cherished her and sated his lusts on her body without actually penetrating her. The next frame showed Laura guiding the magnificent prick towards her unplumbed hole while Lucette stroked the still-virgin vulva with one hand and tickled the girl's arse-hole with the other.

Victoria explained her difficulty. She had begun a drawing in which Laura lay on her side while her guardian took her from behind. Although this was one of the easiest positions in which to copulate, Victoria had simply not been able to get her representation of the point of connection right. She wondered . . .

'Couldn't have chosen a better moment,' the Captain assured her. 'You just get your pencil ready. Mine's already full of lead and well sharpened.'

Without disengaging from the giggling Helen, he clung on to her and rolled over on his right side, pulling her with him. Helen lifted her left leg, bending the knee and flexing the thigh back as far as it would go. In this way she knew she could give the talented artist the best possible view, as well as maximising the Captain's pleasure by increasing the depth of his penetration. He returned the favour by placing his right hand on Helen's left breast and the forefinger of his left hand, which he had passed between the girl's thighs, on her clitoris. She used both of her own hands to draw back the lightly furred pubic mound so that the hood of flesh was pulled back with it, allowing the engorged bud to spring free for her lover's ministrations.

Yielding to the promptings of nature, the Captain thrust furiously in and out of the slight figure pressed against his belly. Such violent action might have been ideal in a video like the one Yglesias had based on Honeymooners material. But it was useless for Victoria's purposes. Landing an angry smack on her employer's bum, she commanded him to keep still while she studied and sketched the conjoined genitals. He bit his lip and forced himself to obey,

160

hoping that this would sweeten the eventual discharge, but Victoria was not satisfied. She leaned forward into the space between Helen's thighs, so close that the Captain felt her breath on his bollocks. Then she used both hands to separate the intermingling bushes until three inches of cockflesh were exposed with the tender inner lips of Helen's cunt clinging round it as if reluctant to let it escape.

Victoria sketched, Helen quivered and the Captain panted, his mouth dry and his balls aching. After what seemed like an eternity, or a good five minutes, the finished drawing was held up for the inspection of the uncomfortable couple. So lasciviously realistic was the depiction that the Captain and his partner were inspired with urgent lust and neither needed to move. The frustrated vagina spasmed furiously; the tormented cock swelled, pulsed and burst, flooding Helen with a second effusion of sperm that foamed inside her and bubbled out to stain the sheet on which the lovers lay.

NINE

GETTING COLD FEET

One week later the Captain eased himself into his swivel
chair and, with a sense of twofold anticipation, sipped the
coffee Helen had provided to ease his labours in the Palace
of Eros. The mid-May weather had improved slightly; even
though a glance through the window revealed eddies of
rubbish whirling around between the market stalls below,
the sun shone brightly. As long as the models turned up,
his planned session of outdoor photography could go
ahead. He had dressed rather cleverly for the occasion, he
thought, in a dark blue sweat-shirt emblazoned in white,
front and back, with the word 'PARKS'. No law against
wearing the garment, surely, even if his means of acquiring
it had not been strictly legal. It wasn't like impersonating
a clergyman. Now that was an idea . . .

The other reason for his feeling of mild excitement was
the envelope on the desk awaiting his attention. It bore
American stamps and could only be from his old friend
Mary Muttock. She had promised, had she not, to submit
a specimen of her writing to find out if it would be suitable
for the Honeymooners Library. He tore it open, glanced at
the covering note, and began to read the rather scrappy
and much-corrected typescript. The offering was headed
'BOUND TO PLEASE: THE INTIMATE MEMOIRS
OF A WHOREHOUSE NOVICE' – presumably the narrative was based on the time the Muttock had served out
west in that Raunch Ranch or whatever it was called.

* * *

On display there, waiting to be picked, waiting and waiting with every heartbeat an eternity of waiting when it can have been no more than five minutes before that busload of drunks rolled in from Vegas. Oh how I flushed with the healthy flush of youth, and how the flush of youth mingled downward from my throat with the flush of shame! To be abused and beautiful, to foam with lust while bridling still with the exquisite reticence of the innocent, the all but untouched. (For who would hold my earliest seduction against me, led astray by the wiles of naked authority? In my ignorance I considered myself fair game, lawfully laid by the long armoury of the law.) My pert young breasts swelled and strained at the pale blue silk containing their flesh but not their lust. And oh my pleasure-mound swelled ripe within the matching scrap of silk secured by flimsy ribbons. Swelled, I say, and foamed. We stood in line, flushed with lust, awaiting the tipsy punters flush from the poker tables. Flushed and foaming. Less than five minutes we stood there, each minute seeming like the lifetime of my lost girlhood. My belly was bare and I so young I trembled still at the thought of men's lascivious eyes hot upon it, bare. Childish games in the English woodland; sunlight dappling bare bellies. And fingers? That came later – those fingers stippling the curves of buttocks, the curves that rhymed with that name of mine and marked me for the beasts between piled blankets in the airless airing-cupboard.

Not to be forgotten the happy woodland hours of shaded innocence, innocence shaded with the cool restraint of chaste thoughts and warmed by the mild heat of pubescent passion. Those distant days when boys were slender, straight and juicy, rigid as rods of marble. The marble fountains they of ever-spilling youth, the creaming fountain-heads of girls' desire. And always tomorrow; tomorrow I will let you see me, let you touch me, let you do it. Today is for me, for me to do it to you. There will always be tomorrow, always another day. But the winds and rains came and the woods were stripped of their leaves. Those sylvan playgrounds, sodden now and mouldy, crawled with maligant maggots. The sleek-coated beasts of lustful guilt now roamed the valleys and rutted in the lanes. Oh, I sheltered in the airing-cupboard but there the beasts lurked lustful for me and my lust burned more beastly between my tremulous thighs.

Insidious and serpentine, worming their sure way through the tangled frondage of my dreams. A girl's dreams of innocent delight, swept into bliss on the back of a great white charger, its nostrils foaming. Rapt into the Castle Perilous and led out by my foaming prince into the walled garden of ecstasy, that *locus amoenus* of panted confessions and secret flesh.

In Texan hats they burst into the gaudy ranch-house, Tex-hatted and discharging phallic Colts into the ceiling. Whoopee, boys! Take your pick, you sons of guns! Horned hands assayed my tender body, kneading the firm dough of desire, tweaking the buds of bliss and crabbing sharp claws through the tangled frondage of my dreams. Insidious. Crablike. I, a mere slip of a girl in the English woodland, my seducer as common as his crime yet more cultured than these high-rolling dudes out to blow their winnings at the Raunch Ranch. Why, he, in those long-lost days, quoted poetry in my ravished ear: something about wishing to be a pair of ragged claws. At that tender age I had not yet perused the Moderns, having been brought up on Ovid, Catullus and cold porridge. Nevertheless, I responded with what he took, or mistook, for native wit. 'But that's exactly what you are, Chief Inspector,' I chuckled. 'I've seen you. You go round pinching ladies' bottoms.'

And now I know all too well how the ceremony of innocence is drowned, and in ways that would have boggled the belief of Harris Hardbuckle, the old groper, even when he clicked into handcuff mode. Two weeks as a Ranch girl and you think you've seen it all, but then a bunch of hard-drinking rednecks like these roll in and you ain't seen nothing, baby.

Three of them selected me to be their sweetheart for the next hour or so. Along with me they chose my arch-rival, that red-headed spitfire Arlene. And it was my room that Arlene led them to. My bed that was to be soiled with the gushes, fluxes and tricklings of their squalor.

I grew up with a horror of zoos. A three-year darling of a pygmy size, they led me between cages a-crawl with obscene monkey-business and on through the reptile house. Travelling home on the top of a bus we passed a grave black statue which in its stillness struck terror into my bones. Months then of writhing in my high-sided cot, struggling against the tendrils of sleep that came snaking between the cage-like bars to drag me into the swamp of nightmare.

Hank 'n' Hairy (doubtless Harry to rhyme with scary) took me, hook, line and sinker, while Big Chuck made out with Arlene. I was being gutted from both ends, reamed and rodded through the forests of my dread. Oh how they swung from the pelmet, red-rodded and blue-capped in their heat! Ripped my scant silk covering asunder, showing all. There in my cage they took me and desire raged hot in my loins, for their desire was my shame and their shameless lust was my desire. Forests of the night.

Arlene and her stud had set the seal on their love knot and yet their mouths were disengaged in their moaning. Two mouths, two tongues, four hands, two thick teats and two pulsing arseholes craved devotion. As Hank 'n' Hairy pranced me through my paces we rolled towards them: two mouths, two tongues, six hands, two thick teats and three hot arses. (Asses, rather, in this zoo of animal passions, this wild American dream.) And so we jostled and jinxed, jutted and juiced until we were linked and mated in a mystic pentagon of copulation.

Bollock-drained and bedraggled, did our big-balled bucks slink off abashed into the jungle, tails drooping slack between their thighs? Did they, heck! They wanted to party with us all the dizzy night. Hank 'n' Hairy bounced out to the waiting bus (driver entertained on the house) and humped in the Buds, six-pack-wise by the dozen, enough for the night of a lifetime. Chuck, meanwhile, had Arlene and me lick his sack and suck his prick back to succulent sufficiency.

Out came the cards, alas, and for end-to-end hours the only big bucks around were the green-backed kind. Back in the rest room Arlene slipped me a shot of something stronger than your regular Bud and I came out blooming, a Venus fly-trap paid for and primed for prey.

Oh the wild hunger of the jungle depths, damp and dripping in their season! Speed up the loves of the plants and they twist horrific in the tropic heat. Slow down the couplings of the beasts and the long gradations of tumidity, the endless-seeming agony of each deep rut, the ripe-to-bursting yearnings of those tortured glands, madden us even as our intellects enlarge to perceive the all-embracing oneness of the evolutionary drive, framed in whorls of purple-pink and studded with silver-sequined starbursts. Evolutionary, I say, mindful of how we came dropping and swooping from the trees of primeval night. When sober, Hank, Hairy and Chuck would have proclaimed themselves anti-Darwinian creationists; drunk, they were surely fundamentalists in the most fundamental, arse-licking sense. Like dogs burrowing their noses into backstreet bitches, this was how they made their natural selection. Back to fundamentals. For this conjunctive urge (the insight pole-axed me then as I swept aside the cards and splayed my womanhood for all to see, for all to taste and for all to use) is truly universal.

Before I left my maternal home I knew no comfort of the flesh save what I drew from the salty droolings of Chief Inspector Harris Hardbuckle and the beefier batterings of my brother. Sun-dappled woodland and steamy airing-cupboard melded in my memory until the humid depths of this tropical rainforest sprang lush and rampant through my dreams. A world well lost for lust.

166

Let the lithe hunters bury their arrows in my quivering cunt! Let the . . .

The persistent buzzing at the street door would not normally have put the Captain off his juicy reading. But he had no intention of missing out on the planned session with Anne and Carla. He put the curious manuscript back in its envelope, reflecting that if he decided to publish it he would need to change the names to protect the guilty. Old Hardbuckle had now attained the rank of Deputy Chief Constable, and the Captain could do without hassle from that direction.

Carla Merryweather and Anne Amory entered the office, accompanied by their two male flat-mates. Although he had met them and seen them in action, the Captain had never spoken to these young gentlemen who were now introduced to him as Bruce and Digger. Bruce was the tall, thin, fair-haired one and Digger the giant with blue stubble and long, greasy hair who had played the part of the biker in Friday night's show. The Captain embraced the girls and nodded curtly at the lads; he was not at all sure he had invited them to this session.

Carla and Anne were delighted to hear that their old college principal was making her literary debut. Helen, engaged in an acrimonious telephone conversation with the printers, was unable to greet them verbally but blew them a kiss. Then Victoria Eisenberg, keeping a wary distance from Bruce and Digger, took the foursome upstairs to be made up and fitted out with suitable costumes from the collection in the studio. Thankful that he had allowed himself the extravagance of a second phone line, the Captain ordered a cab.

The visitors returned some twenty minutes later wearing mid-calf-length black leather coats over knee-high black boots. To complete the effect, all four of them were equipped with black peaked caps, dark glasses and white silk scarfs. 'You guessed right,' Victoria remarked. 'Nothing much underneath.'

His camera and tripod in a professional bag, the Captain

escorted his models down to the street. They picked their way through the garbage and squeezed between the fruit-and-veg stall and its neighbour, attracting dirty looks from the queues on the pavement.

'Hey, Sid,' called Sharon. 'Lady here says she can't do wivvaht a courgette.'

'Fresh ahta courgettes,' came the reply. 'Ask if she can make do wiv a banana.'

The taxi had taken a short cut, zigzagging through the double-parkers in the back streets, and was there even as they reached the kerb. 'Fulham Palace,' the Captain directed.

Bruce and Digger said they had already done the sights, including this one, but the girls had never visited the former seat of the Bishops of London and were impressed by the Tudor architecture of the front courtyard. They sat on a bench, arms round each other's shoulders, as the wind-on mechanism whirred for the first set of pictures, and more were taken under the arched gatehouse. Then they were marched round to the extensive grounds at the back of this historic building. The Captain found a reasonably secluded lawn flanking the Victorian chapel and stood Anne and Carla side by side beneath the dark brick wall. A pair of squirrels darted across the grass to the girls' feet and looked up at them expectantly.

'That's really cute,' the Captain chuckled, firing the camera. 'Open your coats and see if you can get them to run up your legs.'

It was not clear if he was serious about this. Anne was very nervous, having noticed the sharpness of these rodents' claws as they had done a vertical run down the trunk of a nearby tree. Fortunately for her, this sequence of photos had to be aborted before any kind of exposure was possible, as a morose-looking groundsman came trundling a wheelbarrow round the corner of the chapel. The Captain hurried his little party along a gravel path which led between overhanging trees. He no longer felt so confident that the conspicuous 'PARKS' on his sweat-shirt was going to deflect unwelcome attention; it might work with the general public but staff wearing the same garment, like that groundsman, were a different matter.

The public were thankfully thin on the ground this bright but breezy Tuesday morning. The palace grounds were full of fine trees, the heritage of a collection first planted a couple of centuries ago by a botanically inclined bishop and now scientifically and informatively labelled. 'Look,' he said, beckoning the group over to one with little fan-shaped leaves. 'Do you see why this one's called the maidenhair tree? The leaves are very delicate. They remind me more of Anne than of Carla – don't you think so, Bruce?'

Anne blushed and Carla laughed; the two lads affected an air of bored superiority. 'I suppose you're going to tell us this next one's a penis tree,' said Carla, 'though I can't say it looks much like one.'

'Not much like mine, maybe,' the Captain replied. 'But it does look like some kind of *pinus*, all the same. You know, a pine. Let's see what the label says.'

Sure enough, the small rectangle of black plastic attached to the trunk was inscribed in neat white letters with the botanical description 'Pinus Wallichiana'. Even the young men were moderately amused. A lady leading a reluctant toddler by the hand gave the little party a wide berth.

Even Anne had to duck her head as they passed through a low arch in a crumbling brick wall into what could have been taken for a place set aside for secret dalliance. For some reason the Captain remembered the enclosed pleasance or *locus amoenus* of Mary Muttock's memoirs as he inhaled the mingling fragrances of this small but delicious herb garden. He held a sprig of crushed rosemary under Carla's nose, then rubbed a leaf of sage against the underside of Anne's chin. 'A pair of tasty dishes for you here,' he observed to the boys. 'All they need now's a bit of stuffing. Don't know about you, but my mouth's watering already.'

Passing out of the herb garden, they entered a grassy expanse fenced with a neatly trimmed beech hedge. In an

169

angle of this hedge they found a bench. All five of them were struck with the same thought at the same time: they could re-enact the park bench sequence with which they had so recently entertained the party-goers.

Down they sat, Digger, Anne, Bruce and Carla. The Captain found he was trembling slightly and was glad he had brought a tripod for the camera. 'Right,' he said. 'First of all I want you to stand up for a moment and flash them at me, darlings.'

They rose from the bench and unbuttoned. The fronts of the four leather coats were parted. Apart from her cap, scarf and boots, Carla's pale nudity was relieved only by a gold chain around her waist. From the chain hung a heart-shaped locket which dangled suggestively over her dark bush. Bruce and Digger were both tightly packed into diminutive pouches of soft black leather, Bruce's skin smooth and tanned golden and Digger's white but shagged with a mat of tangled black hair. Like Bruce, Anne's skin was tanned, but much more lightly – it was still only the middle of May, so this honeyed tint was probably more the residue of last summer than anything she had acquired this year. A black ribbon had been tied low round her hips. Attached to this and scarcely large or substantial enough to conceal her modesty was a tiny apron of black gauze, not more than four inches square, edged with silver lace.

Pictures were taken of the four of them standing. To complete this series, Anne was instructed to hold up a corner of her little apron with a show of dainty reluctance. Then they were all told to sit on the bench and get petting while the Captain, who now removed his camera from the tripod, closed in and used up a whole reel of film on frank shots of mouths on tits and more teasing ones of fingers playing around covered, partly covered and, in the case of Carla, uncovered genitals.

For a time they had to close the fronts of their coats and sit quietly while the woman with the toddler they had already encountered loitered around this part of the grounds with her young charge. Whenever they seemed to be about to disappear into the herb garden, the child would find

170

some pretext for tottering back towards the Captain's party, and the mother (or more likely nanny) was in no hurry to move on.

At last the coast was clear. The only person in sight was a young man with 'PARKS' on his back, tidying a distant corner of the beech hedge with a noisy petrol-powered trimmer. Now was the time for action. The others followed the Captain as he shifted his tripod across to a kind of shrubbery in the middle of the greensward.

The layout of this feature was formal; essentially it comprised two high, square-cut blocks of greenery, each about twenty feet long and six wide, with a narrow passageway of grass between them. In the summer months, when the outer foliage was enlivened by the blooming of wild roses, this shady strip was a favourite courting ground for the young and hopeful. Now it offered just the right setting for the culminating sequence of photographs.

Ushering his flock into this space between the high shrubs, the Captain supervised their undressing. Total nudity was not the aim. The men retained their caps, sunglasses, white silk scarfs and boots. Only the leather pouches were peeled off. It was interesting to observe that Bruce was already erect, his penis twanging up into a near-vertical angle, while Digger's hung limply over a bulging ballsack. Yet even in its flaccid condition Digger's dick was considerably longer and fatter than his mate's. Not for the first time, the Captain caught himself wondering if these guys swung both ways. Did Digger dig Bruce? And did Bruce bugger his buddy?

Carla, too, was only required to remove her coat, making her a female match for the two lads. But Anne was singled out for different treatment. Off came everything except the silver-fringed little veil over her sex. She was not altogether happy at having to remove her boots, complaining that her feet were cold. 'Don't worry, dear,' the Captain reassured her. 'As long as the cold doesn't spread higher up you'll do just fine.'

The group huddled and cuddled together in the opening between the two blocks of shrubbery for the first few shots of this set. In some of them Anne's apron simply hung over the centre-point of her loins in semi-innocence. In others it was being lifted, at first only slightly but later completely, by Digger's big hand. The Captain asked her to move forward a little so that the sunlight fell on the shiny blonde fuzz with its pink dividing line shockingly visible.

There was no doubt that Anne had become central to this operation. She was, of course, the Captain's favourite and he had often suspected, perhaps unrealistically, that she had a bit of a crush on him. Now that the apron had been lifted he felt the scrap of gauze had become redundant. Time for a quick change. It had better be quick, as the young gardener over there was working his way along the hedge towards them with rather more haste and considerably less care than his superiors might have desired. At this rate he would soon reach a position from which he could turn and look straight across into the gap where the photography was taking place.

Anne's change of costume was minimal. It had to be, as the costume itself was minimal. Off came the apron and its supporting ribbon. Bruce, whose habitual attention to his appearance raised the possibility that he might have had some fashion-house experience, was then asked to pick up the girl's discarded silk scarf and drape it tastefully round her middle. As he did so, the tip of his hardened prong smeared a juicy trail on the outside of her thigh.

There was no need to advise Bruce; he was obviously fascinated by his task, which he executed with the eye of a connoisseur and the hand of an adept. He knotted the white silk about an inch above one hip, letting the loose ends hang halfway down Anne's thigh, just behind the wet streak which he was careful to leave on show. Instead of being wrapped round her in a straight horizontal line, the scarf sat slightly lower on her other hip, leaving exposed just the beginning of the crease separating abdomen from thigh. On this side Bruce opened the silk out so that the full width of it hugged her buttock and the top of her outer thigh. The lower edge of the scarf then traced an oblique line running upwards from a point some six inches below

172

the point of the hip-bone across to the knot on the other side. This meant that the midpoint of the line cleverly intersected Anne's pubic triangle, leaving the plump mound almost entirely bare while at the same time suggesting that she was modestly trying to hide it. To add a final touch of class, Bruce put her cap on the back of her head so that her blonde fringe peeped out from under the peak.

The Captain was delighted with the effect and insisted on Anne stepping out from the shrubbery just for a moment to be photographed posing on the sunny grass. On her emergence the buzzing hedge-trimmer made an alarming swooping sound as if some demented Biggles was looping the loop at a flying display. Then the engine cut out. The silence was hardly noticed.

Now for the big one, the Captain thought; he certainly felt big enough inside his jeans. This would have to be managed tactfully. He ordered Carla to bend forward with her hands on her knees, sideways-on to the camera, and to take Bruce's erection into her mouth. Digger, whose cock swelled up to frightening dimensions on hearing what his role was to be, approached her from behind. He first parted the cheeks of her bottom and then the seeping petals of her cunt, before driving his whole monstrous length and girth up into her fuck-channel. Carla winced at the initial force of the penetration and Bruce's prick was rammed further down her throat. Quickly she became accustomed to what was unlikely to have been a novel experience, sharing a flat as she did with two brisk lads like these. The Captain asked Anne to stand just behind the threesome, her hands resting on the shoulders of the men who stood facing each other with Carla bent forward between them. Bruce and Digger were only too happy to fondle her firm little breasts. The camera whirred away.

But this was merely a preliminary. The Captain now set the self-timing device and dashed forward to join the others in the gap between the slabs of shrubbery. He quickly opened his jeans, struggling to release the well-primed organ on which the garment was caught. The jeans dropped to his ankles. He stood close beside Anne, who instinc-

173

tively turned to face him. This was the potentially dodgy bit. He cleared his throat and addressed Digger.

'Don't mind, do you, old man? We go back a long way, Anne and me.'

Digger remained as impassive as could be expected in a man desperately holding back from orgasm. 'We don't own these sheilas, mate.' he replied. 'We just pay the rent for them. Be my guest.'

Anne closed her hands behind the Captain's neck. He reached down to lift one of her legs, holding it with a hand under her thigh while he used the other one to open the fur-edged furrow thus disclosed. Just as his shining purple plum hovered at her vaginal entrance the camera clicked. The shot must have been pretty much what the Captain had intended, with their imminent joining plainly visible above Carla's downward-sloping back as she took cock at both ends. But this was no time to call a halt to the fun, even if, strictly speaking, the five of them were there for business purposes. He slid in easily. Anne clung tighter to his neck and raised her other leg, grasping him around the hips with her thighs as he supported most of her weight by cupping her buttocks in the palms of his hands. The tips of his two little fingers drifted into the moist, warm groove between the cheeks and found her other opening ready to welcome his probing caresses. The girl released his neck and let her head hang back blissfully, her tight nipples pointing up at the sky. He checked with the others; everything was now in place for a threefold release of sperm.

Before any ejaculation occurred, however, a shadow was thrown upon the statuesque tableau. A powerful figure had materialised at the opening of the gap in which they stood and now loomed up between them and the sun, the word 'PARKS' glaring from across his chest and a dangerous-looking hedge-trimming implement hanging from his right hand. It was only the advanced state of the multiple copulation that kept the Captain's party from falling over in surprise.

The young newcomer smiled, his attention caught by the matching legend on the Captain's sweat-shirt. 'Snap!' he exclaimed, pointing at his own. 'You must be the new amenities officer. Did they tell you in the office? You can start off nice and easy for the first few days. All you've got to do is hang around watching out for shirt-lifters and perverts. But don't let me spoil your fun.'

The Captain had no intention of letting him do so. Barely able to contain himself, he asked the young man to operate the camera while unfinished business was attended to. Even as he gasped out his instructions, the pressurised reservoir of spunk burst inside him. What felt like a solid mass of semen shot up the length of his tightly encunted cock to gush deep into the squealing Anne's belly. While still discharging he fell forward with her across Carla's back. As Carla went down she took Digger and Bruce with her. They too were in the very act of emission, joined to her in coitus and fellatio as firmly as coupling dogs. The pile of bodies seethed, heaved and bubbled with spouting lust, both girls yelling out as they joined their partners in lewd climax.

It could be, the Captain admitted to himself, that none of these pictures would be suitable for Honeymooners covers. But if necessary he would write a book himself to describe this scene of lustful enjoyment and use the photographs to illustrate it.

Miss MacDonald had gone to the college and Derrick had not been round that morning. Melanie had a bath, put on a pretty yellow bikini-bottom as a safeguard against any repetition of the previous day's untoward occurrence and took her diary out into the garden where she chose a seat in a sunny spot. Mac's overnight irritability and lack of tenderness was a sign that she might be getting cold feet; her anxiety was communicating itself to Melanie, even though Melanie was more inclined to see the lighter side. Frowning slightly with worry as well as with concentration, she began to write her account of that rather alarming event.

Thu, May 20
This could be trouble on the way, though I don't think so and even if it is it probably won't be really *big* trouble

175

– nothing so heavy we can't handle it. It was yesterday afternoon, about one. Mac had popped home for a bite of lunch, just the apple and piece of cheese she usually takes with her, but sometimes she likes to get away from the little madams for the lunch hour and be with me. Aren't I the lucky one?

Anyway, I was sitting out here – I'd better say out there, it's just that I'm sitting here again now but I probably won't be the next time I read this. Neither will Posterity if they ever get round to doing my biography.

Where was I? Yes, in the orchard. Much warmer than last few days. That wicked wind's died down and the sun's as bright as ever. I hadn't got anything on except my floppy straw sun-hat but the big fat ginger cat was curled up on my lap. I heard usual popping noise as Mac switched off engine of car and in no time at all she came skipping down the path with her lunch box, all smiles and lithe athletic limbs. Instead of her old track-suit she was wearing her tiny white shorts and a little black top that left her shoulders and tummy bare. I'm surprised she can get away with showing herself like that at Cunlip now they've tightened things up so much. Maybe Mac can get away with anything. Maybe she's going to need to be able to.

MAC: What's happened to your muff, darling? Been using hair restorer?

ME: Can't I stroke my pussy without being made fun of? I feel lovely and warm down there.

MAC: Well, no fleas on Orlando, I hope. But watch out for his claws when he's had enough of lapping up the cream.

ME: He's certainly creaming up my lap. His tongue's as rough as Derrick's thumb.

MAC: But not as rough as Derrick's tongue, dear. I can't think why we put up with a foul-mouthed little peasant like him.

Well, Mac never has liked D, which isn't surprising as I don't go for him that much myself except for a bit of a tumble in the morning when I'm on my own. She came

176

up to me and bent down to stroke Orlando but Orlando jumped off my lap and climbed a tree so Mac was left stroking my ginger fur instead of his.

Just then we heard another car pull up outside and door bell rang. Mac hurried back to cottage and went inside to open front door but meanwhile side gate opened and suddenly garden and orchard were full of police.

A slight exaggeration, that, but that was what it seemed like because of the shock of suddenly seeing both of them there in their uniforms. They came up the path at a trot, as if they didn't want me to escape or get dressed or anything. As soon as they got close I recognised them from those two previous occasions. It was the burly sergeant (spelling?) and busty young WPC who caught me driving dangerously that time on way to picnic and barged in on orgy we were having over at the Muttock's place last year. Sure enough, they recognised me too.

WPC: Look, sarge, you was right – it's the self-same one. Got even less on this time, but it's her cheeky face I recognise.

SERGEANT: Pity, in a way. We could have set up an ID parade with a whole line-up of nude blondes like her.

WPC: Still can, sarge. It's not us what's got to identify her, is it now? It's that old frump – I mean that lady what laid the complaint in the first place.

SERGEANT: Good thinking, Jives. And though we ain't got much more than her face and her tits to go on, our lady witness will have had an eyeful of *this*. Not so many like it, you know – leastways, not in my experience, not when they got it yellow on top. Just look at it. Like a ginger kitten with a little pink mouth. Hope she don't have claws on her.

WPC: You better keep well out of her reach, Albert Raddle, if you don't want your missis creating. She give you a right bollocking that last time you . . .

By this time Mac had joined us, flushed and indignant. Wanted to know what they thought they were do-

177

ing, busting in like that. To cut a long story short, they said they'd come to investigate a complaint. I knew that already.

SERGEANT (*to me*): Where was you last Saturday morning, then, miss?

ME: The Market Street baths.

SERGEANT: Alone?

ME: With some friends.

SERGEANT: Well, we have reason to believe a public order offence was committed, to say the very least. (*To Mac*) And you, madam, I suppose you was the tall, older woman with this lot, though our informant did say something about very fair hair and yours is brown.

I could see Mac was making connections and probably guessing we'd had the Iceberg with us.

WPC: Just had a brainwave, sarge. That old bag – our eyewitness, I mean – said something about a boy got up as a girl with a wig. (*I was now beginning to think that middle-aged woman in the bathing cap swimming up and down while we were at it must have kicked up a fuss about our bit of fun.*) We fished the wig out of the water and kept it as evidence, remember?

SERGEANT: So?

WPC: Well, likely as not this lady was wearing a wig too – a blonde wig, see.

MAC: This is scandalous, officer. I have an alibi.

SERGEANT: Oh yes? So where was you?

MAC (*glancing at me in a rather guilty way, I thought*): With some friends in London. My solicitor can let you have the details.

ME: For heaven's sake, sergeant, there's got to be some mistake here. You've got hold of the wrong end of the stick.

SERGEANT: How's that, miss?

ME: Me and my friends were innocent victims. You weren't there, not when it happened. We were set on by this gang of yobs who tried to rape us in the water. Someone called the police. The guys got away. It was OK – happy ending and everything. Your colleagues looked after us.

MAC: You never told me about this, Melanie. You'll have some explaining to do later.

WPC: Don't let yourself get sidetracked, sarge. Remember what our witness told us. We're looking at a case of blatant provocation. Them boys was led on something disgusting, she said.

Just then me and Mac were surprised to see someone else coming out of the cottage. It was another copper, much younger than these two. Younger than me, in fact. Looked very pleased with himself. He was carrying a plastic Bigbuys bag which seemed to be full of papers.

YOUNG PC: Got all the incriminating evidence we need here, Sergeant Raddle, sir. Tons of it. Listen to this. 'The slap caused Ulv – Ulva to swing forward on her chain. She swung towards the male bonds – the male bondslave and her belly butted against the long – the long . . .' – shall I say it, sarge?

SERGEANT: Get it out, boy.

YOUNG PC (*looking confused at first and fiddling with his flies until penny dropped*): Oh, I see what you mean. '. . . the long fleshcock that had lifted from his hairy bumps and pointed at her when the oiled thing – the oiled thong was removed. Already that fleshcock was weeping its milt. The slave swung away from her . . .'

SERGEANT: That's enough, lad. Don't want to get Jivesy here overexcited, do we? Give us that bag, will you?

Everyone was quiet for a few minutes, though I could hear my own heart beating and thought I could hear Mac's too. Wished I had something on or that Orlando would come back to sit on lap. Young constable kept looking at me sheepishly and sort of bending forward as if trying to hide wagging truncheon in trousers. I could see this Sgt Raddle had found some letters and was reading them.

SERGEANT: This here's more like it, Jives, if it's hard documentary evidence we're looking for. Chapter and verse. Names, addresses and telephone numbers.

Now see here, ladies. We still have reason to believe an offence has been committed, even if it's not quite the one we first thought. But it definitely appears to be related – closely related, and just the sort of thing the Home Office wants us boys in blue to jump hard on. On hard, I mean.

WPC: And girls. You know, girls in blue.

YOUNG PC: Not really blue at all, is it, sarge? More like black if you ask me. Like what the SS used to ...

SERGEANT: You colour-blind or something, sonny?

YOUNG PC: Thought that's what we was supposed to be these days.

SERGEANT (*breathing in and trying to control himself*): So it's like this, ladies. Me and my little team here's going to be pursuing our enquiries up in the smoke with the co-operation of our good friends in the Fulham nick. Or maybe we'll save time and cut that particular corner. And in the meantime I'd be glad if you'd kindly hold yourselves open for further investigations as and when. I bid you good day, ladies.

The three of them plodded off with their bag of 'evidence'. Mac was furious but couldn't help seeing funny side of it.

MAC: Got to work my anger off somehow. Will you kindly hold yourself open for investigation, dear? Just an internal one, you understand. That's the way – hold it wide open. Hurry, now. Pull my shorts down while I'm doing you. I'm nearly there already, but if I work at it really hard I may just get you in the nick.

TEN

HEADING DOWNMARKET

The Captain and Helen waited in their cab while Victoria Eisenberg alighted from hers, which had halted on the brow of a hill some fifty yards ahead of them. She paid off her driver and disappeared into the darkness at the side of the road. The two watchers got out and followed.

Although it was after ten it was still quite warm. This was just as well, as both of them were quite lightly dressed, the Captain in his habitual denims and Helen in her thin black sweater with the red miniskirt of soft woollen material and black tights.

Victoria had left the office some time after seven but made straight for a little restaurant in Fulham Broadway, where she had spent more than two and a half hours, apparently alone. Reluctant to relinquish their quest so soon, the Captain had insisted on stretching out a couple of beers among the Friday night crowd in the Red Lion. Through clear parts of an engraved glass window they were able to keep watch on the restaurant. They had been lucky to stop a cab immediately after Victoria took off in hers, and their driver had managed to tail her all the way to this location somewhere in north London. The Captain was already regretting he had forgotten to ask the driver exactly where they were.

They soon realised that the little hill on which Victoria had vanished was a bridge with a high brick parapet. Helen led the way through a well-used gap in the fence just beyond the parapet and down the uneven stairs to the railway cutting which ran beneath the bridge. It was a dark night, but street lights up above made it possible to make out a surprising number of shadowy figures milling about on the unlit and dilapidated station platform below. Whatever these people were up to, they were not waiting for a train; passenger or (to use the current terminology) customer services had long since been rationalised and there were no longer any rails for the trains to run on.

Helen strode boldly forward, stepping over the weeds that sprouted from the broken concrete of the platform. The Captain did his best to keep up with her, worried that she might be targeted as easy prey if mistaken for an unaccompanied woman. But these men (for they all seemed to be men down here) were hustling for partners of their own sex.

Beyond the platform the hopeful trippers were much thinner on the ground, some walking purposefully in one direction or the other while others just hung around. The sexual orientation also seemed to have changed, unless the females were really transvestites. The Captain was glad he had not come to this place alone; he found it quite surprising that the cool Victoria had done so. So this was her scene . . .

Where exactly was Victoria? Almost certainly among the dark figures up ahead. Helen urged him on. The going was hard, the ground underfoot strewn with sharp stones, and the only lighting was that cast by the odd street lamp on the bridges spanning the cutting at irregular intervals. Under these bridges lurked winos and druggies in various stages of exaltation and disintegration.

Suddenly Helen gripped his arm. 'That looks like her,' she whispered, indicating a pale form some thirty feet ahead of them. 'You can just make out her yellow coat.'

This discovery gave the Captain fresh interest in what he was doing, even though it seemed rather unlikely that Victoria was leading them to the pirates and abusers of intellectual property to whom she has betrayed the trust of the Honeymooners Library. Still, any information they gleaned about her private life would have potential value in the struggle ahead.

The sinister figures lining this section of the disused track were certainly not in the business of abusing intellectual property. It was Victoria's physical appurtenances that were attracting their attention. The Captain and Helen, being a couple, came in for verbal abuse only, apart from the odd grope as they passed between the massed ranks of these undesirables.

Victoria, however, was being tugged about, dishevelled, mauled and felt up with every step she took. From behind, it was hard to see exactly what indignities were being visited upon her under that yellow coat, but the bawdy remarks of her tormentors left little doubt that by now her breasts were exposed and her tights seriously ripped. The Captain noticed with revulsion that some of the hairy creatures between whom he was elbowing his and Helen's way were still holding the bared and stiffened cocks they had just been attempting to thrust at or into her as she passed between them.

And yet the haughty blonde appeared to be deflecting these lewd approaches with some success. The inroads on her modesty could only have been superficial. As far as could be made out from the distance at which her employer and colleague were tailing her, she was resisting the importunities with barbed words and a niftily swung handbag.

Beyond the next bridge the crowds thinned out again. They now seemed to be all female, even if some of the crop-headed horrors who eyed the Captain with distaste and Helen with lust had done everything they could to disguise their femininity. Others, the Captain noted, affected an exaggerated tartiness, all black lipstick and stiff black taffeta leaving everything bare between the tops of their torn stockings and their waists. He wondered if he was being unduly cynical, too far out of tune with the spirit of the age, in wondering whether the return to family values urged by the authorities could do much to change the way of life pursued down here. It would make more sense, surely to re-open this disused railway line. Victoria, to be sure, seemed quite at home. She was no longer hurrying to get past these people – on the contrary, she could be seen to be dallying and flirting with them.

This new turn of events posed a real problem for the Captain and his young companion. If they went on, it was almost certain that the dallying Victoria would recognise them. If they went back, all their detective work would be lost. But if they remained where they were, they could hardly expect these harpy-like denizens of the night to leave them alone. Not Helen, at any rate. It was clear that they had no use for the Captain.

Helen, thank goodness, was willing to play along with them. Her natural lasciviousness goaded her on to tease and tantalise them by raising the front of her black sweater, lifting the hem of her red miniskirt and edging down her tights and knickers to reveal her bottom and cuntmound. A dozen grubby hands and snaking tongues moved in to the assault; the Captain felt himself harden inside his jeans as he watched the plucky girl writhe and weave her way between them. All the time she remained in control of the encounter, setting the pace and calling the shots.

What was being enacted before his eyes, the Captain reflected, might have quickly degenerated into a crude lesbian gang bang, just one more case of an over-adventurous middle-class girl falling into bad company and being exploited by social inadequates whose parents, growing up in the sixties, had never taught them the difference between right and wrong. Thanks to Helen's spirited reaction, however, and above all to her supple athleticism, the performance turned out to be an erotic ballet such as he had not witnessed since Miss MacDonald took him along to the New Vibrations Modern Dance Group's acclaimed nude production, *The Twenty-Fifth Day of Sodom*. Lips and fingers slid over Helen's bare white skin and lingered on the erectile tissue and damp complexity of her erogenous zones. Each lunge of her suitors provoked a corresponding thrust of her pelvis, belly or pert bosom, but every approach to vaginal or anal penetration was nimbly sidestepped and turned into a flirtatious gesture gracefully declined.

Ignored by Helen's fascinated admirers, the Captain strained his eyes to see what was going on a bit further down the line. The scene being enacted there appeared to be more businesslike than erotic. As far as he could make out, Victoria had lined up some eight or ten women and was assessing their finer points, or perhaps their more obvious ones, like a horsewoman intent on buying a mettlesome filly. He actually saw a number of banknotes changing hands; the denominations might have been anything, but even if they were only fivers it was evident that this Ms Eisenberg had no thought of laying out her cash, whether hard-earned or embezzled, on the purchase of rubbish.

Even as he watched the transaction, Victoria broke away from her group, taking a tall woman with her. They were heading back up the track at a brisk pace. The Captain turned to face the other direction and did his best to avoid recognition by burying his features between Helen's little breasts and reaching up to cover her rather corrupt-looking prettiness with his hands.

This behaviour was not well received by the corps de ballet, who used their combined forces to drag him away from Helen and boot him off in precisely the direction from which he was trying to remain hidden. Victoria and her new purchase had advanced to within six feet of this scene. But at the very instant when the Captain was virtually hurled into their arms, they turned and made for a steep flight of steps leading up to the road which crossed the nearest bridge.

He looked directly at their now receding forms. They were walking arm in arm. Victoria was using her free hand to clutch her yellow coat tightly round her abused body. Her partner's appearance differed quite strikingly from that of all the other women he had seen so far in this weird meat-market. She was dressed like a show jumper in white riding breeches, shiny black boots, tailored black coat and hard hat. The hand not engaged with Victoria clutched a riding crop. So she was the rider and Victoria the filly. When she spoke, her accents rang out superior and Sloan-ish.

'I've got a better idea,' she was saying. 'Let's go to my place in Cadogan Gardens, darling. You'll feel more at home there.'

'Are we going to have trouble finding a cab?' asked Victoria.

'We don't need one. I told Manners to wait with the Bentley up there on the bridge.'

The pair of sapphic lovebirds passed out of sight and out of earshot. No point in attempting to follow them now. This was a casual encounter between two strangers bent on a brief bout of sex and violence. The Captain had always suspected that Victoria looked down her nose at him and his associates – she thought they lacked breeding. So this was it. She came to this venue of downmarket sleaze to pick up a bit of real class. Well, they had penetrated one of her shabby little secrets and they would go on tailing her in her off-duty hours until they cracked the other one. But not tonight.

The harpies had lost interest in Helen when they realised she was with the Captain and had left her whimpering on the stony ground. He pulled her to her feet and helped her to rearrange her clothing and brush off some of the dirt. Both of them felt somewhat depressed at losing their quarry like this after giving so much time to the aborted hunt. They looked at each other down there in the feeble light and reached an understanding without needing to speak. Now that they were in this place they might as well make the most of it. To the Captain it seemed that, if Victoria could do so well for herself here, so could they. All tastes seemed to be catered for if only one found the right spot somewhere along the line.

They trudged on down the track but it soon ended at the next bridge. Closer inspection showed that this was probably not a bridge at all but the mouth of a tunnel, sealed off for reasons of safety with a high fence of boards and

186

corrugated iron sheets surmounted by a tangle of barbed wire. Some of the boards had been wrenched aside; voices could be heard echoing in the darkness beyond.

Without much enthusiasm, the Captain led the way into the dank tunnel. Helen clung to his hand, fearful of the scurrying creatures their steps disturbed. The Captain was not too keen on this feature either, but tried not to let his misgivings communicate themselves to his companion.

As his eyes grew more accustomed to the damp, dripping environment he realised that the blackness was not absolute. Electric torches flashed on and off. Here and there, storm lanterns cast their pale light on couples engaged in sexual connection against the curved wet walls.

They had not taken many steps when the Captain felt a tugging at the leg of his jeans. To judge from her reaction, Helen's skirt was being similarly treated. They had walked into someone kneeling in their path. That person now rose between them, embracing them both together. At least, the Captain noted with surprise, no repugnant odour offended his nostrils.

Since the light just here was quite insufficient for them to form any opinion regarding the visual attractions of this creature of the night, the Captain embarked very warily on a manual investigation of the physical attributes on offer. The figure seemed to be enveloped from head to foot in a long, hooded cloak of velvet. This was reassuring – at least, there was nothing so far to repel the sense of touch. He drew the form to his body. The top of the head just reached his chin and the contours to be felt through the velvet were almost certainly female, though rather less developed than Helen's (and Helen was not exactly what he would have called a well-grown lass). Yes, these somewhat bony hips had to belong to a girl. And the chest, he now discovered, was not totally flat. The bumps beneath his palms were hard and prominent; it was just that they were even smaller than Helen's.

Helen had been using her own hands to make the same discoveries. She would have happily clinched the deal there and then but the Captain insisted on taking the girl over

187

to the nearest lantern to get a look at her face. You couldn't be too careful.

At first sight he recoiled in horror. Then he realised that the unfavourable impression he had gained had been caused partly by the unconducive atmosphere of this spooky place and partly by the fact that the girl's pale features were lit from below, lending her an unduly ghoulish appearance. He stooped and lifted the lantern.

What he now saw was more than pleasing. This young girl was undeniably pallid but by no means emaciated. She was smiling, evidently relieved, he flattered himself, that both her prospective clients were so personable. Her eyes were dark and sparkling, her teeth regular and her looks both saucy and surprisingly bashful. The Captain kissed her forehead and turned to Helen. 'What do you think?' he asked.

Helen needed no time to consider before replying. 'Just the thing,' she said. 'But not in this awful place.'

Mindful of his responsibilities towards his employees if not himself, the Captain hesitated for a moment. He looked into the girl's eyes, then looked down. 'How do we know . . .' he began, 'well, how do we know you're *clean*?'

When she spoke, the girl's voice was deeper than he would have expected. 'I'm not just clean,' she explained. 'I'm a fucking virgin. If we go somewhere a bit brighter you'll be able to see for yourselves before we get properly started.'

'But in that case . . . It's just that . . .'

'I know exactly what you mean, sunshine. They all wonder if it'll be worth their while. And they all end up telling me they'll be back for more. And for you it won't be a problem at all, will it? If you like, you can finish off in your girlfriend's cunt.'

Helen threw the girl a glance that might have been conspiratorial. 'Fine by me,' she said. 'Only, like I say, I can't do it in a place like this.'

'Hardly any of them can,' the girl replied. 'I've got a room just round the corner. Come on.'

Leaving the tunnel the three of them hurried back along

the cutting to the nearest bridge and up the steps used by Victoria and her equestrian pick-up. Soon they were climbing the stairs of a shabby terraced house and entering an attic room full of junk. Wall posters of Blake paintings and Ché Guevara. Overflowing ashtrays and packets of cigarette papers. Empty bottles. Guitars. Unwashed dishes. Books, more unwashed dishes and discarded clothes, the whole untidy scene illuminated by a naked bulb. A faint but unmistakable smell of illegal substances hung in the air. The Captain felt himself caught in a timewarp. 'Don't mind the mess,' said the girl. 'You'd better sit on the bed.'

Shaving tackle on the cluttered draining board and a large pair of boots under the sink suggested to the Captain that the room was shared with a man. The girl noticed what had caught his attention and explained, at the same time filling three large mugs with instant coffee. 'My boyfriend, see. I've just moved in with him. But don't worry – he won't be back for a while.'

'Pimps for you, does he?' the Captain enquired in a matter-of-fact tone of voice.

'No, he's a poet. Writes erotic verse but can't get it published.'

The Captain expressed polite surprise. Then an embarrassing thought occurred to him and he felt in his pockets doubtfully. 'Look,' he began. 'Before we go any further I'd better ask what you charge. We won't be staying the night.'

The girl seemed to be put out, but observing Helen's raised eyebrows and realising she had an ally who might share something of her own feminine sensibility she smiled and touched the Captain's face. 'I'm not after money,' she assured him. 'Of course, a tip or a little present's always welcome. That's entirely up to you and your girlfriend. We're students, you see.'

'But . . .'

'That's just for fun, what I do down the tunnel and when I bring blokes back here. Well, mostly for fun. You know how it is with these student loans. Sometimes we need a bit of extra for – well, for fags or something.'

'Or rent?'

'Well, no – we're sort of squatting.'

She handed the visitors their coffee and stood before them with her feet slightly apart as they sipped it. Her hands moved to the front of her midnight blue cloak with its monkish hood; suddenly she parted the front to reveal, against the red silk lining, a vision of dazzling white nakedness from her throat down to the neat little black boots which, with the long hooded garment, were all she had on. She let the cloak fall back into place. This, however, was merely to allow her small hands to find and unfasten the clasp at her throat. The cloak fell to the floor. She grinned saucily and posed with her hands behind her neck.

The Captain caught his breath and Helen, too, seemed agitated by the sight exhibited before them. Now that the girl's head was no longer hooded, the velvety cap of blue-black hair could be appreciated. It was cut short, neatly, even expertly, like a boy's. Apart from the different colouring the Captain was reminded of Darcy's brother Tim. He noted that the resemblance was not confined to the hairstyle but extended to the snub nose and, interestingly, to the general appearance of her legs as she stood with them slightly parted.

But what caught his eye between those legs bore no resemblance at all to Timmy's boyish endowments. The Captain gasped his admiration. 'Oh yes. I really like them that way, you know. Helen here had hers like it for a while last year, didn't you, love? There's something so lewd about it. Such a suggestion of – what can you call it? Corrupt innocence, or innocent corruption.'

He was referring to the fact that apart from her armpits, which sprouted luxuriant black tufts, the girl's body was absolutely hairless, with no trace of prickly stubble, telltale shading or soreness to mar the perfect whiteness of her genital area. Her outer cuntlips were smooth and shining. Their plump curvature was divided by a vertical double line of delicate pink which ran down to disappear between the soft curves of her buttocks, just visible through the opening of her thighs.

Soon, he knew, this exquisitely pretty quim, or at least

its outer defences, would become the temporary centre of his universe. But before abandoning himself completely to uncontrolled lust he cast an appraising eye over the rest of her body.

'Look,' he murmured to Helen, who seemed to be equally awed by the delights displayed before her. 'Just look at those pale pink nipples. Amazing they're so big and stiff and stick out so much when her tits are just like little apples. My God, what an interesting contrast with yours.'

The posing girl's amber-coloured eyes lit up. 'Let's see hers, then,' she demanded. Without hesitation, Helen drew her thin black sweater up and pulled it off over her head.

'They're not that much bigger than mine,' the girl observed. 'No cleavage there. What they call pert, I suppose – mine aren't even pert. Well, maybe the actual nipples are, but not the boobs.'

The Captain clarified his previous remark. 'That's what I'm talking about. It's mainly the difference in the nipples and the bit round them, the areolas. Yours are pink and pretty big; hers are brown and tiny, not much bigger than these little moles on her. But you're wrong, you know, if you think your breasts aren't pert. Know the only difference there? Yours are like apples and hers are more pear-shaped.'

'Here's another difference, while we're on the subject of fruit,' laughed Helen. She had pulled up the hem of her skirt and eased her tights down over her thighs. 'I've got a nice downy split peach and hers is a smooth-skinned nectarine.'

'Both of them nice and juicy,' quipped the Captain, who wished busty Sharon from the market could have overheard the conversation. 'Ripe for the, er, plucking, you might say.' He laid a cool hand on the girl's behind. 'Your boyfriend's poems,' he said. 'Any chance of having a look at them?'

At first she seemed reluctant, impatient to get on with the business in hand and particularly to enjoy Helen's body, now extended on the bed in full nudity. 'Most of them are too long. He expects people to spend hours not

191

just reading them but analysing them. A perfectionist, he is, my brother – I mean my boyfriend. You might think he's old-fashioned, not hip. Calls himself a traditionalist. Says he's inherited the mantle of Dante Gabriel Rossetti.

The Captain's eyes fell on the contents of an ashtray and moved to a syringe he had noticed on a dirty plate. Poetry was not the only bad habit this boyfriend had inherited from the founder of the Pre-Raphaelite Brotherhood, it seemed.

Helen was looking puzzled and rather bored but the Captain knew better than to put this interesting girl off. So far, there was no verse on the Honeymooners list. 'Quite a Rossetti fan myself,' he lied. 'I like that one he wrote about a whore called Jenny – "fond of a kiss and fond of a penny".'

Wouldn't get much of a kiss for a penny these days, he mused, now regretting he had mentioned the poem in case it brought them back to the question of payment for services soon to be rendered. What he still had in his pocket would be needed for the fare back to Fulham. He thought of something else to say about Rossetti. 'Had a thing with his sister, didn't he?'

'Not his sister – his girlfriend, I think. His model.'

'That's right. I remember now. He married her, she killed herself, he buried his poems in her coffin and had to have her exhumed so he could get them published. Hope your brother won't have to go to such lengths.'

'My boyfriend.' The girl thumbed through an untidy pile of papers and fished out a crumpled, beer-stained document, dog-eared and dark with angry deletions. 'I'm fond of these,' she said. 'A sonnet sequence – well, just three sonnets actually. No, they're too scrappy for you to read. Let me. By the way, I've been thinking. I might let you have me for free later if you let me do your girlfriend.'

She sat on the bed beside Helen. Holding the paper in one hand, she allowed the other one to rest lightly on Helen's pubic mound. The Captain lay back, taking in the scene with relish.

'This first one's called *Girls Missing*. It goes like this.

192

Girls Missing, by Mick Maddox. That's his pen name. Here we go again – *Girls Missing*:

> *Where are those girls? The temptresses have fled*
> *But still their fingers haunt my turgid dreams.*
> *The moonlight laps their thighs, and wetly gleams*
> *On bellies where my longing's load is shed.*
> *One sucks my softened prick. I dip my head*
> *To lick both bellies dry. The moon's cold beams*
> *Draw down my eyes; I furl my tongue, which reams*
> *Each cunt in turn. Their juices soak my bed.*
> *But now, awakening in the morning light,*
> *I flail about and feel for them in vain.*
> *Is this a hardening nipple? Next I hunt*
> *For lovesick mouths, eager to kiss and drain*
> *My cock. I search the sheets, soiled in the night,*
> *And spill my spunk, but not in mouth or cunt.*

When he reads it himself he doesn't quite sing but sort of chants it and strums chords on his guitar. What do you guys reckon?'

'Very nice. I like it. What about you, Helen?'

Helen frowned for a moment. 'I don't go for poems that rhyme,' she complained. 'All that *thee* and *thou* stuff leaves me cold.'

'Hang on,' the Captain objected. 'I didn't notice any of that what-d'you-call-it – poetic diction. No *thees* or *thous* there, surely.'

For a moment Helen seemed surprised. 'That's just because he hasn't got the girls speaking to each other,' she explained. 'But yes, apart from that it's not bad.' She turned to their hostess. 'A bit of a wanker, is he, your boyfriend or whatever he is?'

'A bit of a dreamer, you might say. A wet dreamer.'

Helen might have been left cold by the poem but the girl's finger was bringing about a dramatic rise of temperature in her cunt. Her face flushed. Her small breasts swelled and their nipples tightened. The flush raced down from her neck to her lower abdomen. The fine and rather sparse fuzz

193

on her pubis bristled, the hairs standing up on end. And now the girl shifted her hand slightly so that her thumb rested on the flesh just above Helen's clitoris while her forefinger slipped into the vagina and the other three fingers curled round under her bottom, exploring the moist groove between the trembling cheeks.

Suddenly Helen stretched her legs out straight, brought them firmly together and clasped the girl's caressing hand between them. 'Oh, stop!' she cried. 'I can't take any more of . . .'

Her screams were stifled by her tormentor's lips and tongue. Wave after wave of lewd spasms racked her body until finally she melted in the girl's arms.

The Captain had not taken his eyes from the performance enacted on the bed while slipping out of his lower garments. Now he could barely control himself. He was hard, painfully tight, and slick with the clear lubricant sluicing from the tip of his penis. Yet he was determined to wring every last drop of enjoyment from this piquant situation before surrendering his charge of lust. He picked up the sheet of untidy scrawl. 'What's this next one?' he asked. 'Ah, this seems promising – *Girls Kissing*.'

The girl snatched the paper from his hand, insisting on reading the sonnet herself. While she did so, the Captain rested a cheek on the inside of Helen's thigh, his ear cradled by her pulled-down tights, and idly bathed his tongue in the juices trickling from her fragrant sex. Clearing her throat, the girl began in her deep, velvet tones:

'I raised the curtain, hoping for the best,
And thought they rested in the midday heat,
Half-lying on their bed, murmuring sweet
Endearments. They were not yet quite undressed –
One looked immodest in a childish vest;
One still had socks upon her pretty feet;
She asked her friend to touch the lengthening teat
That crowned the creamy smoothness of her breast.
Face covered glowing face in bright eclipse,
While nimble fingers strove to penetrate

194

And plunder nectar from each orifice
That longed for love. Then, trailing honeyed drips
From thirsty mouths no girlish tongues could sate,
Lips clamped on cunts in throbbing twofold kiss.

I don't know how he manages it,' she continued. 'OK, he likes to watch me doing it with other women. But where do the *words* come from?'

The Captain lifted his head to reply. 'I know what you mean. I often get the same feeling with writers whose work I publish. It just seems to come gushing out as if they were talking cocks.'

'Talking clocks?'

'Cocks, as in pricks.'

'You mean you're a publisher? You publish erotic poetry? Any chance you could bring out a slim volume of my – of these poems? When he's finished them, I mean.'

Affectionately smoothing Helen's pubic hairs, the Captain frowned. 'We haven't taken on any verse yet, have we, Helen? But I might consider doing a really handsome limited edition on hand-made paper. With line drawings by our first-class illustrator. On the other hand, it might be much too expensive – too much of a risk for a commercial outfit like ours.'

For the moment he had quite forgotten that the original purpose of this outing had been to track down and nail Victoria's shameless flouting of copyright and, even more galling, of his trust. Referring to her as his illustrator reminded him. Of course, until they caught her red-handed or extracted a confession from her, condemnation might be premature. The painful thought crossed his mind that if the culprit was not Victoria it would almost certainly be Helen. Well, one step at a time. In any case, the girl, who was now cupping his testicles in one hand while still holding the sheet of paper in the other, was speaking again.

'Look, I know it's hot stuff. Sometimes he gives readings down the tunnel – I've seen how it gets them turned on down there, even old tramps you wouldn't think had it in them any more. Here's the last one: *Girls Pissing*. That title

195

shows you he's not just another of your wishy-washy late romantics.

> I turned the woodland corner, hot and lewd;
> There, underneath an oak, those girls long missed
> Lay in each other's arms and fiercely kissed;
> Apart from socks and knickers they were nude.
> I heard the tender nothings which they cooed
> And, as their passion rose, I saw each twist
> Of slender neck. I strained to catch the gist
> Of whispered words. One giggled, 'No – that's rude.'
> Her sweetheart stood and, baring all her bum
> (Her back was turned to me), bent down and stripped
> The other's pants off, moist with love's sweet stain.
> Cunt over mouth, she slipped a wagging thumb
> Up in young flesh that, pink in sunlight, dripped
> Lovedrops at first, then spurted its golden rain.

Would we get any sort of advance if you decided to take them?'

'I hope I haven't been raising false hopes,' replied the Captain, whose manhood had been raised to balloon-like proportions by these pornographic texts and the circumstances in which they had been read out. 'Much too early to be talking about payment. I'd need to speak to my accountants and literary advisers, not to mention our lawyers.'

'Tell you what I'll do. Say yes and write a check for a small advance on royalties – a couple of hundred, say – and I'll let you go all the way with me. Both of you, if you're both interested. You can have my cherry. Can't say fairer than that.'

If the Captain had doubts about this offer as the basis of a business deal it was in all other respects an offer he could hardly refuse. And he could see that Helen was game.

Instead of waiting for a considered reply or for the production of the chequebook the Captain had not brought with him, the girl lay back across the bed, her feet dangling on the floor and her hairless vulva flaunted in the eager faces of her visitors. Helen began to suck fiercely, first on one pink nipple and then on the other. The girl sighed, closed her eyes and spread her legs wider.

To the Captain's fingers the outer lips of her cunt felt like silk. He parted them gently, then used the point of his tongue to slit open the tender petals of girlflesh from which, in the words of her boyfriend's or brother's sonnet, 'lovedrops dripped'. A probing finger encountered resistance. When he brought his thumbs to bear, prising open the pink, unused passage, he saw the shiny film of membrane which sealed the entrance to her secret receptacle of lust. 'How are we going to do this?' he mused aloud.

'We'll start by using our tongues,' Helen suggested. 'Then our fingers. And then, when we think she's stretched to the limit, you can put your thing in and rip through in one sharp shove.'

The Captain thought that one sharp shove with no preliminaries might be the kindest way of dispatching this virginity but he said nothing. That way he could hardly be blamed for the inevitable discomfort attending on the process.

Helen was already kneeling on the floor between the girl's hanging legs. The Captain took the booted ankles, lifted them and laid the thighs gently over Helen's shoulders so that the calves and feet hung loose behind her back. In this position Helen's ears and cheeks were clasped very firmly between the girl's thighs. Her chin was pressed into the soft moistness just below the clitoris. When she stuck out her tongue, the underside rested on the smooth mons. A radical rethink was required.

Helen did the thinking for herself rather than leaving it to the Captain. She stripped off her remaining clothes, jumped up on the bed and knelt over the girl's white body, placing her knees on either side of the ribcage and her hands beneath the mounds of her bottom. Her head dipped down. With mouth wide open she enclosed the entire cuntal area within her lips and began to suck and prod. After a moment she raised her head to speak, a dreamy look in her eyes. 'Mm!' she exclaimed. 'This is so yummy! And you wouldn't believe what a difference it makes to have it all smooth and silky like this.'

The experience might have been new to Helen but her boss was well aware of the difference hairlessness made. After all, it was this same Helen who had kept herself bare-quimmed for him when she came to work at the motel the previous summer.

As the cunnilingual caress was resumed, the girl drew out her arms, which had been trapped under Helen's calves. Resting the upper arms upon the soft cushions of the calf muscles, she ran her hands up the outsides of the thighs, reaching round to the front as she pulled Helen down towards her face. From behind, his view dominated by Helen's taut, shiny buttocks and the dividing rift with its hidden treasures displayed, the Captain could see the lightly bearded pussy as it dipped down to meet an agile tongue. The two girls were at each other now from both ends. Up at this end the contact was superficial and teasing. Down below, Helen seemed to be launching a fierce, all-out assault. Or all-in, perhaps.

It was always difficult for the Captain to witness scenes of this nature without feeling the urge to participate. As the girl's tongue flicked away at Helen's fanny he lowered his head to the provocatively raised behind. The girl oblig-ingly parted Helen's buttocks to allow him to plunder the puckered pinkness that winked obscenely as if demanding to be plugged. His tongue darted out. Forget your sonnets, he thought. This was *real* poetry, right down to the rhym-ing of the two licked cunts and the rhythm of his probing tongue. None of your emotion recollected in tranquillity, either; more like that Keatsian definition of the poetical – every rift loaded with ore.

He was dizzy and needed to breathe. He reared up on his knees, gulping the air, and as he did so his erection swung almost accidentally into Helen's cunt. The aching weight of his balls was taken by the face of the girl beneath him. The whole fullness of his sac slipped into her mouth. For a moment it throbbed and swelled in her saliva; then she, too, was on the point of choking and wrenched her head to one side. As soon as the inrush of oxygen had brought some colour to her pretty cheeks, however, she craned her head upwards and began to play the tip of her tongue over the intimate seal of Helen's cuntlips around his hard thickness.

His fingers dug into the soft flesh where Helen's hips folded against her thighs. Completely out of control, he powered into the seductive sleeve of flesh while the girl's tongue flickered along the bursting tube on each outward stroke.

Suddenly the girl yelped and rose on her elbows, butting the Captain forward. His battering ram drove Helen down off the bed to the floor between the girl's legs, which were now stretched out stiff and quivering. His cock sprang free, still frustrated and pulsing with pent-up fury.

Her sudden movement had been caused by the sharp sensation of having her hymen ruptured.

Apparently none the worse for this abrupt termination of her virginal status, she lay back again, smiling. She brought her knees up, rested her boots on the edge of the bed and let her thighs hang wide open until her knees were almost touching the rumpled bed cover. 'Go ahead,' she breathed, looking up at the Captain with an air of bravado. 'Be my guest. A limited edition, remember. On hand-made paper.'

Half standing on the floor and half lying on her youthful body, he pressed against her. The blunt head of his weapon butted and blundered about, skidding against the tantalising smoothness. Helen came to his assistance, reaching up from behind under his bollocks, one hand on either side. She slid one finger of each hand into the girl's newly opened channel and stretched it wide. His cock seemed to glide in, between the guiding fingers, until about half its length had entered. Helen then withdrew her fingers but remained in her position kneeling behind him on the floor. She ran her tongue up and down the groove of his arse and used both hands to fondle the heavy ballsack.

Now that it was no longer widened by those helpful fingers, the girl's cunt tightened voraciously around the Captain's prick as it delved maddeningly into the seething flesh. This tightening, in its turn, enraged the straining member into even fiercer tumidity. The Captain's scrotum also tightened as the juices which had been distilling inside him for almost half an hour gathered for the imminent explosion. Sweat trickled from his hair and dripped on the girl's left breast as his tongue reached down for the puffy nipple. She whimpered beneath him.

In a desperate attempt to hold back and prolong his pleasure he lifted his lips from the teat. 'What exactly are you studying, dear?' he enquired.

'Did-did-didn't I tell you? Hairdressing. Aaargh – this is too much.'

'Am I hurting you?'

'I – aaargh – I love it. Just keep that cock of yours boffing away at me. Go on, give me a proper fuck. Do it to me!'

He lurched forward and then took the whole apple of her breast into his mouth. His hot cockhead ploughed into her, the first to have forced its way through the creaming young flesh that now gloved it and apparently loved it.

At this instant the door swung open. A huge, barrel-chested giant strode into the room, all hair, black leather, beard, metal studs and chains. Terrified, the Captain was quite prepared to see him produce a live chicken and bite its head off. Or, failing a live chicken, his lively cock.

'That's cool, Sis,' the intruder chuckled. He raised a hairy paw and patted the Captain playfully on the rump. 'I dig, man,' he went on. 'Know something? This crazy chick's been keeping her legs closed for days now, ever since I shacked up with her. Ain't that right, Cicely? Correction – ever since we were both knee-high to a flea. Seems to think I like my women the way I like my poetry – yup, I'm a wordsmith, man – thinks I'm into that romantic stuff, all yearning and wanking. Am I right, Sis? Ride her, cowboy!'

This time he brought down his ham of a hand more heavily on the Captain's buttocks. Looking back under his arm, the Captain saw that the boyfriend or close relative (for such he seemed to be) had produced a massive ramrod, seized Helen by the haunches and plunged the tool into her from behind without as much as a by your leave, let alone a word of introduction or explanation.

By now the Captain was far beyond self-control. He screwed powerfully but briefly into the newly-broached cunt, relishing the only thought he was capable of, the thought of his wiry pubic bush dragging against the girl's smoothness at the top of each upbeat. His teeth closed on her left nipple, his buttocks clenched and his whole body shuddered as the hot load of sperm burst exultingly into her belly, wave after wave, until he lay on her, soaking in pools of sweat and overflowing spunk.

Almost simultaneously the bearded giant let out a howl of triumph as he emptied himself into the astonished Helen. 'Way out!' he cried, somewhat predictably. 'That was the real thing for a change. And do I dig a change! Don't get me wrong, friend. No way am I going to get tired of young Sis here. Wow – the cat even gets off on my poems. But know what I mean? No change for days on end and it gets kind of incestuous.'

ELEVEN

UNDER PRESSURE

A week later the Captain was no nearer to plugging the costly leak. Alone or with Helen, he had dogged Victoria's footsteps relentlessly for the last four nights. Once she had gone straight to her flat in Islington. A couple of times she led them again to the disused railway cutting, where they had not bothered to follow her. And once, without Helen, he had ended up peering through the little windows in the door of a classroom. In there he saw Victoria sketching with other keen evening students while a naked redhead splayed her legs shamelessly, but with no obvious signs of arousal, on a couch in the centre of the circle of easels. Now Friday had come round once more. Altogether a pretty unsatisfactory week since that encounter with the hip, hirsute sonneteer and his smooth-quimmed sister or girlfriend.

The Palace of Eros was so cramped these days that Helen had to perch on a stool in the little tea kitchen with a typewriter on the draining board. Her proper desk and chair as well as most of the floorspace were cluttered with stacks of virgin paperbacks, hot from the press and priced at £3.99 to undercut the opposition. Most of the distribution had been farmed out to specialist contractors. But the Captain had made the unwise decision to take delivery of a few hundred copies of each new title in the hope of finding local retail outlets in his lunch breaks. So far he had been unsuccessful, although Helen had persuaded a couple

202

of newsagents to display those with the least lurid covers on their racks of best-sellers. Maybe, he told himself, he ought to set up a Saturday stall down in the market. He would have a word with Sharon.

Victoria Eisenberg was working away at her desk in front of the window as if her only ambition was to do the best possible job for Honeymooners. And the job she did was unquestionably good. Could he be mistaken about her?

At least there was no mistaking the extraordinary physical attraction this cool blonde held for men, whom she despised, as well as for women, whom she adored. Today her flaxen hair (perhaps augmented with someone else's to give it added bulk) was piled on top of her head with a few loose tresses dangling in front of her ears in artful negligence. The Captain noted that she was wearing a crisp white blouse, mauve skirt and black woollen tights or stockings. He focussed his attention on the nape of her long neck.

The door burst open and in charged a wild and furious Alison Absalon, unannounced and unexpected. Alison Absalon was the professional name of the retired headmaster and aspiring pornographer who had attended the Captain's launch party three weeks before in the guise of Old Nick. However friendly and appreciative he had seemed on that occasion, he was now in a towering rage. Sweeping books and papers from a corner of the Captain's desk, he sat down on it, pulled a heavily corrected typewritten draft from his briefcase and spat out his grievance.

'It only took me three weeks to write,' he began, in menacingly level tones. 'That's because I knew exactly what I was going to say. Before the first sentence was written I'd got the whole book up here in my head, down to every last word and comma. I am a man of culture and wide experience, after all. These short stories were my life's work, sir. And what have you or your confounded copy editors done?' He paused, drew a deep breath and screamed out the answer to his question. 'Mutilated them! Savaged them! Neutered them! Raped them! You have raped my artistic integrity.'

203

'Steady on, Dr Absalon,' the Captain replied. 'It's quite possible . . .' (he lowered his voice so that Helen would not hear him out there in the kitchen) '. . . it's possible that my editorial assistant errs on the side of caution from time to time. We need to operate within the law, and even more importantly for commercial reasons, within the parameters of public taste. *Advanced* public taste, I hasten to add. But observing those parameters is vital to our survival.'

Absalon was furiously unconvinced. 'You have the gall to lecture me on public taste?' he exploded. 'I am an educator. For forty years I was an arbiter and moulder of public taste. Do not have the impudence, sir, to insinuate that I don't know what the public can take and what they want. I know damn well what goes on in their smutty little minds. I put it there myself in their formative years. It was I who sowed the seeds and now the time has come for me to harvest the fruits, unhindered by your piddling censorship.'

This arrogant bastard needed cutting down to size. The Captain considered for a moment while Absalon fumed. 'Let me be brutally frank with you,' he said, 'and let me remind you of the terms of your contract with us. My objection to your work falls under three main heads and all three are covered by the clause in the contract which says that in the event of our being displeased or unsatisfied with any aspect of your work we have the right to insist that you re-write it to our specifications. You have signed the contract, Dr Absalon. Either you accept our editorial advice or you will have to avail yourself of that other clause which allows you to withdraw from the contract on repayment of your advance. With interest – the advance is to be treated as a loan.'

'Who the devil are you to be displeased or unsatisfied with the work of a master – a headmaster?'

'Well, you may have been a headmaster and I may have been a blockhead in my schooldays. But what are we now? You're a pensioner and I'm the paymaster. My paymaster's chequebook wields more clout than your headmaster's cane ever did, buster. You're the piper and I call the tune.'

For a brief moment this appeal to economic reality succeeded in silencing the irate author, though not in calming him. He sat shaking on the edge of the desk, his knuckles white. Narrowing his eyes, he made an effort at controlled utterance. 'Why don't we get down to specifics. There may be something useful for you to learn if I take you through your quibbling criticisms point by point.'

'No need for that, doctor. As I say, there are three main areas of objection. They can be dealt with very briefly, and apply to all the stories in this collection. First, your spelling. I have to say that it's quite appalling. I'm surprised.'

Here the Captain had certainly got his teeth into the ex-headmaster's Achilles' heel. Absalon's premature retirement was officially down to disagreement with the Department on matters of received orthography, although the underlying and unspoken reasons were of a more damaging nature. Ruinously damaging, in fact, and based on criminal allegations. But knowing that the spelling of every other word of his book had been corrected in this office he was not unprepared.

'Look,' he said, 'these are just drafts. Preliminary sketches, rough impressions. Accuracy comes later. First, the important thing is to catch the spark of inspiration before it dies away. What's more, I've got a semi-literate narrator as a device to unify the stories, and that's meant to be the way he thinks. He can't stop to consult a dictionary every time he has a thought. It would take hours, especially as he doesn't even know his alphabet very well.' The learned or semi-learned doctor was warming to his theme. 'In any case,' he continued, 'it's different with the last story, the longest one. You may have noticed that it's set in the seventeenth century. A lot of the spelling's what you might call archaic.'

The Captain laughed unkindly. 'I suppose you might call it archaic if you knew how to spell the word. But that brings me to the second class of criticism. A lot of these stories are what you might call historical romance. I've no objection to a story set in the time of the Civil Wars, like the one you want to finish with. But I can think of at least two good reasons why you can't call it *The Naseby Nexus*. In the first place it's just not sexy enough. The other problem's a legal one.'

'I did have a reserve title: *The Fair Sex Sucks Fairfax*.'

'That's an improvement. Better still, call the story something like *The Civil Whores*. Then split it into two parts – *The Fair Sex Sucks Fairfax* and *Fairfax Fucks the Fair Sex*. That's pretty much what it's meant to be about, isn't it? But listen, Absalon. These details are just cosmetic; the real faults are more radical. OK, we've all got a soft spot for those laughing cavaliers, if not for the grim-faced round-heads. But what have you given us? Page after page of boring historical drivel – lists of dates and battles, just lists, pages and pages of them. If the punters want a bit of background they can get that out of the library. What they want from our books is strictly the hot stuff. The story's just an excuse. All right, you can have your odd battle as long as it doesn't take more than a couple of sentences. But we all know what soldiers need the night before risking their lives, don't we? And we know what they get up to with their enemies' wives and daughters after they've won the battle. We want more of that and less of the academic stuff, in a proportion of roughly ten to one.'

`Absalon calmed down marginally as he thought he saw a window of opportunity. 'As I say, this is just a draft, an outline. I really must keep most of the history because it's essential to our understanding of motivation and psychology. But I'll see to it that there's ten times as much sex if that's what you want.'

'In that case you'll have to re-jig that particular story as a full-length novel,' the Captain sneered. 'There's a limit to the number of pages you can squeeze inside a paperback cover, especially if it's going to stand up to the kind of one-handed treatment our books are likely to get.'

'Any other complaints?'

'Yes. That brings me to the third and most serious problem. I thought I warned you in the strongest possible terms to keep clear of taboo areas. All characters well over the age of consent, I said, their ages to be clearly spelt out as seventeen or more if there's anything childish about their behaviour or appearance. I'm warning you, Dr Absalon, from personal – well, I'm warning you that if you end up behind bars you won't exactly be flavour of the month with the other inmates. What you've given me here, especially in your title story . . .'

Absalon, whose face had twisted into a close likeness of the diabolical mask he had sported at the party, rose from the desk and seized the Captain by the shoulders. The Captain was alarmed to see a vein throbbing grotesquely in his right temple. 'Are you insinuating . . .?' Absalon spluttered.

His strangulated voice tailed away as his attention was caught by the resourceful Victoria, who had swung round on her swivel chair and was slowly unbuttoning the front of her blouse. When she had opened it all the way, she parted it just wide enough to reveal the generous curves of her bra-less breasts while keeping the nipples covered. She stood up, winked and worked the hem of her tightish mauve skirt up until it was plain that her legs were sheathed in self-supporting black stockings. She exposed her white flanks up as far as the slightly concave sides of her buttocks, taking care that the front of the skirt remained looping down over her sexual parts.

`But when she perched her bottom on the corner of her desk and raised one leg to roll the stocking down, her two male spectators were vouchsafed a brief eyeful that promised to banish their mutual animosity. Victoria had given them a tantalising glimpse of scarlet silk; just a flash of a scanty triangle between the smooth white thighs and the soft mauve of her skirt. She removed the other stocking more modestly, keeping that leg crossed over the first one as she peeled it off. Then she stood up, turned her back on them as if wishing to look out of the window, and stepped out of the skirt. Instead of knickers, they now understood that the flash of red was a tiny G-string. Its vertical thong could be seen disappearing between the dimpled cheeks of her bottom.

If the Captain had been implying, before this interruption, that Alison Absalon was only interested in under-age sex, what happened next proved him wrong. So successful was Victoria's ploy to deflect Absalon's violence from her boss that the frustrated author now sprang at her, spun her round towards him and forced the white blouse back over her shoulders.

Victoria struggled violently. 'Don't you dare touch me!' she screamed. 'You men are all the same – give you an inch and you take a metre. Keep your grubby paws to yourself. I was going to let him have a wank while he watched me,' she said to the Captain, 'but now he's put me right off my stroke.'

While she spoke and struggled, the Captain had managed to restrain the author of *Behind the Bike Sheds and Other Cautionary Tales* and had forced him down into a chair. He stood behind Absalon and held him firmly by the shoulders as Victoria gallantly slipped her blouse right off and pirouetted about in her diminutive red G-string. In one swift movement she straddled Absalon's thighs, whipped his zip down and drew back to resume her erotic dance. A fiery, rock-hard rod shot out of the opened fly, pointing straight up at her and wagging in time with her undulations or his own pulse – the two rhythms were as one.

'Right,' said the Captain. 'Isn't that big of her? And of you, I have to admit. Just feast your eyes on those bouncing tits and let yourself go. I'd say you're running at dangerously high pressure. You need to let off steam.'

Indeed, so worked up was Absalon and so hugely tumid his cock that it would not have surprised the Captain to see steam issuing from the gaping slot in its tip. Instead, the enlarged opening wept a continuous stream of clear lubricant. This ran down the underside of the shaft and disappeared into the trousers, which began to show traces of dampness as the fluid seeped through from the inside. The Captain had never seen anything like it. He wondered whether this copious flow of pre-come was a portent of a truly phenomenal ejaculation of semen. Perhaps there would be no fluid left in the man's loins. But this was not to be counted on and he wished he kept something like a rubber sheet in the office . . .

208

At this moment all three participants in the tense scene froze as they were joined by a fourth performer. The Captain had forgotten Helen, who had been out of sight in the tea kitchen all the time. But Helen had been fully aware of his difficulties and was determined to render all the assistance in her power. Now she came dancing into the office in nothing but a little pair of pale blue cotton knickers.

First she embraced Victoria, engaging the cool blonde in a suggestive waltz in which mouth battened on mouth, breasts jostled breasts, cuntmound ground against cuntmound and fingers spidered over bottoms. Then, pretending to notice Absalon for the first time, she broke away from Victoria and bent forward wide-eyed until her open mouth almost touched his pulsing organ. She licked her lips. The Captain had to tighten his grip on Absalon's shoulders as he strained forward in lustful fury, heaving his hips up from the chair.

Helen straightened up and backed away. She reclined on the Captain's desk, her bare feet dangling on the floor and the upper part of her body propped up on her elbow. In this position her white belly was flat and tensed, the velvet-skinned points of her hips prominent and her tightly knickered sex presented for attack. The Captain realised that Victoria was casting an artist's eye over the widely splayed upper thighs and the covered area between them. No doubt she had been struck, as he had, by the way the tendons in Helen's groins, a pair at the top of each inner thigh, stretched the knicker elastic so that a little opening appeared on either side, almost large enough for an inquisitive finger.

'There it is,' Helen declared in strident tones. 'No point in all this fuss. Just let him get stuck in and help himself – that's all he needs to calm him down.'

Absalon required no further encouragement. Breaking from the Captain's restraining grasp he fell on his knees in front of the desk and launched his mouth at the pale blue panties. The Captain's own mouth watered and his prick leapt painfully in his underpants as he imagined the contrast between the initial crispness of the hairy padding as

Absalon's tongue felt it through the cotton material and the soft squishiness as the plump labia fell apart. If only Victoria would lie down alongside Helen and allow him a similar liberty with her G-string . . .

By now Absalon was quite carried away and unable to hold back. All his anger had been converted into lust and all his lust was concentrated in his great blue-knobbed bludgeon and swelling balls. Suddenly he jumped to his feet and brought the bludgeon blindly to bear against the knickers where his tongue had pushed the thin fabric into Helen's cleft. His face was purple with frustrated libido as he butted into what must have felt like a stubborn hymeneal membrane. The Captain wondered if he would actually puncture the garment with his fierce weapon. But by now the girl's assailant had reached down and found the narrow elasticated strip encircling her hips. He withdrew his tool, inflamed from its struggle, dragged the now sopping blue triangle to one side and thrust back in. This time he was welcomed by naked, engorged cuntflesh, slick and well lubricated. He sank in, up to the hilt, and rested a moment to recruit his strength before hammering into Helen with such violence that her head shook from side to side.

`The door opened and three newcomers burst upon the scene. A middle-aged man in a brown suit led the way, followed by a slightly plump young woman and an even younger man trying to look older by smoking a pipe. The leader addressed the Captain.

'Honeymooners Library, I presume, sir. And this lady and gentleman would be the honeymooners, I take it. Me and the missis had ours a bit more private but times are changing, times are changing. No, don't get up, you two. Just finish what you're doing if you're as nearly finished as you seem to be. Wouldn't you say they was nearly finished, Jives?'

The young woman stepped forward and stared brazenly at what was going on between Absalon and Helen. 'Can't have far to go now, sarge,' she replied. 'His doodahs have gone all tight, like.'

Sure enough, Absalon had frozen in his fucking and his scrotal sac had tightened as he braced himself to inject his lascivious wrath into Helen's compliant body. The floodgates opened. With a long, sobbing sigh he voided himself. Then he rose, dripping, from the desk, tucked his limp length back into his trousers and made as if to leave the office.

Detective Sergeant Raddle (the Captain had now remembered the brown-suited officer's name from their encounter at the motel) fingered the detumescent writer's lapel. 'Yes, you can go now, sir,' he said. 'We won't be needing you, leastways not for the moment. We'll be in touch through this office if we need to interview you in connection with our ongoing enquiries.'

Absalon took his life's work and briefcase and slunk off without a word. In an attempt to gain the initiative, the Captain turned to Raddle and addressed him in his blandest manner. 'Nice to see you again, officer,' he began, calculating that after the favours he had laid on for the sergeant and his plump young WPC there would be no need for him to worry. 'Last summer . . .'

Sergeant Raddle cut him off, raising a finger to his lips and rolling hs eyes in the direction of his smooth-faced male understrapper. The young man, as if to emphasise his temporary plain-clothes status, was still fiddling with his pipe near the door and evidently somewhat out of his depth. 'Not just now, sir, if you don't mind,' Raddle continued. 'We're following up a lead in quite a different matter. Or matters, for that matter. You can consider the file closed on that business last year. Muttock, her name was, if my memory serves me aright.'

'With the Met now, are you?'

'Well no – still at Upchester. But certain evidence what came our way in pursuance of investigations following a complaint laid by a member of the public . . .' He broke off, turned to the WPC and pointed at Victoria, who was standing with an arm lightly round Helen's shoulders. Both girls were still minimally attired. Victoria looked magnificent in her red silk G-string but Helen's knickers, now

211

heavily stained in front, seemed to have shrunk so much that fine yellow curls were visible along all three sides of the triangle.

'What do you think, Jives – is that the one?'

After considering for a moment, the young woman replied. 'Could well answer the description. Maybe we should take her in for questioning.'

'Can't do that,' said Raddle. 'Not on our own patch here, are we?' He turned to the Captain again. 'Let me explain, sir. Three weeks ago . . .'

Jives interrupted. 'Saturday the eighth of May, to be precise, at eleven thirty-seven.'

'Three weeks ago, like I said, this incident at the public baths in Market Street was reported. No need to shock innocent parties with the sordid particulars, but to be frank with you, sir, a certain lady accompanying a party of young people incited this gang of yobs – this group of local youths – to have sexual relations with her young charges, or something like that.'

'In the water,' Jives added. 'To the detriment of public health and safety.'

'And the scandalisation of public morals.' Raddle advanced on Victoria Eisenberg. As she had no collar for him to finger, he laid a hairy hand on her chest, between and just above her breasts. She shuddered and clasped Helen harder to her but managed to stand her ground.

'May I ask, madam, where you was and what you was doing at eleven thirty-seven on the morning of Saturday the eighth of May?'

Victoria was about to speak but the Captain intervened. 'We've been hearing a lot lately about oppressive police interviewing and about the right to silence. Has that been abolished yet? This lady was attending a party given on these premises. Our launch party. It went on right through the weekend. More than a hundred people must have seen her here.'

During this exchange the young constable had abandoned his struggle to get the pipe burning and had picked his way over piles of books into the centre of the room. A hot flush had lit up his face as he thumbed through the

212

paperbacks nearest to him and the piles of typescript littering Helen's desk.

He spoke. 'This is it, Sergeant Raddle, sir. This is the big one, like.'

'What you on about, Clunton? Can't you see we got this case just about tied up? Lady's got a cast-iron alibi. We can be getting back now to claim our expenses.'

Constable Clunton was the tenacious kind of recruit who would go a long way in the service if he kept his nose clean. He was not to be deflected. 'No, sarge,' he insisted. 'We was right all along about them documents we picked up in the cottage. Know what we've walked into here? Looks like we're on the point of cracking a major vice and pornography ring. Listen to this:

> *All three of us were recalling the film we had been shown in Madame R's establishment that glorious afternoon in Paris, the film in which the cunning hermit, Father Rustique, had delighted the charming and naive little Alibech by showing her how he put his 'devil' into her 'hell'. This had been Nora and Evelyn's graphic initiation into the secret of copulation and the lewd sensations it aroused in them as well as in me had been satiated as far as possible by an afternoon of debauchery in which everything had been accomplished save the actual ravishing of the little darlings.*

What do you think of that, then?'

Laying the book aside he glanced shyly towards the almost naked Helen and Victoria. They were giggling. He had found the passage he had just read distinctly arousing and had a shrewd idea that the girls were not unaffected by it. He took up a sheaf of papers from the desk. 'Here's a typed one:

> *The crop swished down and stung her across both buttocks. Patience swung forward on her chain. The bulbous head of the masked ad collared man's cock nudged against the lips of her cunt. Her cunt refused to*

213

*open. She went swinging back while the man was held
firmly in place by Komiko's hands and tongue.*

Cor! I reckon that must be what they call S and M.'

Blushing but emboldened, he leered at the two girls.
Helen tilted her hips jauntily and ran the tip of her tongue
over her lips. Clunton opened a paperback at random. 'Oh
yes,' he began. 'Maybe this one's more to your taste, sarge:

> *Each of my hands was clasped between a pair of girlish
> thighs. I wriggled the fingers and simultaneously
> pressed into the two young cunts, one on each side of
> me. A third vulva, more generous in its ripe, thick-
> fleeced maturity, masked my nose and mouth. As my
> tongue plunged into the hot channel, the tip of my erec-
> tion was touched by moist flesh. For a moment I lay in
> sweet uncertainty as to whether those gloving lips were
> the gateway to a mouth or to a fourth vagina.'*

Clunton perched on the edge of the desk to hide the stiffness in the front of his trousers. He snatched a glance at
Helen, who winked at him. Flicking through the pages of
the next book to come to hand, his eye fell on another
likely passage. 'Hey, this one looks a bit dodgy, age-of-
consent-wise:

> *She stood behind her friend and, for the briefest mo-
> ment, lifted the girl's white vest up to reveal the plump
> little pink-topped protuberances. Then, just covering
> them again, she rolled the bottom of the vest tightly so
> that it fitted snugly below the breastlets. These she
> squeezed through the cotton, making the nipples stand
> out hard and well defined in the sunlight. "She's all
> yours to look at for a moment, mister," this amazing
> girl went on, "but she's very shy and doesn't want to
> be fucked – not until she's married. I'm her special
> protector."*

Reckon we could . . .'

The Captain interrupted the zealous young officer. 'Not one of ours,' he said. 'Look at the cover and you'll see it's published by our main competitor. Close that outfit down and you'll be doing us all a favour.'

But young Clunton was not to be deflected from the line of duty, especially as Helen, apparently enjoying his performance, was now stroking the base of her belly just above the elastic of her skimpy blue briefs. He picked up a sheet of paper from the desk. 'And what do you make of this handwritten one?

> My pert young breasts swelled and strained at the pale blue silk containing their flesh but not their lust. And oh my pleasure-mound swelled ripe within the matching scrap of silk secured by flimsy ribbons. Swelled, I say, and foamed. We stood in line, flushed with lust, awaiting the tipsy punters flush from the poker tables.

And look – there's something looks like it's meant to be a poem:

> I turned the woodland corner, hot and lewd;
> There, underneath an oak, those girls long missed
> Lay in each other's arms and fiercely kissed;
> Apart from socks and knickers they were nude,
> I heard the tender nothings . . .'

'All right, sonny,' Raddle cut in. 'We don't need no more of that muck, leastways not while there's ladies around. Maybe we'll just impound some of these paperbacks for forensics to run their eye over.'

'But surely it's obvious these must be obscene libels or whatever they call them? You know – obscene within the meaning of the act? Liable to deprave and corrupt – ain't that so, Jivesy?'

'Well, I . . .'

'Calm down, everyone,' said Raddle. 'You might well find, young Clunton, that the solid burghers of Upchester would be depraved and corrupted by this filth – leastways,

215

some of the older ones, like my old mum. Heavens forbid! But we're up in the wicked city here, lad. Pretty far gone already, this lot, just from reading the papers and watching the electric television. Why, the courts here . . .'

At this point WPC Jives, tired of being marginalised, managed to get a word in. 'You saying, then, sarge, we can be getting back now? It being Friday, like, my Kev'll be, you know, ready and waiting for me.'

'What, before dinner time even? Pity your Kev can't find a proper job like the rest of us. Take his mind off it, that would.' He turned to the Captain. 'Tell you what we'll do, sir. You play ball with us and we'll play ball with you.'

'Scratch each other's backs?'

'That sort of thing, sir. Not so much scratching backs as greasing palms, if you take my meaning. It's a regular scandal, what we gets paid for a trip like this when we don't get no results. Performance – that's the name of the game these days. You ask the boys down the Fulham nick. Well, maybe you won't be chatting to that lot after all if we settle things amicably between us up here. What we'll do, we'll take some of your more interesting specimens with us for further perusal, like I said. Nothing like a good read when the missis is snoring. You can pick out a selection for us. Don't forget to put bookmarks in the juicy bits. Used bookmarks'll do, and nothing smaller than tens. They're stiffer if you clip them together in half-dozens, know what I mean? Oh, and while you're doing that, me and my colleagues might as well be passing the time of day with these charming young ladies. Don't seem to have too much to say for theirselves, do they? That's the way I likes them. You can join us as soon as you've finished.'

The Captain took Raddle by the elbow and led him aside. 'A word in your ear, sergeant,' he whispered. 'We might have a bit of a fuss if you try to poke the tall one. Best leave her to me. She's having this thing with me, you understand. Probably remember the one in the blue knickers, don't you?'

'Course I remember her. She's the one I done from behind that motel of yours. She were all dressed up in

216

bride's togs. Tight as a monkey wrench. But keep it quiet – this young constable here don't need to know nothing about that little episode.'

The young constable had inched his way across to the girls and was laying a tentative palm on Helen's bottom. Raddle pushed him aside and seized the girl by the hips, butting his head into her back to bend her forward until her small breasts were flattened on the Captain's desk. He drew the pale blue cotton knickers down over her thighs. 'This one's reserved,' he growled. 'So's the other one. You best look after yourself, constable, in the best traditions of the force. Use your initiative, lad.'

At first PC Clunton thought his superior officer was referring to Helen's buttocks. If they were both reserved, he reasoned, there should still be other parts, no less desirable, for his enjoyment. Yet this could hardly be what was meant. Raddle had wriggled his hammy hands under the girl's breasts and was tweaking the nipples. At some point he had managed to unfasten the trousers of his creased brown suit and his businesslike truncheon was already whipping in and out of her foaming cunt.

Happily for Clunton, his female colleague had grown lewd from listening to his readings and watching the two girls. She came to his rescue, hitching up her skirt, unzipping him and allowing him free access to the contents of her loose silk drawers. They got down behind Helen's desk, forgetting themselves and the others for the next twenty minutes or so while they attended to the matter in hand.

Meanwhile, as Sergeant Raddle subjected Helen's juicy tightness to the most vigorous battering he had dished out for some weeks, the Captain opened a safe and busied himself counting out notes for the backhander that had been demanded. 'Might get mislaid if I put them inside books,' he remarked. 'A brown envelope OK for you?'

Raddle paused in his pistoning for a moment. 'Done this before, sir, have we? That's the way. Oh, and this young lady here – she's grown a nice little bush of yellow fuzz since I last – since, well, since that incident we was discussing just now. Most becoming, it is. Why don't you come and join in? The other lassie seems to be at a bit of a loose end.'

All this time poor Victoria had been hanging about by the window, seemingly indifferent to the occasional catcalls and wolf-whistles directed up at her from the market below. 'How much is that pussy in the window?' some wag was singing. 'Hey, Sharon, you got competition today,' another bawled. 'Bet yours ain't nothing like as luscious and juicy as what's on offer up there!'

Although it was quite a warm day, Victoria's white skin, all the whiter on account of the scarlet G-string at her crotch, had come up in goose pimples. The almost invisible fair hairs on her arms and legs were bristling, as if begging for a brisk rub. The Captain strode straight over to her and took her in his arms. She was a fairly tall woman with long legs but he released her, piled a couple of phone books on the floor and made her stand on these before renewing his embrace.

Although Victoria flinched and trembled she made no real effort to break away. Perhaps she didn't like being left out of things. Or maybe she felt safer and less exposed with her boss hugging and pressing up against her. He brought his lips to her ear and whispered reassurance: 'Don't worry about these oiks – I won't let them touch you. Just try to relax. We'll let them think I'm doing it to you, but really I'm going to stay outside. OK?'

The quivering blonde said nothing, but the Captain thought he noticed a slight slackening of the tension in her muscles as he gripped her strongly with one arm and used his free hand to release his half-erect prick. He let his jeans and underwear fall to his knees and tucked his clothes up to expose his hairy abdomen. Holding the organ upright, he pulled her to him so that it was squeezed and trapped by their embracing bodies, or rather by his eager body as it embraced her semi-reluctant one. It stiffened and began to climb up between their bellies. He felt the thick base pressing into the silk G-string, through which the fleshy labia swelled to fold his engorged rod in their moist, involuntary clutch.

Victoria turned her head sideways to avoid his kiss but blushed and smiled when he thrust a hand between them to cup a breast. The nipple was as hard as a dried pea but perhaps it had already been in that state before he touched her. None the less, even if he found that this talented young woman had betrayed him, the Captain felt he would almost be able to find it in him to forgive her – on suitable terms.

A kicking of heavily shod feet against Helen's desk, accompanied by a high-pitched squeal, indicated that Clunton and Jives had reached a satisfactory conclusion. As if triggered by this preliminary explosion, Sergeant Raddle's weaponry was detonated into a protracted heaving chain reaction which in its turn sent Helen into a series of seismic shock waves.

And now the Captain's other hand, which had been gently stroking the soft down in the small of Victoria's back, drifted downwards. His middle finger curved itself down the line of red silk between the cheeks of her bottom; the groove felt warm and damp. Two other fingers joined it. The hand reached down further, right down, round and up until the two outer fingers rested on the elasticated edges of the silk where they nestled in the creases dividing her crotch from the tops of her soft thighs. The tip of the middle finger probed the red silk and found the concealed bud of lust. Victoria's belly rippled in orgasm against his upright cock and his knees gave way as a great tide of sperm flooded up between their two bodies.

Victoria, whose left cheek had been pressed against the Captain's right one, drew back and looked him in the eye. 'Treat me as nicely as that,' she murmured, 'and I might let you do it properly one day.'

TWELVE

BIG IS BEAUTIFUL

Thu, June 10

Dear Diary – It's been such a hectic day I'd better try
and jot down what happened before I forget bits of it.
We'd had this phone call from the Captain asking us to
join him in a sort of detective job he was doing. Idea
was to trail this Victoria Iceberg woman in hope that
she'd lead us – well, he didn't say where she might lead
us, but apparently he'd been trying to track her down
for nearly three weeks, just with Helen's help, and
thought we'd have a better chance if there were four of
us.

This was supposed to be something like professional
sleuthing. Disguises, that meant. Easier for men because
they can have false beards and things. Mac got herself
up in traffic warden's uniform she 'borrowed' from one
of the Cunlip girls whose mum's a meter maid in Upchester. Wouldn't have recognised her. A bit silly, I
thought – Iceberg probably wouldn't have recognised
Mac anyway in her usual tracksuit. And this uniform
was going to make her much more conspicuous. She
said this was the whole idea. If one of people following
the Iceberg was really obvious she wouldn't notice the
others so much.

I decided to disguise myself as schoolgirl so I put on
old Cunlip gear – short, pleated grey skirt, white shirt,
striped tie, plum-coloured blazer and long white socks.

Didn't bother with regulation knickers – Mac wanted both of us bare-bottomed. Had hair in two plaits tied with black bows. The old straw boater as crowning glory. Uniform still fits quite well. Haven't had it on for two years, of course, but I really don't seem to have put on any weight worth worrying about. Think my hips are just a teeny bit fuller and my thighs more, well, more powerful. Captain used to call them slender – rounded would be more the word these days. And I suppose it was quite hard to button shirt over tits (no bra, of course). So although my body's hardly changed since I was eighteen, just those tiny differences seem to add up enough to make quite a big difference to overall effect. Instead of looking like a sixth-former, you could see, if you stared hard enough, I was actually mature, attractive young woman squeezed into kid's clothes. Not exactly busting out all over but definitely ripe for the plucking, as Captain would say.

Instructions for this morning were to go straight to address in Islington where Iceberg has flat. Today's her day off so it seemed quite likely she would make trip to wherever it was she got up to her dirty tricks, whatever they were supposed to be. Captain and Helen were to make own way there. To avoid arousing suspicion if she was looking out of window or anything, we were not supposed to talk to the others or show signs of recognition. No problem. Because of their disguises we didn't recognise them anyway among all the people hanging about in street.

Mac parked on meter. Bold as brass, she marched straight up to a sour-faced traffic warden, a genuine one probably, who was slamming tickets on cars. After a bit of a chat she came back, all smiles, and said she'd fixed it so we could stay there all day for free.

Anyway, we sort of loitered about in case Iceberg came out of house. Mac's outfit ideal for this part of operation except that one angry motorist thought she'd put ticket on his car and said he was going to push her teeth down throat. But he calmed down and drove off when she tore ticket up. My Cunlip clothes attracted a bit too much attention with me standing there on corner, so Mac told me to wait in car.

At about ten thirty front door opened and Iceberg came out looking really smart in purple cord trouser suit over white blouse with big floppy collar. Me and Mac kept fairly close together as long as we could. We followed her on bus to King's Cross, where this bloke nearly shoved me into waiting car, but I broke away and we headed for Underground. Everyone seemed keen to talk to me but I knew important thing was to keep Iceberg in sight – luckily she's quite tall. I caught up wth Mac at ticket machines. I wanted to try and pull Captain's usual scam but she persuaded me it wasn't a good idea on unknown route. She got two of the most expensive fares to cover all possibilities.

Purple trouser suit quite easy to spot in crowd. We ran after her and more or less caught up with her on Circle Line platform. Somehow we managed to squeeze into same carriage as her. My bottom kept getting pinched by men in dirty raincoats but when they saw Mac glaring at them and looking all official they tended to lay off.

Iceberg got off at Baker Street and we followed her up one lot of stairs and then down again to Metropolitan Line. Not so many people about now, though still too many for us to spot Captain or Helen. It was an Amersham train she got on – where's Amersham, I wondered, feeling all confused. Baker Street was end of line and we could see from indicator board that train wouldn't be going for twenty minutes. Well, we didn't want to be too obvious so after a while we separated and got in carriages on either side of one Iceberg was in. When I looked through window in door at end of carriage I could just see top of her head.

Quite a few more people piled in just before train left but it still wasn't crowded and most of them got out at Harrow-on-the-Hill. Wondered what sort of welcome

I'd get in my Cunlip uniform if I dropped in on the well-known boys' school I think they have up there.

It was after this that I started to get a bit rattled. There was this bloke in seat opposite on other side of aisle (spelling?) – looked like one of the guys. in raincoats who'd been pestering me on the other train. Had Groucho Marx type moustache and bushy eyebrows, NHS specs and one of those middle-aged tweed hats which he'd pulled down low on forehead. I didn't really take much of this detail in because he'd opened front of raincoat and was stroking big white plonker with knob on it like purple plum. A flasher, believe it or not. Well, I felt a bit disgusted but sort of fascinated at same time. Flattered, almost. Then I realised the way I was sitting he could very likely see my twat.

I crossed my legs and stared out of window. Looked quite rural out there but I couldn't concentrate on scenery. Out of corner of eye saw flasher move across to sit on seat facing me. He laughed.

FLASHER: Feeling a bit hot under the collar, Melanie?

ME: Hey, it's you!

Yes, I might have guessed – it was the Captain, disguised as a dirty old man. He came and sat next to me.

CAPTAIN: I'd loosen that tight collar for you if I thought we had time. But we're on a mission, aren't we? Done pretty well so far but mustn't lower our guard.

ME (*touching his stiff dick*): Don't know about lowering my guard but you've already raised my expectations, among other things. Think we might have time for something quick and to the point?

CAPTAIN: Well, maybe. After the next station, as long as our suspect doesn't get out.

ME: Not sure I can wait. Where's Helen?

CAPTAIN: Up the other end of the carriage where she's got a better view through into the next one. Ah, this is Moor Park.

Train stopped. One or two got out, but not Iceberg. As soon as we were moving again he made me pull up skirt and sit astride his lap facing him. Didn't go for cold feeling of raincoat on bum but that was made up for by lovely hot sensation as I let myself down on his biggie. Seemed to stretch me as much as if I hadn't been had for a week. By the time I'd got all of him into me he'd undone three of my shirt buttons and had one of my boobs in his mouth. That false moustache felt like a hard-bristled broom and sent prickles right down to my pussy.

Just as he got hand on other tit, train started to slow down and one or two passengers got up to go to doors. Lifted bottom slightly and Captain sort of slid out of me, using raincoat to hide his wet sausage. Hope no one got view of bum before I pulled hem of skirt down. Would have looked a bit obvious if I'd started buttoning up shirt again so I just made sure everything was more or less inside and pulled blazer round me.

Station was Rickmansworth. Never heard of it before, or if I had I thought it was in Yorkshire or somewhere. First thing we saw was Iceberg hurrying past window, followed by Mac the meter maid and then Helen. Knew it was Helen from her disguise. Guess what? She was in her Cunlip uniform, same as me, with boater and blazer, except that she'd chosen the light blue summer dress instead of grey skirt. I don't think old Muttock would have allowed the sunglasses she had on, though, with their heart-shaped pink frames.

Captain and me jumped out just as doors were closing and followed everyone through subway and out into car park, just in time to see Iceberg drive off in minicab. Mac had already bagged one for us – she climbed in front and rest of us piled into back seat, Captain in middle with his hands up our skirts. Driver had difficulty keeping his eye on road as we hurtled down leafy lanes in hot pursuit of Iceberg.

We pulled up when her cab turned into a drive and a security guard opened gate for them. Captain paid off our driver. We walked on up lane, probably looking a bit suspicious – two overgrown schoolgirls, a traffic warden and an old perve in a dirty mac. A hundred yards or so past driveway we found small opening at bottom of high holly hedge. Mac led way and we all crawled through. Very painful, especially for me with my unbuttoned shirt.

Found ourselves in dense shrubbery. Worked our way through, getting more and more scratched and untidy, till we came to a stretch of long grass between us and a sort of factory or barn-like kind of building and a big house beyond that. We were wondering how to get to house without being seen when lo and behold – Iceberg appears round corner of barn, slides a little door open and steps inside. Captain told us to lie low and give him ten minutes. If he hadn't shown by then we were to go in and get him, he said.

Much too tired to write any more tonight and I know Mac wants me. Think I can hear her coming upstairs now. Will finish this tomo

Sally Nugent held up her mouth to let Yvonne Yglesias retouch her makeup. With all the kissing and sucking demanded by the endless takes and retakes under the hot lights of the set, this retouching seemed to be needed every few minutes. It tended to take some of the excitement out of the performance. On the other hand, Sally had to admit that it made the pleasure last longer, and in the end the longer the critical moments were deferred the more intense they were when they arrived.

Her golden hair had been cut shorter to give her that nineteen-twenties look. Yvonne had got them to curl it in tight ringlets instead of the natural ripples Rod was so fond of. He would have had a fit, Sally thought, if he knew what she was getting up to.

She just hoped Rod never started bringing adult videos home for them to watch in bed – Talbot had said this one was going to be all the rage and the word would go round so everyone would be looking out for it. A heavily cut version would be released for general hire. Talbot had explained what would be in it and she knew even that version would make poor old Rod see red. But if he ever clapped eyes on the more explicit one for sale in licensed sex shops, let alone what Talbot called the director's cut, which had to be sold in shops pretending to specialise in kiddies' annuals and biographies of the prime minister . . .

No, she just couldn't bear to think of what her Rod might do to her. He might even go right off her. She did so hope she was doing the right thing. Well, in the end it was bound to be for the best, what with no signs of any real upturn in the market. As long as she held on to what she thought of as her own natural innocence her husband might be able to overlook what she had let them do to her own natural hair.

She admired herself in the mirror Yvonne was holding up for her. No denying they'd got her looking really pretty and quite a bit younger than her eighteen years. How did they do that? She'd have to ask Yvonne one day when the film was nearly finished and there was less pressure. Maybe it was something to do with that funny round pudding-basin hat – had Yvonne called it a *cloash* or *closh* or something like that? – which fitted snugly over the tops of her ears and sat low on her forehead.

Although Sally's breasts were quite a decent size, and had even filled out a little since she'd been married, the dove-grey satin tube they had dressed her in made her look flat-chested and almost bottomless, if that was the right word in this connection. Yes, that was one of the things that gave her such a young appearance. You would think a dress like that would do nothing for a girl. It could hardly be said to flatter her. Instead of being flattering it was flattening. Nevertheless, it had an undeniable something about it. It gave her this gift-wrapped look, as if the whole point was to get her unwrapped as quickly as possible.

And that, of course, was the point, if not the whole point – if it had been, the movie would have been pretty tame by the standards of Yglesias Enterprises. It was called *Little Darlings*, and was based, they said, on *Two Flappers in Monte Carlo*, a book Sally had never heard of. She thought the change of title was a good idea – if they hadn't told her

226

what a flapper was she would have guessed she was co-starring in a film about performing seals. The thought of seals reminded her of one distressing moment when she feared she was going to be made to appear with a snake round her neck. Yvonne had laughed and pointed out the difference between a boa constrictor and a feather boa.

Her co-star, the other flapper or little darling, was an auburn-haired twenty-year-old with lots of pretty freckles on her face and body. Although Sally had been working with her for six or seven weeks now, ever since they had performed in the Yglesias production of *Girlie Delights*, they were not really hitting it off with each other except in front of the cameras. This Gina always seemed preoccupied with her unpleasant and uncouth boyfriend Joker, who was playing the part of a randy French servant in the scene they were doing today. It was a funny conicdence that Gina and Joker knew Sally's old friend the Captain – not from the Honeymoon Palace Motel but from the time when he was working at that weird college near Upminster or Upchester.

Right now Gina, dressed just like Sally but with a green hat and dress and black stockings instead of Sally's matching grey ones, was impatient to get on with the filming. She had announced loudly that she wanted to get this scene out of the way as soon as possible, and hoped they could do it without too many retakes. It was the scene where she had to wander into the bedroom and find her best chum being fucked by this gross servant. In the movie Evelyn (Gina) was supposed to be angry because she didn't want to share Nora (Sally) with anyone but Uncle Jack (Talbot). But in real life she was furious that Sally was getting to fuck Joker. The whole occasion was a bit fraught today.

'Quiet, everyone,' Talbot bellowed. '*Little Darlings*, scene fifteen, take twelve. Cameras. Action.'

Sally strode across the floor in her unaccustomed high heels, this time managing not to trip on the edge of the rug. She stood at the window, remembering not to touch it in case it fell over again. Bracing herself, she drew on her long cigarette holder and collapsed in a fit of coughing.

'Cut!' yelled Talbot. 'All right, darling – try it again without inhaling.'

After a few more false starts Sally was standing quite calmly, looking out of the window and really feeling herself into the part of young Nora. She laid the cigarette holder in an ashtray, removed the cloche hat and languidly patted her tight blonde curls. 'How I wish Uncle Jack would come back early,' she sighed. 'He seems to spend all his time at the casino. And now Evelyn's slipped out to buy a new hat. What's a girl supposed to do, left on her own like this?'

She felt pleased with herself for having delivered such a long speech without fluffing it – more difficult than one might think, she told herself, even though a stage hand on the other side of the window was holding up an idiot card for her to read from. Then, just as she was getting carried away in contemplation of her own burgeoning talent, she remembered to let her hands drift down the silky front of her dress, one of them lingering on a breast while the other one settled on the level of her pubis. Resting the heel of this hand on the mound and reaching down with her fingertips she was able to hook the hem of her short dress and draw it up.

The hem rose, as did the denim-clad manhood of the camera operator who had taken the place of the stage hand on the other side of the window. Nora's crimson garters and the tops of her grey silk stockings were uncovered and the whiteness of her thightops came into sight. But at this moment the door swung open and Joker entered the room, uncharacteristically dapper in black trousers, white bumfreezer jacket and little pill-box cap. 'You rang, mademoiselle?' he enquired, his native Cockney masked by an overdone Gallic accent.

'No, Gaston.'

'Then perhaps there is something I can do for mademoiselle? Mademoiselle is alone this afternoon, *n'est ce pas?* Monsieur makes a promenade? *La p'tite amie de mademoiselle* she take the siesta? Mademoiselle Nora – what jolly name! – will become victim of the *mélancolie* if she passes her time in – how to say? – idless.'

'Idleness.'

'*Exactement*. I pray you of it, young lady, permit that I pleasure you with my grand *zob*.'

Even if Yvonne had not translated this crude term in rehearsal for the benefit of the players, Sally could have had no doubt as to its meaning. Joker had released his rampant *zob* from the confinement of his trousers and advanced on her menacingly. She screamed, ran into a corner, turned her back on him and hid her face in her hands. This was a totally futile defensive measure; Joker took three strides across the floor, seized the top of her dress and simply ripped it from top to bottom. The cleverly concealed Velcro parted and the dove-grey garment settled round Sally's ankles, ready to be reconstituted for any further retakes of the scene.

Sally was now completely bare apart from her silk stockings, supported by the pair of crimson garters just above the mid-point of her pretty thighs. For a moment Joker, and the camera, admired her firm, round buttocks. Then he pressed himself to her, running his hands down the hidden front of her body.

Once more the door opened, this time to admit an indignant Gina. In these circumstances it was easy for Gina to give a convincing enactment of indignation. 'Nora, darling!' she cried. 'What is this peasant doing to you? Do you require assistance?'

Warming to the intracrural proddings of the yob's *zob*, Sally answered with disdain. 'You can just sit down and watch, Evelyn. If you will go off and leave me to my own devices, then you can't blame me if Mother Nature takes her course.'

'But what would dear Uncle Jack . . .'

'Uncle Jack isn't my father – he's not even your uncle, is he – or is he? And he's not exactly married to me either, so I don't see what it's got to do with him.'

Gina had flopped into a brocaded armchair. In sulky fascination she watched as Sally, all her fear overcome, dragged the servant lad over to the bed. Gina raised her bottom from the chair and pulled her green dress up until all the nudity was exposed between her belly button and the tops of her black silk stockings with their eye-catching orange garters. Her hand dropped to her vulva, fringed with coppery curls, but although the dew that glistened on those lips showed that the flesh was more than willing, her heart was not in the job. Gina was jealous.

Joker had stepped out of his trousers and was now kneeling between Sally's thighs on the bed. He stooped right down to kiss her on the mouth. A camera positioned to the side was registering the lengthening and upcurving of his already stiff prick in the space between their two bellies until the swollen tip was almost digging into his navel.

Talbot made frantic signs to Gina, who was now supposed to approach the bed and assist the servant's penetration of her chum. With deliberate malice she sat right between the camera and the lovers and gave Joker's erection a squeeze that subdued it to half its size. 'Look, I just can't do this bit,' she whined. 'I can't bear to watch him screw her. Couldn't you use a body double and just show it in close up?'

Talbot frowned as he ordered the camera crews to cut. 'This guy's dong's a character actor in its own right,' he growled. 'See that corkscrew twist? And the way those veins make a kind of net round it like ivy on an old oak tree? We're not going to find a stand-in for that one.'

His wife was not so sure. 'I know one gorgeous man who looks like a corkscrew and fucks like a corkscrew and he's standing right here in front of me. Get stuck in, Talby – a nice slice of action for the director's cut.'

But Talbot was having none of it. He would be able to play about with Sally Nugent as much as he liked after the shooting. Right now he was keen to get this scene wrapped and in the can. It was authenticity he was after. This young ruffian's cock was something else again and it was this cock he wanted to film stretching the engorged pink leaves that pouted out so temptingly from Sally's young slit. He grasped Gina by the shoulders. 'Just you listen to me, miss,' he began. 'If we bring on a substitute for anyone it'll be for you. I've no time for a starlet with an attitude, do you hear me? Now, just watch while Yvonne here shows you what we want you to do.'

Yvonne Yglesias sat on the end of the bed. While Joker stooped once more to kiss the more than willing Sally, Yvonne placed a cool hand on his behind. 'Watch how I do it, dear,' she said reassuringly. 'I've got his balls resting in the palm of my hand. I press up slightly, but not too hard, and grip the root of his dick between two fingers. See how it hardens up as soon as he feels the pressure there? And then I start using my thumb and that should really get him going.'

Gina watched in a state of horrified titillation as the pad of Yvonne's thumb teased away at Joker's puckered anus. 'That's enough by way of demonstration,' Talbot interrupted. 'We don't want to waste a come shot at this stage. And when we do it for real, Miss Wootton,' he added for Gina's benefit, 'make sure your thumb doesn't slip in. Just get him primed but don't bring him off – OK? Get the cameras rolling and we'll take it up from where Evelyn comes and sits on the bed while Gaston's kissing Nora.'

This time things went fairly smoothly until Gina, her right hand engaged in the way Yvonne had demonstrated, used her left one to force Joker's distinctive cock down towards its target. At the same time she pulled down with her right hand so that his loins and whole package of sexual endowments lunged into the succulence between Sally's thighs.

The great glans was still throbbing in Gina's fingers. The other girl's open flesh was wet on the back of her hand and it was into this gaping wetness that she was supposed to guide the hot manflesh. Her stomach heaved at the thought.

Sally, too, was having a slight attitude problem at this point. Once things really got under way she was usually OK. But the moment of penetration in these movies always found her agonising, torn between her sense of affectionate loyalty as a young married woman and her desire to supplement Rod's inadequate income. And on top of that there was this other desire, the desire to wallow in the sensuality that had been so long suppressed and for her body to leap joyfully in response to its ravaging by as many fierce pricks as she could lure into its tight clutch. This filming lark was just the thing, of course. She could, and did, tell herself she wasn't being shagged for real – it was only a video and didn't count as proper adultery.

Just as Joker clenched his buttocks in preparation for his impaling thrust Gina's jealousy got the better of her. In jabbed her right thumb and her boyfriend's loins jerked wildly. She felt the stem thicken between the upcurling fingers of her right hand to accommodate the spunk racing along the hot tube. At the same time she cupped her left palm over the bursting knob to block its entrance to Sally and to catch most of the creaming sperm that gushed from the tip. The surplus trickled stickily from her hand to puddle Sally's pussy and inner thighs.

'Right, we'll find some way of editing that shot into the finished sequence,' said Talbot. 'But listen to me, Miss Wootton. This kind of temperamental behaviour won't do at all. It's completely unprofessional and unacceptable. Still, no use crying over spilt body fluids. As you're so fond of this young man you'd better do what you can to get him on red alert again. And no more time-wasting.'

Yvonne was already repairing Sally's makeup, cleaning her quim and thighs with tissues and using a hair-dryer to restore the fluffiness of the pretty yellow bush. Meanwhile, Gina complied with Talbot's instructions.

It took a good five minutes for her tongue-work to restore Joker's cockstand to something like its former dimensions and solidity. A wicked gleam lit up her eyes as the fresh taste of his pre-come juices tempted her to take him over the top once more and thoroughly spike his guns where Sally was concerned.

Just as his testicles tightened in her hand and the point of her furled tongue darted into his oozing little slot, proceedings were interrupted by a new arrival on the set. All eyes turned, attracted by Victoria Eisenberg's striking purple trouser suit and the immaculate flaxen hair cut straight across her shoulder-blades.

Knowing the script as well as anyone, she immediately realised that the action was deviating from it and asked Talbot what they were up to. He explained the little local difficulty they were experiencing. As anxious as the rest of them that the film should not only be a hit but a cheaply and therefore quickly made one, Victoria threw herself into the task of pacifying Gina, a girl she found quite lovely, and scandalously wasted on Joker.

To take Gina's mind off the object of her jealousy she peeled off her own trouser suit and the expensive black underwear she wore beneath it. Naked, Victoria presented a sight that drove men mad with lust and filled women with melting desire. Yvonne had to restrain Talbot when he said he felt like taking out his excited dick and coming all over the tall blonde's gleaming limbs. The air of the studio was already rank with the smell of spunk, she pointed out, and if the shoot were to degenerate into an all-out orgy they might as well shut up shop for the day.

Victoria cuddled Gina, stroked the auburn curls that framed her freckled, tear-stained face and then moved her hand down to stroke the other auburn curls, the ones framed by white flesh framed in its turn by the raised hem of her green dress, the orange garters and the black silk of her stockings. As she stroked, it soon became obvious that this principle of framing worked inwards as well as outwards. The pubic hair framed the musky flesh now exposed as her outer labia fell open. This in turn framed the tender petals which clung together at first but soon parted, bringing into sight the pale pink juiciness framing a small, inviting aperture that winked invitingly at everyone on the set until it was plugged by Victoria's soothing finger. Sally, still lying on the bed in her stockings, felt as if she was going to get off on just watching this little show. At least it seemed to have achieved its purpose; Gina, if only temporarily, had lost all interest in Joker's affairs.

Talbot thanked Victoria for the effectiveness of her intervention. He now judged that the time was right to resume filming and gave orders for the action to be taken up at the point where Evelyn was sitting on the armchair with her fanny exposed, watching Gaston prepare to mount Nora. The cameras rolled.

Once again operations were disrupted. Commotion broke out as a strange man stumbled across the studio floor. He blundered into the lighted area of the set at such an angle that he pulled up immediately in front of Gina with her blatantly spread legs. He rubbed his eyes, dazzled first by the lights and then by what he saw beneath him.

Sally thought there was something vaguely familiar about this intruder behind his hat, moustache, eyebrows, glasses and raincoat. And she gathered from his gasps of delight that the astonished Gina was by no means unfamiliar to him. He was shouting Gina's name as he tore off the shabby mac.

The figure he now struck was a bizarre one even by the standards of this production team. He still wore the little tweed fishing hat and National Health spectacles. Above the waist he was clad in a navy sweat-shirt decorated with the word 'PARKS' in white capitals. But below the hem of this garment he was bare as far as just above his knees. From that level down his legs were covered in the lower portions of cut-off pin-striped trousers held up by tape tied round his thighs. Sally vaguely recollected Rod describing something like this as a typical flasher's outfit, but she had thought he was pulling her leg.

As Sally watched, the member that had swung loose but long between his legs sprang to attention. Although he had recognised Gina he was confused, disorientated by the dazzling lights and the even more dazzling spectacle of his old flame apparently offering herself to him on the armchair. He fell to his knees, dragged Gina forward until her bottom was on the edge of the chair and stabbed into her proffered sex.

After half a dozen lusty heaves he stopped pumping and raised his head from the breast he had been mouthing through the thin green material of Gina's dress. The girl's loins continued to quiver as if had not paused. As soon as Sally heard him speak she knew it was the Captain from the Honeymoon Palace Motel, who had done so much to

234

get her marriage off to a reasonable start. In fact, she now realised she had known it was him the moment his dick had come into sight.

He gazed into Gina's eyes. 'We're alone, are we?' he enquired uncertainly.

Unlike everyone else on the set, Joker, primed and ready to go, had been totally unaware of this interruption. Sally's view of the unscripted action was suddenly obscured as he flung himself upon her and drove his love bludgeon urgently up her cunt.

Even as the Captain asked Gina if they were alone, two things happened. The realisation rushed in upon him that they were certainly not alone, and at the same instant the sperm rushed out of him. His mind had gone blank in the first seconds as he had emerged from darkness but now it was crystal clear. This was a film set and the whirring he could hear told him he was performing on camera. He had flooded the lovely Gina's cunt not while energetically rogering her but in the moment of slackness as he lifted his head to look around him. He now lay panting on her belly, his spent prick clasped warmly in her flesh and bathing in the spunk that was beginning to leak out of her and trickle down over his balls. The sound of creaking bed-springs testified to a bout of fucking going on just behind him.

What an impetuous fool he had been. On the very point of completing his mission to nail the offenders and assert his legal rights, he had landed himself up to the neck – well, up to the neck of his cock – in this incriminating situation. Unless he was mistaken, he had just made an appearance in a pirated video based on one of his own novels!

The same ludicrous insight must have struck his three female accomplices, who now skipped out of the shadows and broke down in uncontrollable laughter. Laughter is infectious. Seeing these two delectable schoolgirls and the glamorous, athletic traffic warden shaking hysterically and thumping each other on the back, everyone on the set dissolved in mirth. Everyone, that is, except Sally Nugent and

235

Joker Jennings, who were on the bed working their way towards orgasm, oblivious that the cameras had ceased to roll.

Mac was the first to get a grip on herself. Her features hardened into a motorist's nightmare. Waiting only for Joker to dump his load into Sally's belly and roll wetly off her, she marched over to Talbot and Yvonne, who were hovering to one side of the set. She addressed them cuttingly.

'Mr and Mrs Yglesias? I believe you know me, both of you. I put on that little show at our friend the Captain's motel last summer, remember?'

Yvonne smiled with relief. 'What a turn-on that was,' she gushed. 'Why, Talbot here . . .'

Mac interrupted her. 'I'm sure that you and your husband derived great pleasure from that performance. And I'm also sure that many thousands of enthusiasts will get off on the movie you're making here. Should be a nice little earner.'

Talbot beamed. 'We hope to gross . . .'

Again Mac broke in. 'Oh, I've no doubt we can arrange things so that you get a percentage, Mr Yglesias. I don't think the Captain will insist on his right to have this pirated production suppressed. His solicitors will be in touch – they're big on copyright law. It shouldn't be too difficult to agree terms.'

Talbot was no longer beaming but fuming. 'Go stick your ticket on some other car, lady,' he shouted. 'Don't talk to me about copyright. This outfit operates outside the law, well outside. Believe me, we're in the jungle. What you're trying to do, it's like fining bank robbers for parking their get-away car on a yellow line. You just try it. Think we haven't disappeared before and re-opened somewhere else a couple of weeks later?'

The enraged director seemed to be on the verge of violence. Thankfully, Victoria Eisenberg stepped forward in her naked loveliness and for the second time intervened to pour oil on troubled waters. 'Surely we can reach a settlement on this little matter of copyright,' she began.

236

Before Victoria could explain what she had in mind, Yvonne's face lit up triumphantly. 'You guys don't know what you're talking about,' she said. 'Copyright? What copyright? Miss Eisenberg here told us the book of this movie – *Two Floozies in Monte Carlo* or whatever – had been copied from some unpublished manuscript in the British Library. That means it's in what they call the public domain. Part of our national heritage. Up for grabs.'

The Captain, who had harboured some nagging doubts himself on this aspect of the matter, was so dismayed that he hardly noticed Helen and Melanie flirting shamelessly with the detumescent Joker, lifting the hems of their schoolgirl skirts to flaunt their knickerless pussies. If the Yglesiases realised there was no copyright to be infringed, it would obviously not be so easy to intimidate them.

His old friend Mac came to the rescue. 'Sorry to disappoint you,' she purred. 'What makes you think it's in the British Library, this hitherto unpublished novel?'

Victoria replied. 'You're Muriel MacDonald, aren't you? I saw you in that daring chain-mail dress at the Honeymooners launch party and I've heard all about you from Helen Lascelles – from this pert young would-be schoolgirl. She said it was you who copied the manuscript. That's how we know.'

'Oh no,' Mac rejoined. 'That's how you think you know. But look in the BL catalogue and you'll get a surprise. Strictly between ourselves, I wrote the book myself. Public domain? You try to sell that to my lawyers.'

The Captain was vaguely aware that Helen and Melanie, their skirts still lifted, had moved round behind Gina's armchair and that Joker's eyes were fixed on them as he knelt between Gina's thighs to lick her cunt. The sight did little for the Captain. He was confused now. This was the first he had heard of Mac's authorship of *Two Flappers in Monte Carlo*. Hadn't he discovered the title himself in the catalogue and commissioned her to make the transcription for him? This must be a bold bluff on her part, and to judge from the Yglesiases' and Victoria's dropped jaws it seemed to be working.

Or was it Mac who had told him of the manuscript's existence and had offered to transcribe it? In that case, he was the one she was bluffing. Just when he had been congratulating himself on the cheapness of this publication compared with the specially commissioned ones, she would be upsetting his budget by demanding a proper author's contract.

Either way, though, her ploy had done the trick with Talbot and Yvonne. And in any case, there was still the matter of their infringement of the *Fucky Days* copyright by filming *Girlie Delights*, about which there could be no argument. Talbot, of course, was right in saying that they carried on their business outside the law. And the Honeymooners operation itelf was only just inside; it was hard to imagine any jury sympathising with a claim for exemplary damages by the Honeymooners Library against Yglesias Enterprises. Helen's suggestion of blackmail was a likelier bet, or maybe protection from exposure would be a better way of putting it. How much was Talbot good for?

The Captain had not quite completed this train of thought when Victoria spoke. 'I've never been convinced myself,' she said, 'but you know what they say? Big is beautiful. I know Mrs Nugent here agrees with that – from what she tells me she can't get them big enough. Well, in this particular case it may be true.'

'In what way?' Talbot demanded.

'In the way of business. Maybe this recession hasn't hit the hot video and book industries as hard as some. The Captain here thinks it's hardly affected demand. In fact, he thinks people want even more of our stuff to cheer them up between giros. But the trouble is, everyone's trying to get a foot in the door now. Second-hand car market stagnant? No problem – knock off a crude fuck scenario on the garage's word processor, get the cashier to pose for a few open crotch shots, warm up the photocopier and bingo! You'll shift them like ringed BMWs. Oh, and while you're about it get out the camcorder and let the mechanic screw the cashier before she pulls her knickers up again. A few thousand copies and you're away. They're all doing it. The only safety's in size.'

Talbot was pondering her words. 'Go for growth, you mean?'

'I mean we shouldn't be squabbling over professional ethics but thinking realistically about a merger. A commercial partnership. If we're not going to be gobbled up by the big boys in Ladbroke Grove we need to set up shop as Yglesias Eisenberg Honeymooners.'

'A multimedia concern,' said Talbot. 'Yes, I see your point. What do you say, Captain?'

The Captain paused for a suspenseful moment, admiring Victoria's nerve in putting herself at the apex of this projected triangle. Yet it wasn't just nerve she could bring to such a set-up – the woman had talent. 'It's worth thinking about,' he said. 'OK then, I've thought about it. Make this movie and we'll market it alongside the book. If that works, we've got ourselves a deal.'

'You're on.'

'Just one condition. If Sally and Gina here are playing Nora and Evelyn, I insist on making my screen debut as Uncle Jack.'

Reluctant though he was to relinquish that role, Talbot had little choice in the matter and complied. 'Be my guest,' he said, dismissing the technical crew but instructing them to leave the cameras running.

Elated, the Captain sprang into action. Big is beautiful, he thought. Lying on the bed in her gartered stockings, Sally Nugent was indeed beautiful and by now he was certainly big. His tongue found her wet mouth as he drove his prick lustily into a cunt he had often recalled with longing in his masturbatory fantasies. And now his pleasure was enhanced by the thought that he was the lecherous Uncle Jack and Sally, with that innocent-looking oval face, was the deliciously naughty Nora. He peered back for a moment beneath his armpit and saw Joker pumping away into Gina as she sprawled in her chair. Talbot and Yvonne, meanwhile, had both shed their jeans and were getting into a standing clinch.

Suddenly Victoria clapped her hands and called a halt to the fucking. 'Hold it, you men,' she cried. 'We all want a slice of the action. You're leaving three of us ladies out in the cold. Now just do what I say and everyone will be satisfied. We're going to celebrate this merger with what you might call appropriate symbolism.'

The Captain pulled out of radiant young Sally with some reluctance. His tool stood wagging in the studio lights and gleaming with her juices and those deposited in her by Joker. Talbot disengaged from his wife and Joker from his girlfriend. Victoria took three pillows from the bed and laying them end to end on the floor stretched out on them, her naked beauty displayed to the other nine as they gathered round.

She looked up at them enigmatically and spoke. 'First I want the ladies to jerk these gentlemen off over me. Yes, all over me. Spray it about, but mind my hair. When you've done that, ladies, you're going to lick it off me while the lads frig you and fuck you. By my reckoning that should be two girls to a guy. Get as much variety into it as you can, right? OK then – enjoy!'

Having discarded his pill-box hat and bum-freezer jacket, Joker got into position standing at Victoria's left side, Talbot at her right and the Captain between her legs. At Mac's suggestion they dropped to their knees. After some argument and jostling, the lovely auburn-haired Gina knelt to the Captain's left and Melanie, trying not to spoil things by laughing at his ridiculous flasher's gear, to his right. He felt cool fingers on his cock and bollocks. The tip of a girlish finger wormed its way into his arse. Mac and Sally attended to Talbot, on his right and left respectively, with Yvonne and Helen on Joker's left and right.

All three males were already so worked up that it took no more than half a dozen strokes to bring them off. The Captain thrust his hips forward involuntarily as he squirted his hot come. Three pulsing fountains sprayed their thick cream over Victoria's belly, breasts, face, thighs and snatch. Spunk splashed against spunk in mid-air, exploding in sticky globules over the smooth white flesh and saturated flaxen bush below. The thinner constituents of the spilt fluid began to trickle down Victoria's sides, leaving her upper surfaces coated with pungent jelly.

The men were elbowed aside and six female mouths went down on their more than willing victim, lapping and slurping at this freshly delivered feast which added a whiff of the salty spice of heterosexuality to their shared lesbian thrill. Six white bottoms were raised around the recumbent figure and the men made sure that any concealing skirts were lifted to allow free access.

The Captain now moved from between Victoria's thighs to a position above her head. He asserted his prerogative by laying hands on Helen, to his left, and Sally, to his right, and pulling on their buttocks until they got the idea. They moved their knees so that they were planted to the sides of Victoria's head. He now had a full view of two enticing bottoms. His left hand lay on a seeming schoolgirl, still clad above the waist in her light blue summer dress, and his right one on a young woman naked except for the dove-grey silk stockings with their crimson garters. The sex pouches of both these charming partners were oozing, Helen's with the juices of her arousal and Sally's with the overflow of Joker's recent spillage mingled with her own full discharge.

It was unnecessary for Yvonne, Melanie, Mac and Gina to move from the positions in which they had wanked their men. Joker and Talbot swapped sides, moving over to the right and left of Victoria respectively, so that Talbot could work on Yvonne and Helen's rear quarters while Joker devoted himself to Mac and Sally's.

For the moment, the eager cunts of Sally and Helen had to be contented with the ministrations of two deft hands; the Captain's dick, though still heavy and engorged, hung down over his ballsack like a half-inflated balloon. But as his thumbs sank into the girls' moistly clinging flesh and his fingers wiggled upwards to fondle their mounds, scratching the pubic fluff and teasing the swollen clits, his glans began to throb and lift itself until it stuck out horizontally in front of him. He used his plundering hands to draw the two cunts, and with them their youthful owners, together. His cock was now held between the softness of Sally's left flank and the firmness of Helen's right one. He

used their quims as handles to frig himself to full hardness
as Victoria, whom he had almost forgotten, entered a series
of shattering and continuing climaxes which communicated themselves to the six girls working on her. By
now, he realised, most of the spunk which had coated her
body would have been replaced with spittle. It was time to
give them, or as many of them as possible, a dose of cock-
cream administered at the other end.

Joker and Talbot were already well on the way to doing
this. They were working furiously, shafting one of their
women for a few strokes while finger-fucking the other and
then pulling their dripping cocks and fingers out and
switching over. The Captain followed their example, first
thrusting into Sally's mushy channel and relishing the silky
warmth of her buttocks against his shagginess while he
continued to handle Helen. Then it was Helen's turn to be
fucked. He appreciated Helen's tight muscular clasp as his
right hand explored the contrast between the textures of
Sally Nugent's buttocks, her mound, her gaping cunt-
leaves and her silk stockings, smearing her creamy exuda-
tions all over the area of exploration.

Helen's cunt began to gulp and ripple in orgasm. He felt
the tell-tale twitching deep in his own loins; he was close
to coming. At the same instant, Helen lifted her mouth
from Victoria's nipple and flung herself backwards. The
Captain collapsed on his back with the girl on top of him,
his dick still trapped inside her.

Quick as a shot she sat up and without relinquishing her
cuntal grip on him turned herself around so that she straddled him face to face. He grabbed the collar of her Cunlip
dress and ripped it open down the front. His eyes moved
up over her lewdly large navel, the taut white skin of her
belly with its scattering of moles, the pinkish brown of the
mole-like nipples that capped her pert little tits, and finally
the cute, saucy face with its fringe of light brown hair.
Normally, Helen's mouth had a tendency to droop at the
corners. But now it curled upwards in a lascivious grin and
the tip of her tongue flickered in and out in response to
those muscular waves that were taking over her whole

body. Her nose and chin, he noticed, were still shining with the spunk they had gleaned from Victoria's body. He pulled her down and kissed her mouth deeply. His erection now felt huge inside her.

Even as his balls tightened and the sperm gathered in readiness to be propelled into the hot young cunt he remembered Sally, whose fate seemed so often to be deprived of the spunk with which she longed to be filled. This time it could not be helped. There would be plenty for her later. In the meantime he extended his right hand and gloved its fingers in the quivering velvet of her cunt. Sally was such a lovely girl. Her husband was indeed a lucky man!

Just as the throes of lust were about to deprive Helen of all control, she lifted her mouth from the Captain's and spoke. 'Oh *yes*!' she cried. 'Go on fucking me with that huge cock of yours. Fuck me harder. Oh, that's so good. Like Victoria said – big is beautiful. Come on, give it to me. I want my belly full of your spunk.'

The Captain's cock started to gush uncontrollably. As he was carried away on the oblivious flood of his lust he was just able to rave incoherently into Helen's ear. 'Anyone told – told you – told you you're a first – a first-rate fuck?' His words were lost in the welter of their thrashing limbs as the deluge of hot sperm filled her to overflowing and went on spouting until she lay sobbing quietly on his chest.

'You're not so bad yourself,' she said contentedly. 'Or so I've heard . . .'

243

NEW BOOKS

Coming up from Nexus and Black Lace

The Palace of Eros by Delver Maddingley
May 1994   Price: £4.99   ISBN: 0 352 32921 1
In this, the fourth in the popular *Palace* series, the wily, randy
Captain ventures into the world of erotic publishing. Once his
licentious editorial team is assembled, their activities make the
books seem tame by comparison.

Emma Enslaved by Hilary James
May 1994   Price: £4.99   ISBN: 0 352 32922 X
Emma's apprenticeship in servitude continues. Taken by her
cruel but beautiful mistress to a North African harem, Emma
discovers the sweet torment of being denied her own pleasure
while forced to attend to the needs of her superiors.

Melinda and Esmeralda by Susanna Hughes
June 1994   Price: £4.99   ISBN: 0 352 32923 8
Just as she thinks she's found her life's happiness with her
domineering lover Walter Hammerton, Melinda is sent to
Spain to give pleasure to a new master. Far from home and
victimised by her lord's cruel stepmother, the green-eyed
blonde finds comfort in the arms of her beautiful fellow slave
Esmeralda.

Lure of the Manor by Barbra Baron
June 1994   Price: £4.99   ISBN: 0 352 32924 6
At Chalmers Finishing School for Young Ladies, Miss Petty
rules with an iron hand. All who step out of line face severe
punishment – especially the pretty ones. From the manor house
across the fields, Lord Brexford watches with interest, plotting
to add his own brand of sexual depravity to the proceedings.

Outlaw Fantasy by Saskia Hope
May 1994   Price: £4.99   ISBN: 0 352 32920 3
Recovering from the sexually hypercharged events of *Outlaw Lover*, Fiona suffers a setback – the disappearance of a valuable sexual fantasy disc. The trouble is, the disc is so good that it will take some powerful persuasion to get it back.

Handmaiden of Palmyra by Fleur Reynolds
May 1994   Price: £4.99   ISBN: 0 352 32919 X
The author of the successful *Odalisque* brings us a third-century tale of lust and ambition. Samoya has been chosen to be the wife of the Palmyrene chief, Prince Alif: but the marriage seems endangered when she meets a man who awakens her innermost desires . . .

Black Lace Summer Blockbusters

River of Secrets by Saskia Hope & Georgia Angelis
June 1994   Price: £4.99   ISBN: 0 352 32925 4
Sexy young reporter Sydney Johnson is covering an archaeological expedition along the Amazon river. With several rugged men in the team, the trip through the jungle is steamy enough; but the action really hots up when a supernatural force begins to exert its libidinous influence.

Velvet Claws by Cleo Cordell
June 1994   Price: £4.99   ISBN: 0 352 32926 2
In the 19th century, it just wasn't done for delicate young
ladies to strike out on exotic voyages of discovery – but that's
precisely what Gwendoline does when she hears that anthro-
pologist Jonathan Kimberton is going to Africa. Once the
voyage is under way, the spirited adventuress begins discover-
ing her own sexuality.

The Silken Cage by Sophie Danson
June 1994   Price: £4.99   ISBN: 0 352 32928 9
When university lecturer Maria Treharne inherits her aunt's
Cornwall estate, she enters a strange new world. The mansion,
steeped in mystical and erotic legend, has attracted the atten-
tion of others – notably the diabolically handsome Anthony
Pendorran. But it's not just her house he's interested in . . .

THE BEST IN EROTIC READING – BY POST

The Nexus Library of Erotica – almost one hundred and fifty volumes – is available from many booksellers and newsagents. If you have any difficulty obtaining the books you require, you can order them by post. Photocopy the list below, or tear the list out of the book; then tick the titles you want and fill in the form at the end of the list. Titles with a month in the box will not be available until that month in 1994.

CONTEMPORARY EROTICA

AMAZONS	Erin Caine	£3.99	
COCKTAILS	Stanley Carten	£3.99	
CITY OF ONE-NIGHT STANDS	Stanley Carten	£4.50	
CONTOURS OF DARKNESS	Marco Vassi	£4.99	
THE GENTLE DEGENERATES	Marco Vassi	£4.99	
MIND BLOWER	Marco Vassi	£4.99	
THE SALINE SOLUTION	Marco Vassi	£4.99	
DARK FANTASIES	Nigel Anthony	£4.99	
THE DAYS AND NIGHTS OF MIGUMI	P.M.	£4.50	
THE LATIN LOVER	P.M.	£3.99	
THE DEVIL'S ADVOCATE	Anonymous	£4.50	
DIPLOMATIC SECRETS	Antoine Lelouche	£3.50	
DIPLOMATIC PLEASURES	Antoine Lelouche	£3.50	
DIPLOMATIC DIVERSIONS	Antoine Lelouche	£4.50	
ELAINE	Stephen Ferris	£4.99	Mar
EMMA ENSLAVED	Hilary James	£4.99	May
EMMA'S SECRET WORLD	Hilary James	£4.99	
ENGINE OF DESIRE	Alexis Arven	£3.99	
DIRTY WORK	Alexis Arven	£3.99	
THE FANTASIES OF JOSEPHINE SCOTT	Josephine Scott	£4.99	

Title	Author	Price	Month
FALLEN ANGELS	Kendall Grahame	£4.99	Jul
THE FANTASY HUNTERS	Celeste Arden	£3.99	
HEART OF DESIRE	Maria del Rey	£4.99	
HELEN – A MODERN ODALISQUE	James Stern	£4.99	
HOT HOLLYWOOD NIGHTS	Nigel Anthony	£4.50	
THE INSTITUTE	Maria del Rey	£4.99	
JENNIFER'S INSTRUCTION	Cyrian Amberlake	£4.99	Apr
LAURE-ANNE TOUJOURS	Laure-Anne	£4.99	
MELINDA AND ESMERALDA	Susanna Hughes	£4.99	Jun
MELINDA AND THE MASTER	Susanna Hughes	£4.99	
Ms DEEDES AT HOME	Carole Andrews	£4.50	
Ms DEEDES ON A MISSION	Carole Andrews	£4.99	
Ms DEEDES ON PARADISE ISLAND	Carole Andrews	£4.99	
OBSESSION	Maria del Rey	£4.99	
THE PALACE OF EROS	Delver Maddingley	£4.99	May
THE PALACE OF FANTASIES	Delver Maddingley	£4.99	
THE PALACE OF SWEETHEARTS	Delver Maddingley	£4.99	
THE PALACE OF HONEYMOONS	Delver Maddingley	£4.99	
THE PASSIVE VOICE	G. C. Scott	£4.99	
QUEENIE AND CO	Francesca Jones	£4.99	
QUEENIE AND CO IN JAPAN	Francesca Jones	£4.99	
QUEENIE AND CO IN ARGENTINA	Francesca Jones	£4.99	
SECRETS LIE ON PILLOWS	James Arbroath	£4.50	
STEPHANIE	Susanna Hughes	£4.50	
STEPHANIE'S CASTLE	Susanna Hughes	£4.50	
STEPHANIE'S DOMAIN	Susanna Hughes	£4.99	
STEPHANIE'S REVENGE	Susanna Hughes	£4.99	
STEPHANIE'S TRIAL	Susanna Hughes	£4.99	Feb
THE TEACHING OF FAITH	Elizabeth Bruce	£4.99	Jul
THE DOMINO TATTOO	Cyrian Amberlake	£4.50	
THE DOMINO QUEEN	Cyrian Amberlake	£4.99	

EROTIC SCIENCE FICTION

Title	Author	Price	Month
ADVENTURES IN THE PLEASUREZONE	Delaney Silver	£4.99	

RETURN TO THE PLEASUREZONE	Delaney Silver	£4.99	
EROGINA	Christopher Denham	£4.50	
HARD DRIVE	Stanley Garten	£4.99	
PLEASUREHOUSE 13	Agnetha Anders	£3.99	
LAST DAYS OF THE PLEASUREHOUSE	Agnetha Anders	£4.50	
TO PARADISE AND BACK	D. H. Master	£4.50	
WANTON	Andrea Arven	£4.99	Apr

ANCIENT & FANTASY SETTINGS

CHAMPIONS OF LOVE	Anonymous	£3.99	
CHAMPIONS OF DESIRE	Anonymous	£3.99	
CHAMPIONS OF PLEASURE	Anonymous	£3.50	
THE SLAVE OF LIDIR	Aran Ashe	£4.50	
DUNGEONS OF LIDIR	Aran Ashe	£4.99	
THE FOREST OF BONDAGE	Aran Ashe	£4.50	
KNIGHTS OF PLEASURE	Erin Caine	£4.50	
PLEASURE ISLAND	Aran Ashe	£4.99	
WITCH QUEEN OF VIXANIA	Morgana Baron	£4.99	Mar

EDWARDIAN, VICTORIAN & OLDER EROTICA

ADVENTURES OF A SCHOOLBOY	Anonymous	£3.99	
ANNIE	Evelyn Culber	£4.99	
THE AUTOBIOGRAPHY OF A FLEA	Anonymous	£2.99	
CASTLE AMOR	Erin Caine	£4.99	
CHOOSING LOVERS FOR JUSTINE	Aran Ashe	£4.99	
EVELINE	Anonymous	£2.99	
MORE EVELINE	Anonymous	£3.99	
FESTIVAL OF VENUS	Anonymous	£4.50	
GARDENS OF DESIRE	Roger Rougiere	£4.50	
OH, WICKED COUNTRY	Anonymous	£2.99	
THE LASCIVIOUS MONK	Anonymous	£4.50	
LURE OF THE MANOR	Barbra Baron	£4.99	Jun
A MAN WITH A MAID 1	Anonymous	£4.99	
A MAN WITH A MAID 2	Anonymous	£4.99	
A MAN WITH A MAID 3	Anonymous	£4.99	

Please send me the books I have ticked above.

Name   ....
Address   ....
              ....
              .... Post code ....

Send to: **Cash Sales, Nexus Books, 332 Ladbroke Grove, London W10 5AH**

Please enclose a cheque or postal order, made payable to **Nexus Books**, to the value of the books you have ordered plus postage and packing costs as follows:

UK and BFPO – £1.00 for the first book, 50p for the second book, and 30p for each subsequent book to a maximum of £3.00;

Overseas (including Republic of Ireland) – £2.00 for the first book, £1.00 for the second book, and 50p for each subsequent book.

If you would prefer to pay by VISA or ACCESS/MASTERCARD, please write your card number here:

Please allow up to 28 days for delivery

—— —— —— ——   —— —— —— ——   —— —— —— ——   —— —— —— ——

Signature: _____